CRAFTY CAT
and the
GREAT BUTTERFLY
BATTLE

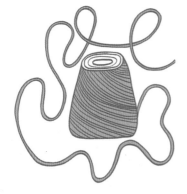

Crafty Cat and the Great Butterfly Battle

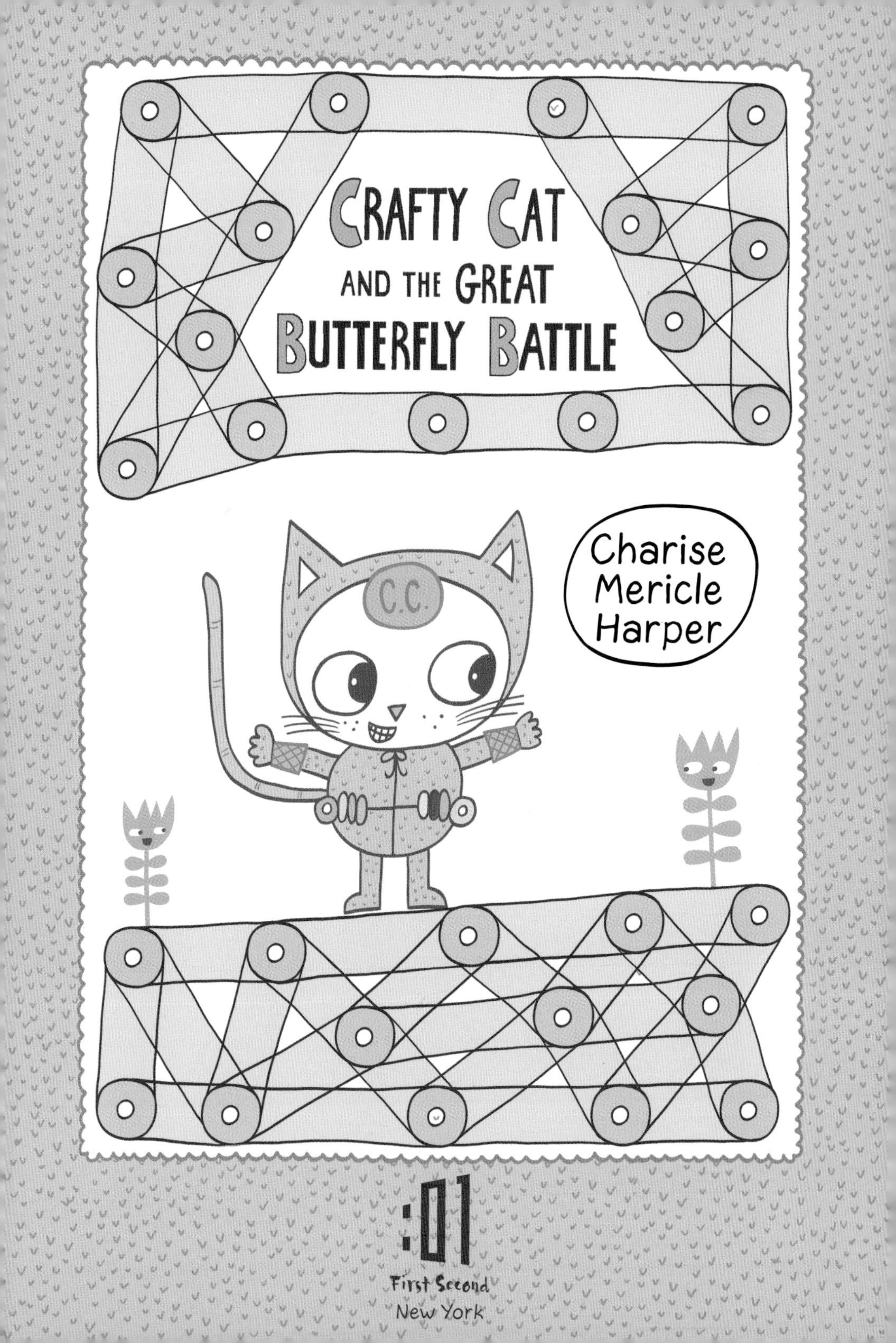
C.C.

Charise Mericle Harper

:01
First Second
New York

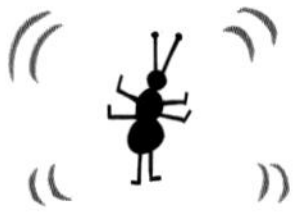

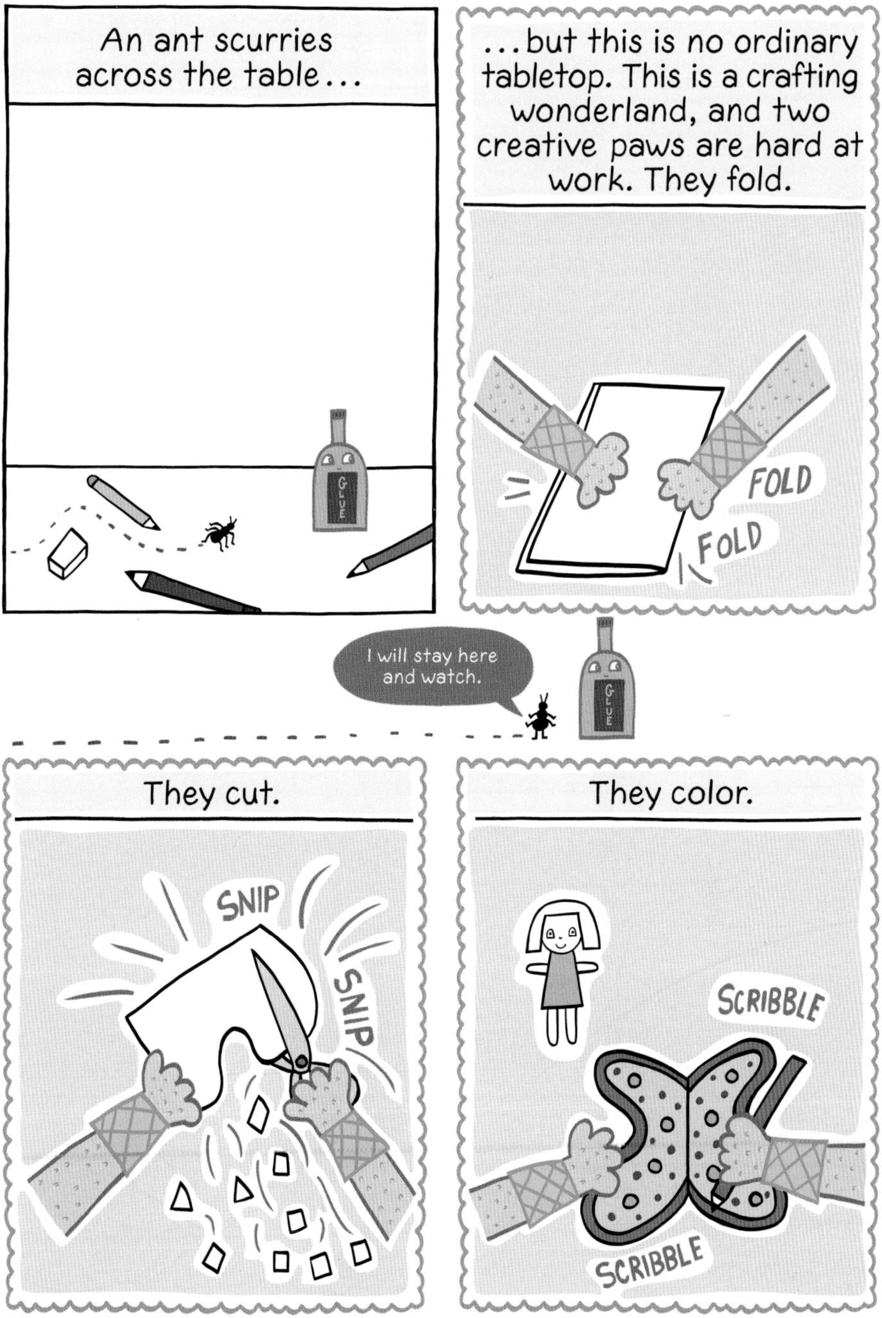

An ant scurries across the table...
GLUE
...but this is no ordinary tabletop. This is a crafting wonderland, and two creative paws are hard at work. They fold.
FOLD
FOLD
I will stay here and watch.
GLUE
They cut.
SNIP
SNIP
They color.
SCRIBBLE
SCRIBBLE

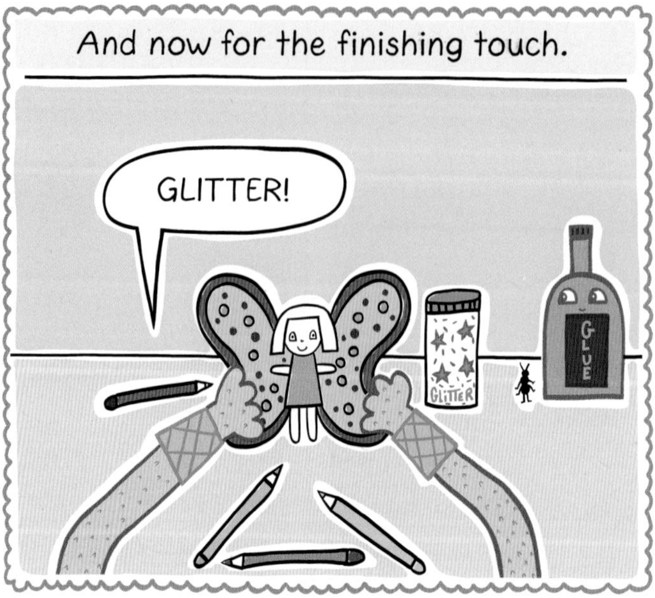
And now for the finishing touch.
GLITTER!
GLITTER
GLUE

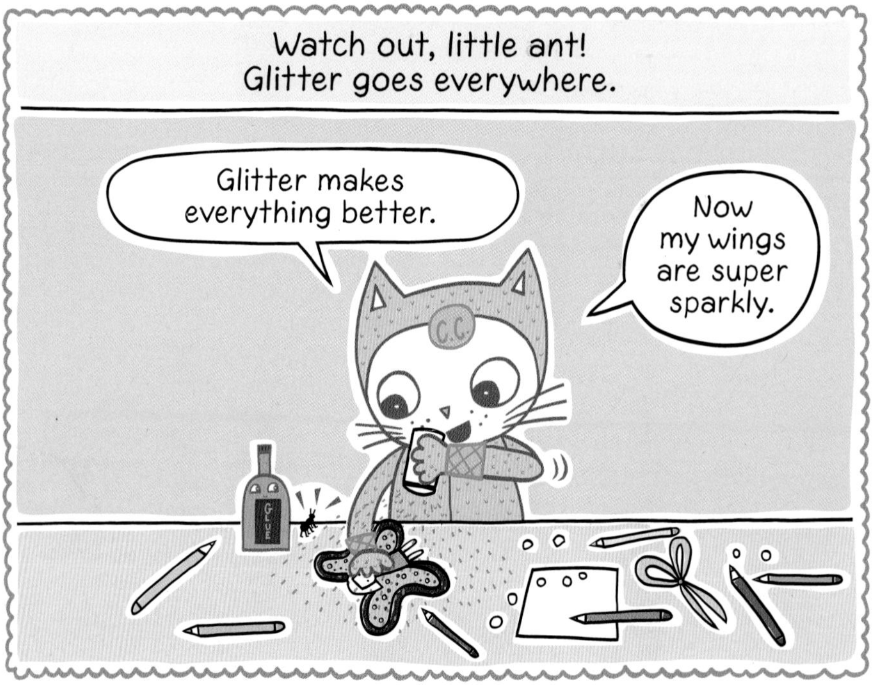
Watch out, little ant!
Glitter goes everywhere.
Glitter makes everything better.
Now my wings are super sparkly.
C.C.
GLUE

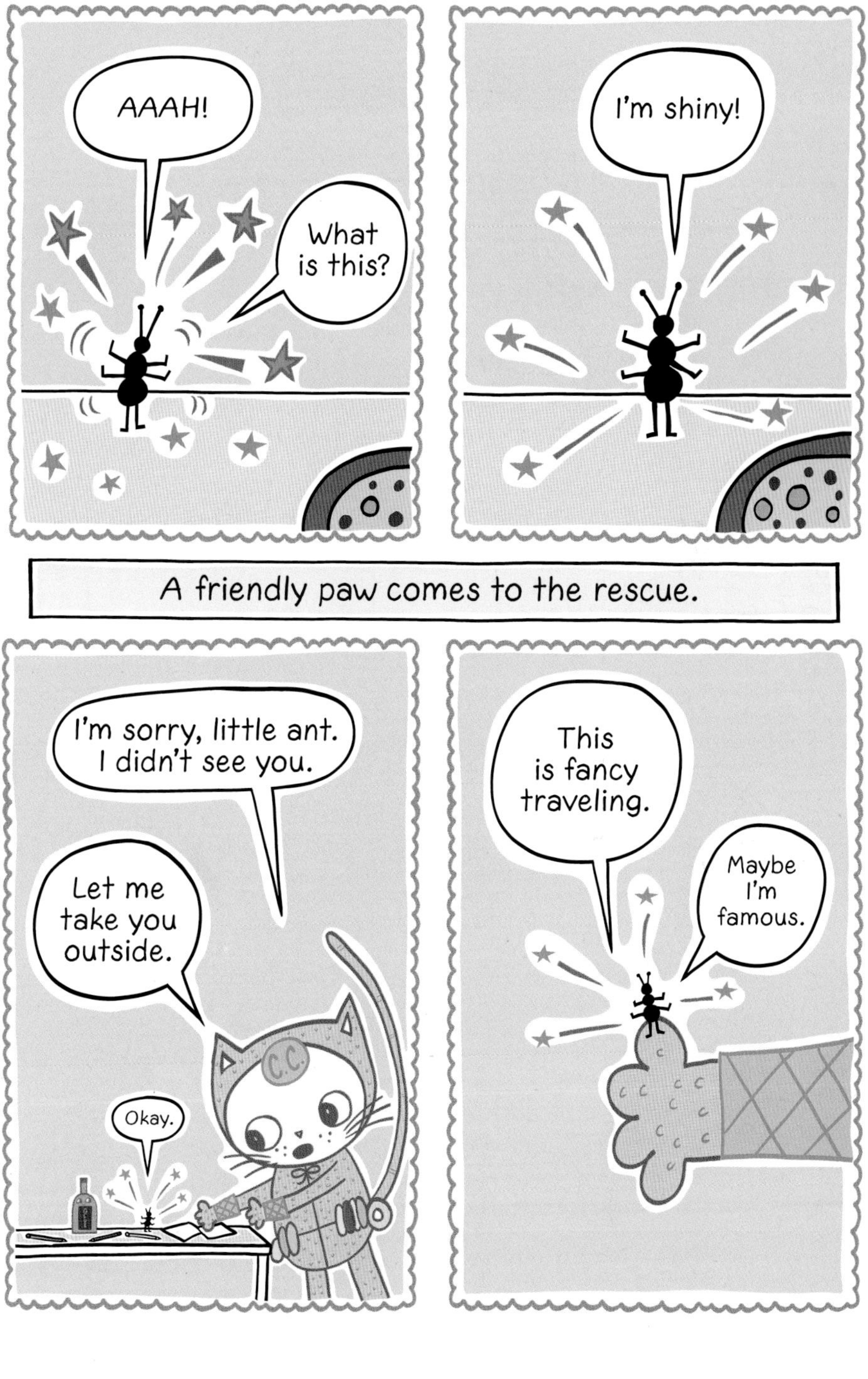
AAAH!
What is this?
I'm shiny!
A friendly paw comes to the rescue.
I'm sorry, little ant. I didn't see you.
Let me take you outside.
Okay.
This is fancy traveling.
Maybe I'm famous.

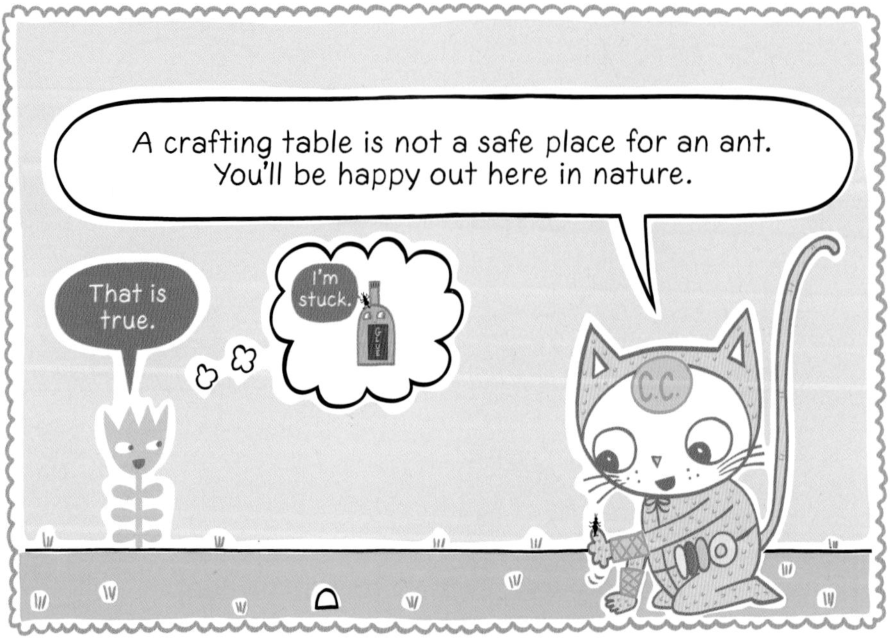
A crafting table is not a safe place for an ant. You'll be happy out here in nature.
That is true.
I'm stuck.
C.C.

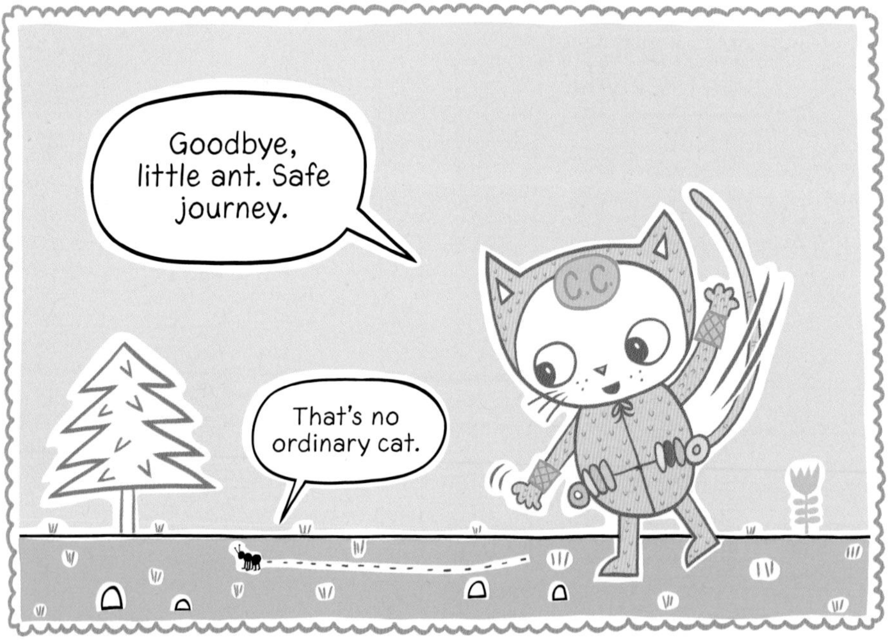
Goodbye, little ant. Safe journey.
That's no ordinary cat.
C.C.

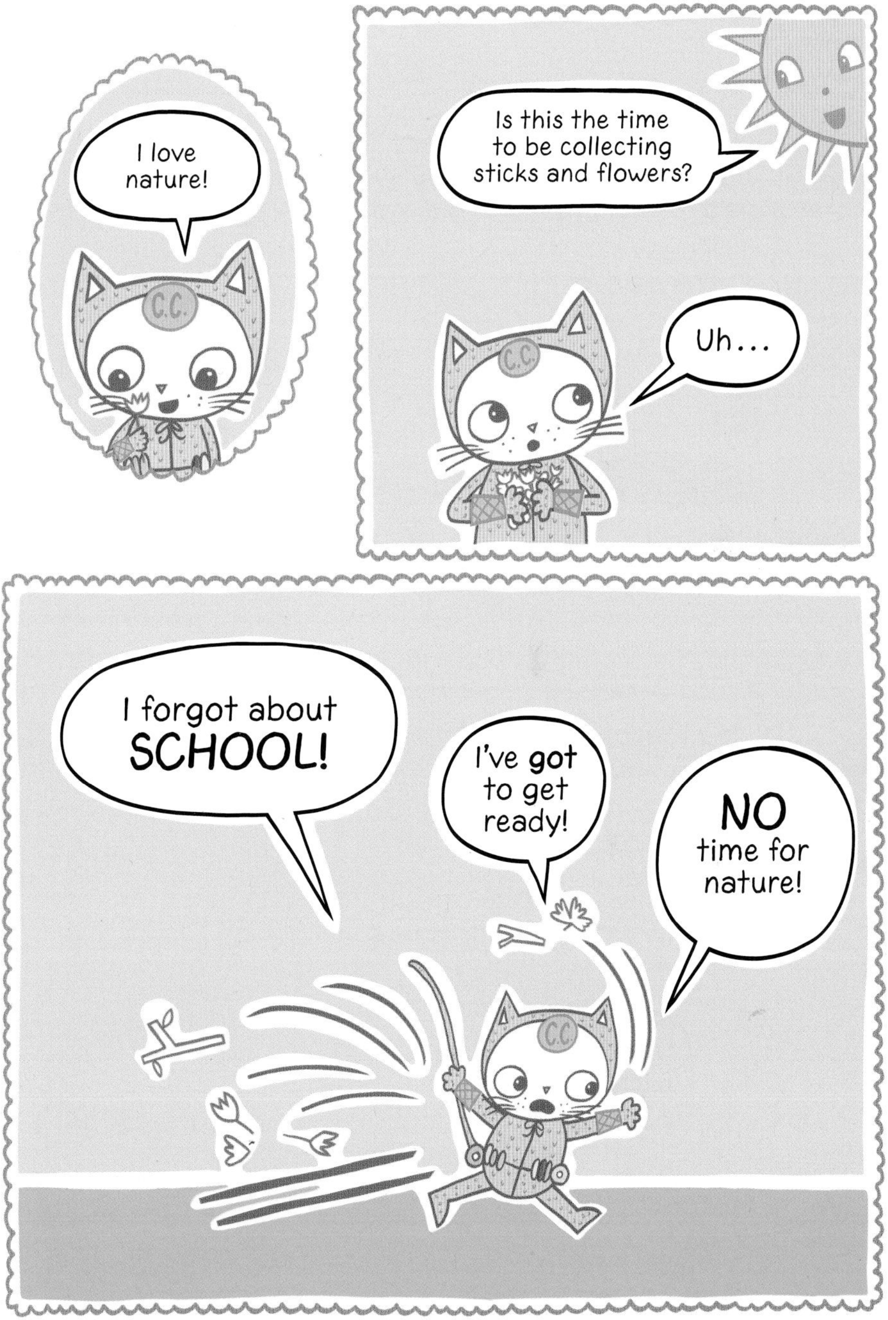
I love nature!
Is this the time to be collecting sticks and flowers?
Uh...
I forgot about **SCHOOL!**
I've **got** to get ready!
NO time for nature!

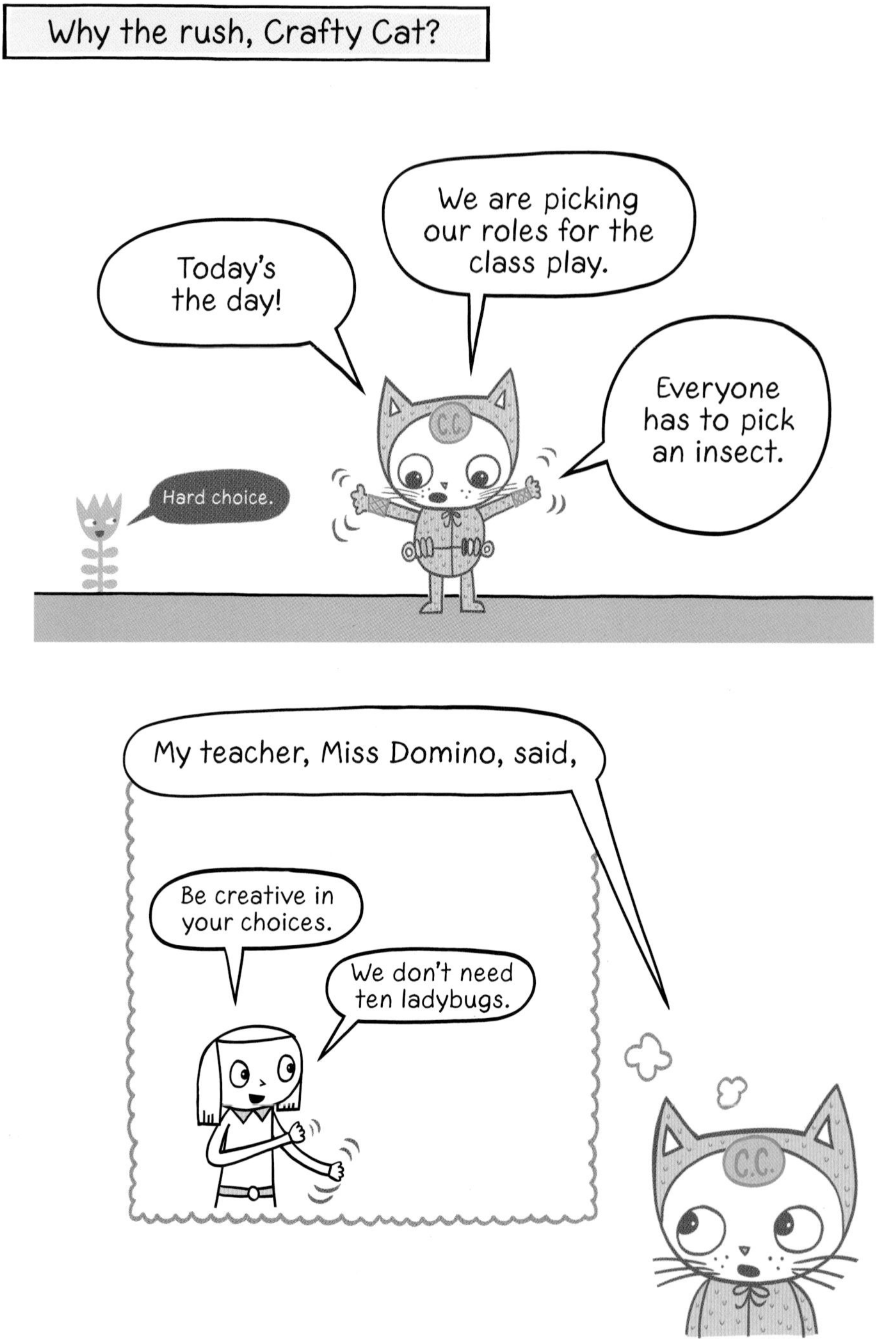
Why the rush, Crafty Cat?
Today's the day!
We are picking our roles for the class play.
Hard choice.
Everyone has to pick an insect.
My teacher, Miss Domino, said,
Be creative in your choices.
We don't need ten ladybugs.

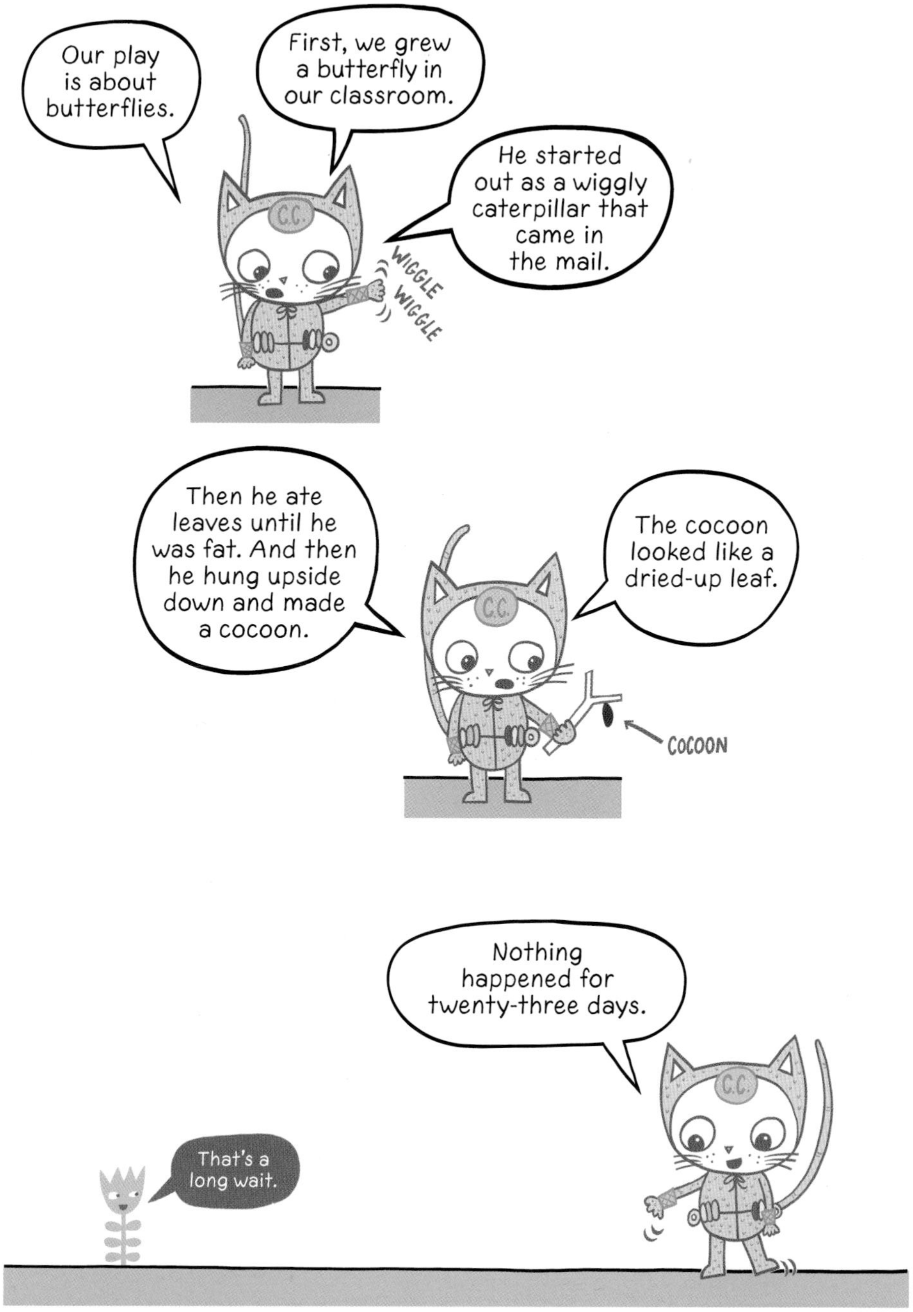
Our play is about butterflies.
First, we grew a butterfly in our classroom.
He started out as a wiggly caterpillar that came in the mail.
WIGGLE WIGGLE
Then he ate leaves until he was fat. And then he hung upside down and made a cocoon.
The cocoon looked like a dried-up leaf.
COCOON
Nothing happened for twenty-three days.
That's a long wait.

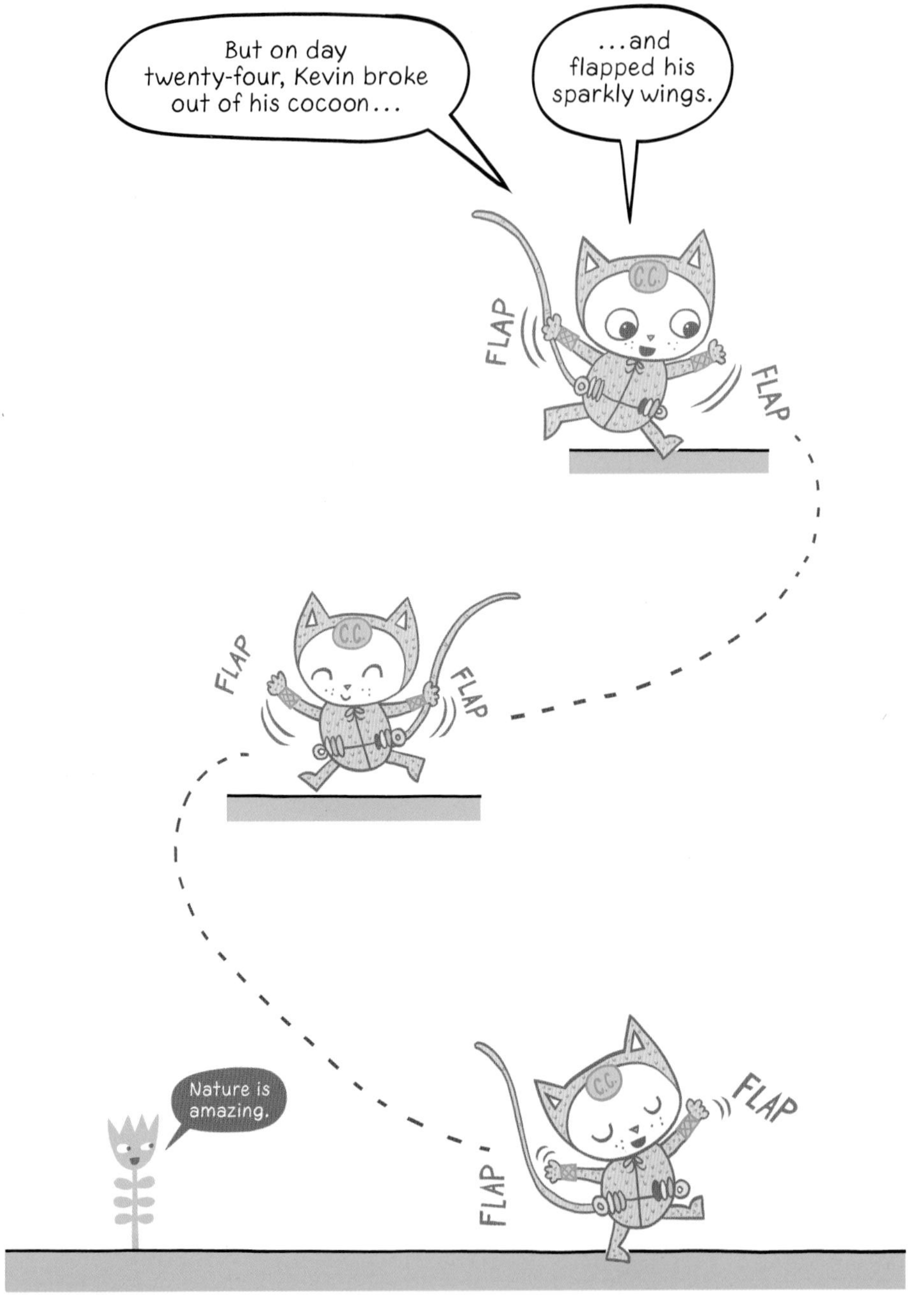
But on day twenty-four, Kevin broke out of his cocoon...
...and flapped his sparkly wings.
FLAP
FLAP
FLAP
FLAP
Nature is amazing.
FLAP
FLAP

Crafty Cat quickly checks left and then right. She has a secret to share.

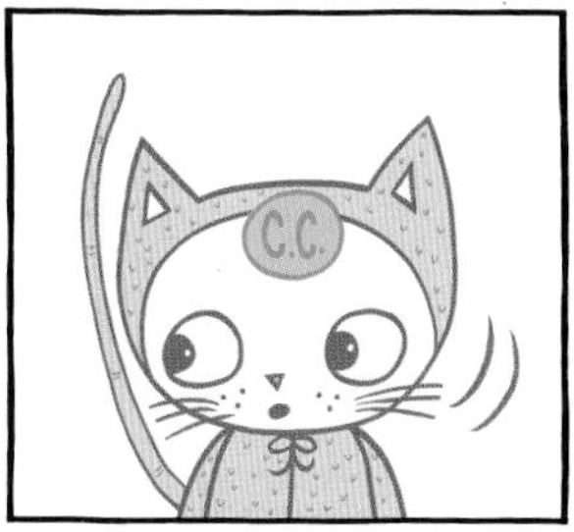

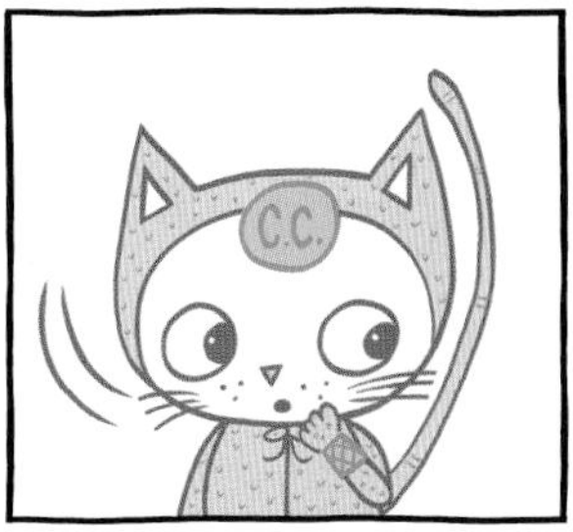

What is it, Crafty Cat? Tell us.

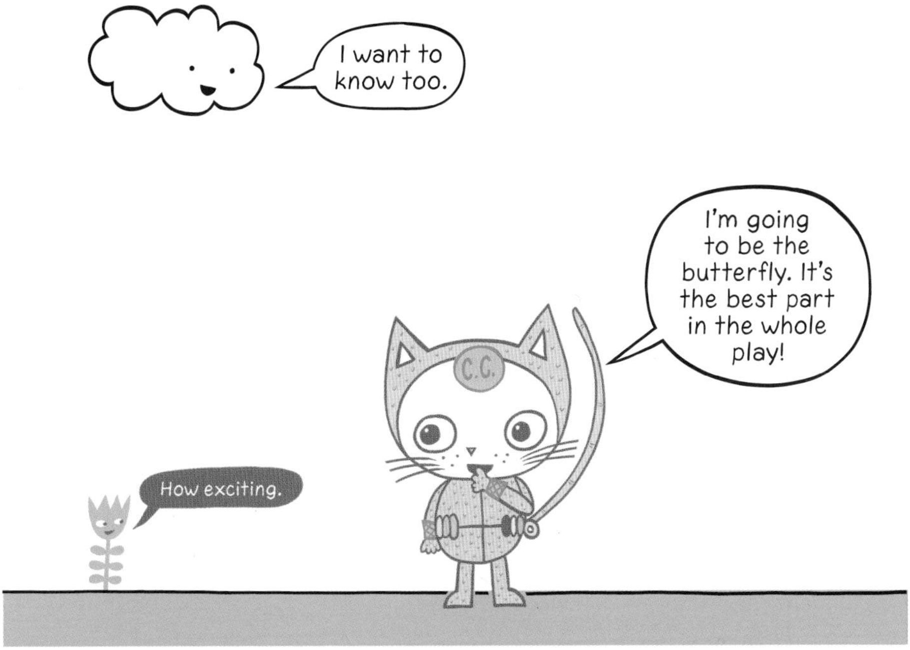
I want to know too.
I'm going to be the butterfly. It's the best part in the whole play!
How exciting.

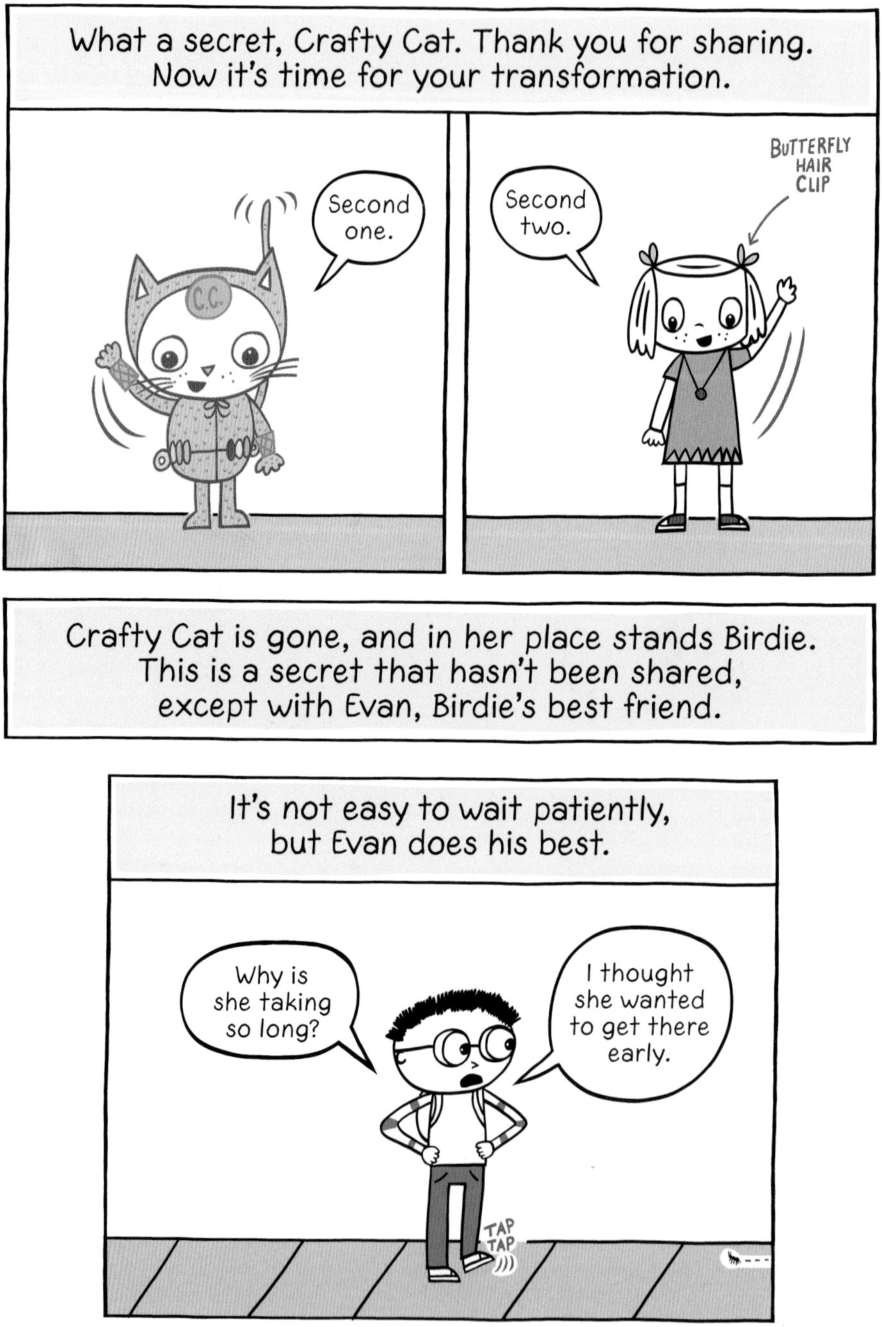
What a secret, Crafty Cat. Thank you for sharing. Now it's time for your transformation.
Second one.
Second two.
BUTTERFLY HAIR CLIP
Crafty Cat is gone, and in her place stands Birdie. This is a secret that hasn't been shared, except with Evan, Birdie's best friend.
It's not easy to wait patiently, but Evan does his best.
Why is she taking so long?
I thought she wanted to get there early.
TAP TAP

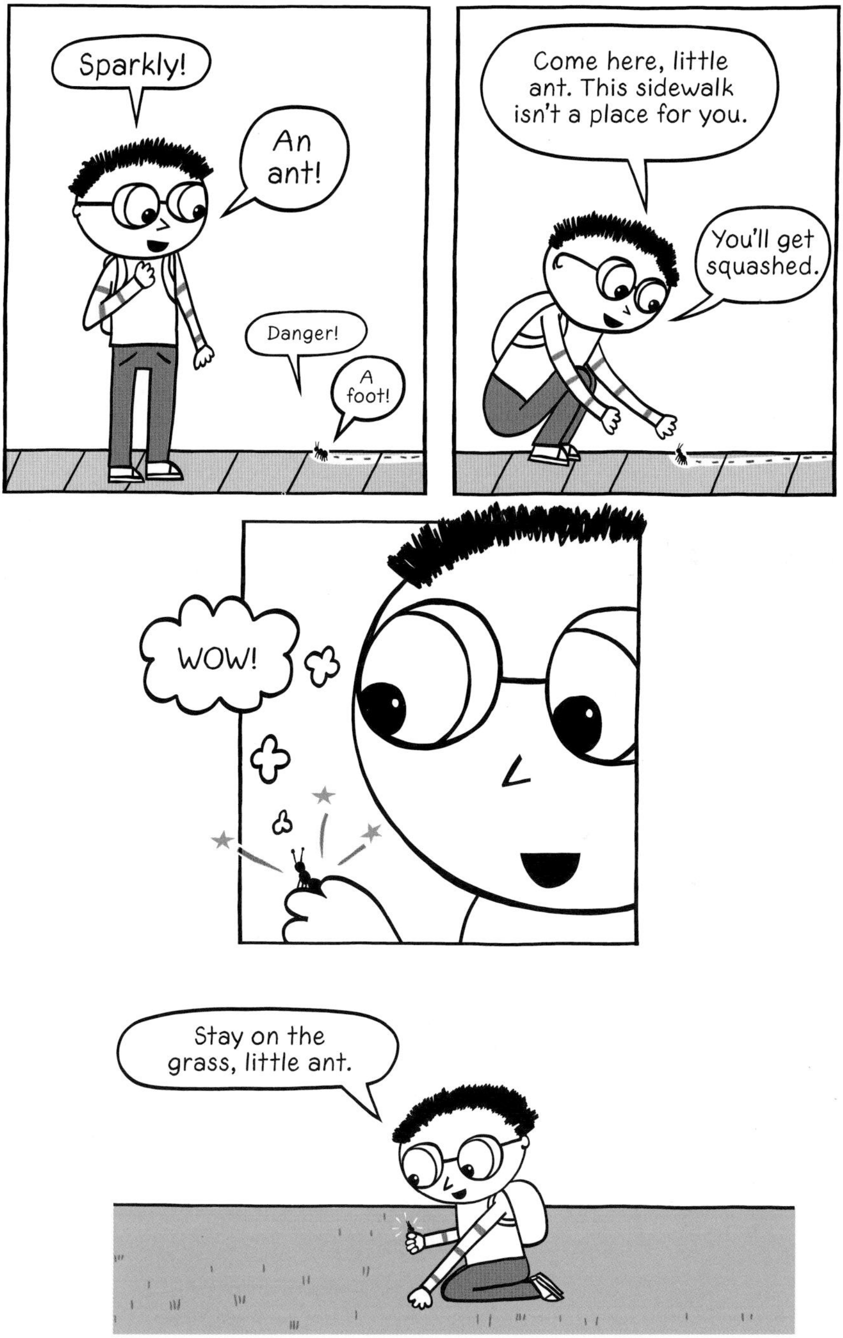
Sparkly!
An ant!
Danger!
A foot!
Come here, little ant. This sidewalk isn't a place for you.
You'll get squashed.
WOW!
Stay on the grass, little ant.

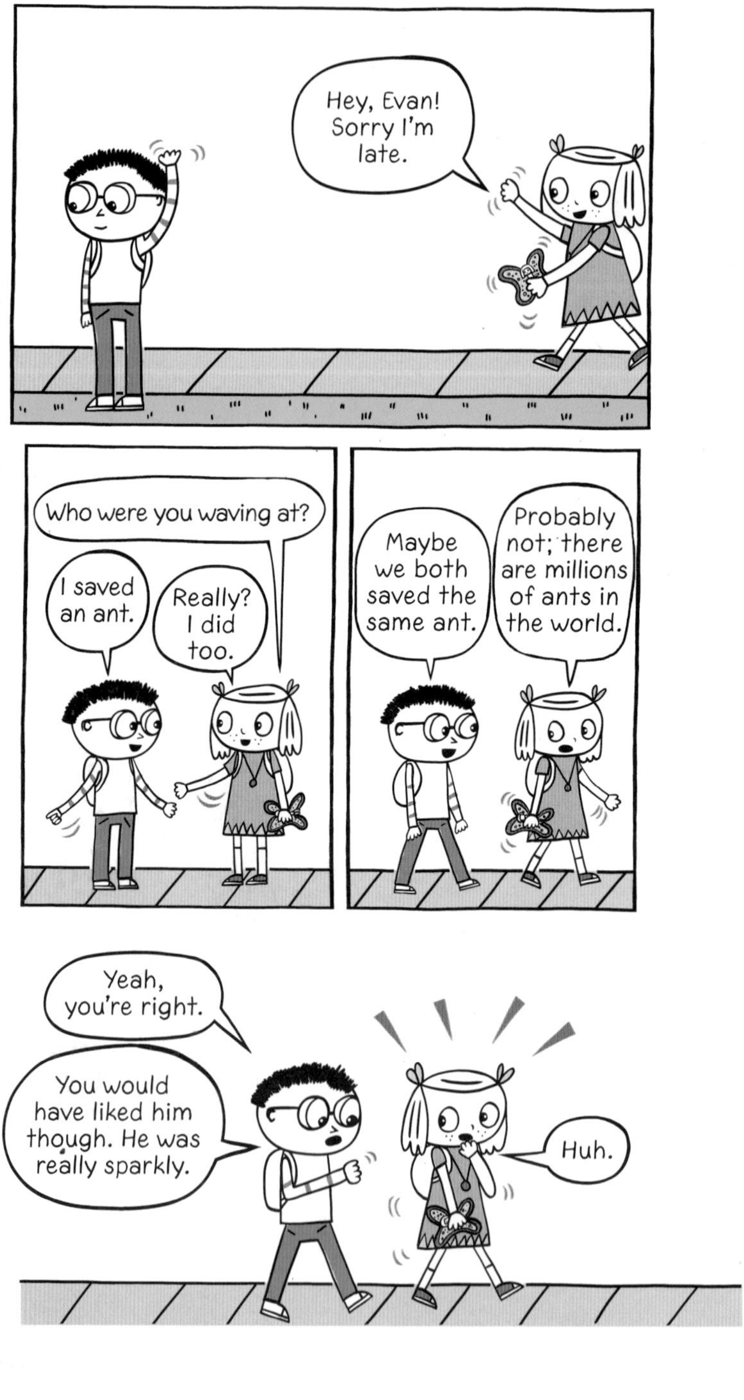

Hey, Evan! Sorry I'm late.
Who were you waving at?
I saved an ant.
Really? I did too.
Maybe we both saved the same ant.
Probably not; there are millions of ants in the world.
Yeah, you're right.
You would have liked him though. He was really sparkly.
Huh.

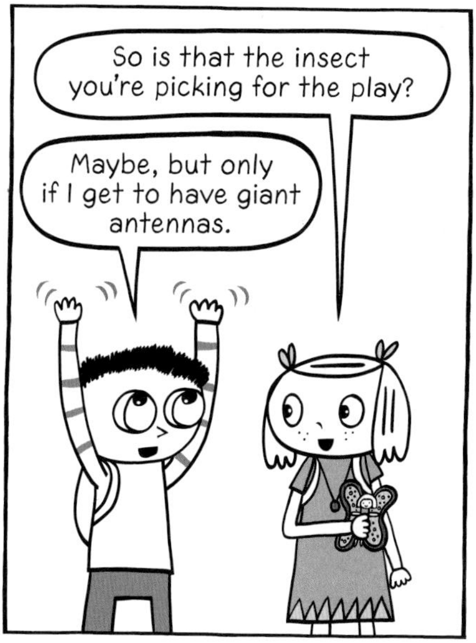
So is that the insect you're picking for the play?
Maybe, but only if I get to have giant antennas.

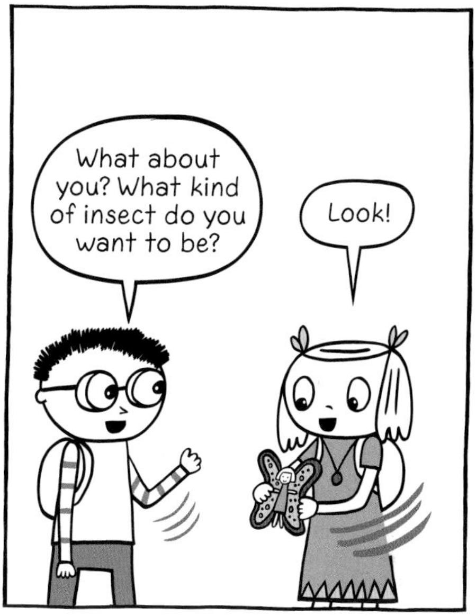
What about you? What kind of insect do you want to be?
Look!

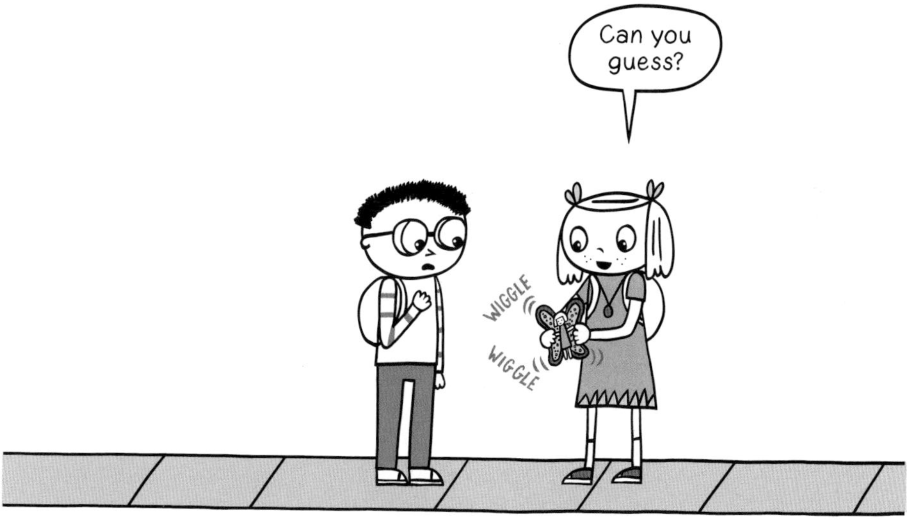
Can you guess?
WIGGLE
WIGGLE

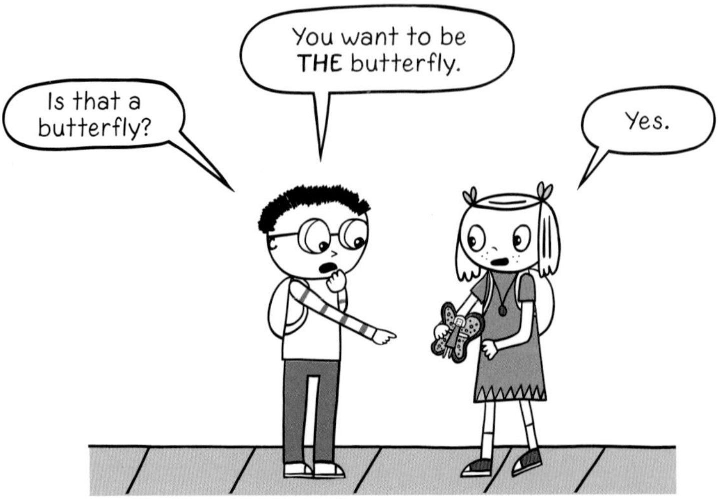
Is that a butterfly?
You want to be THE butterfly.
Yes.

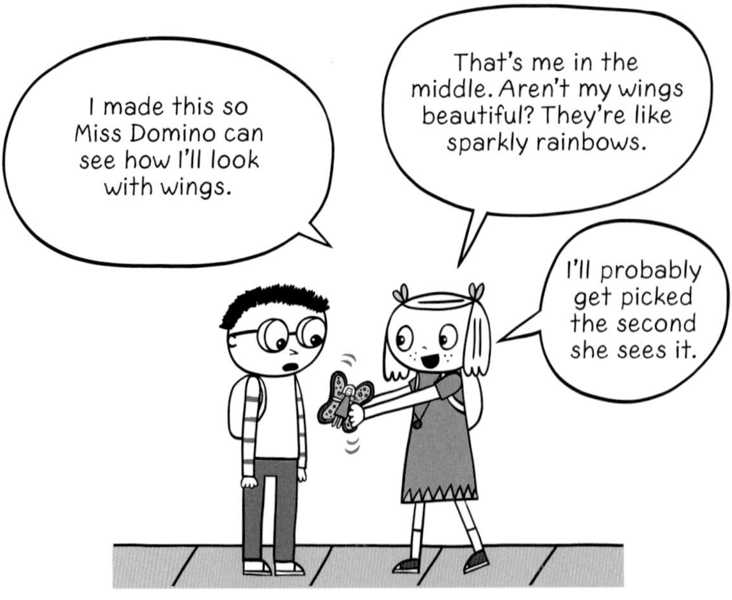
I made this so Miss Domino can see how I'll look with wings.
That's me in the middle. Aren't my wings beautiful? They're like sparkly rainbows.
I'll probably get picked the second she sees it.

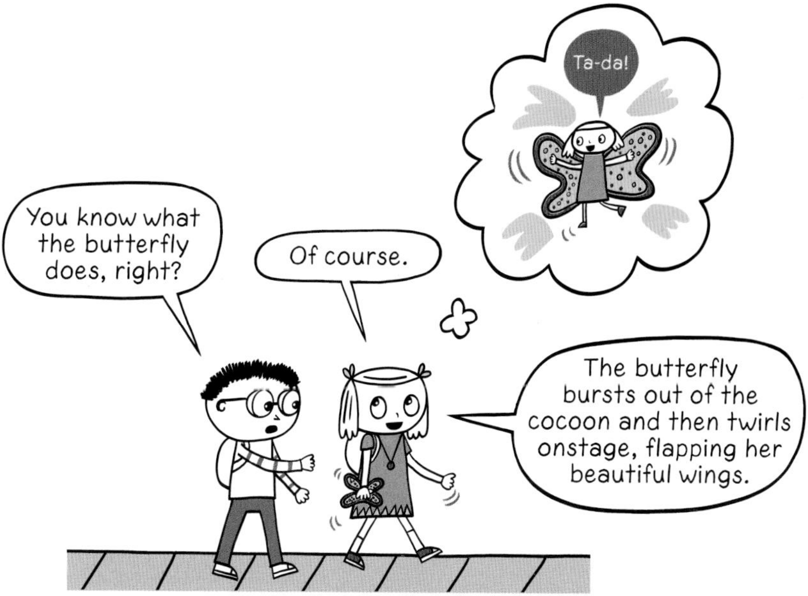
You know what the butterfly does, right?
Of course.
Ta-da!
The butterfly bursts out of the cocoon and then twirls onstage, flapping her beautiful wings.

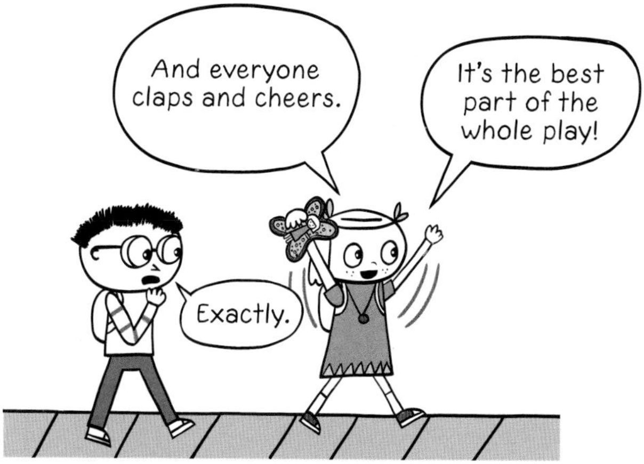
And everyone claps and cheers.
It's the best part of the whole play!
Exactly.

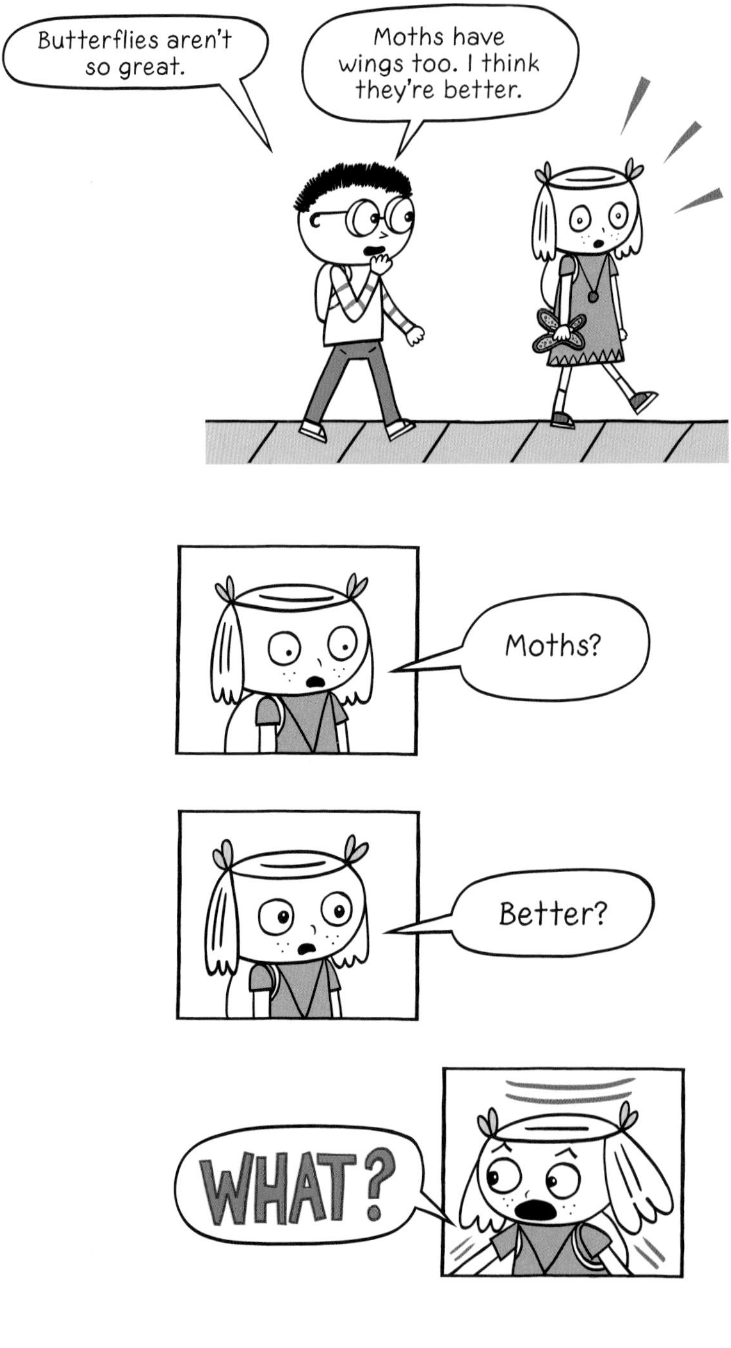
Butterflies aren't so great.
Moths have wings too. I think they're better.
Moths?
Better?
WHAT?

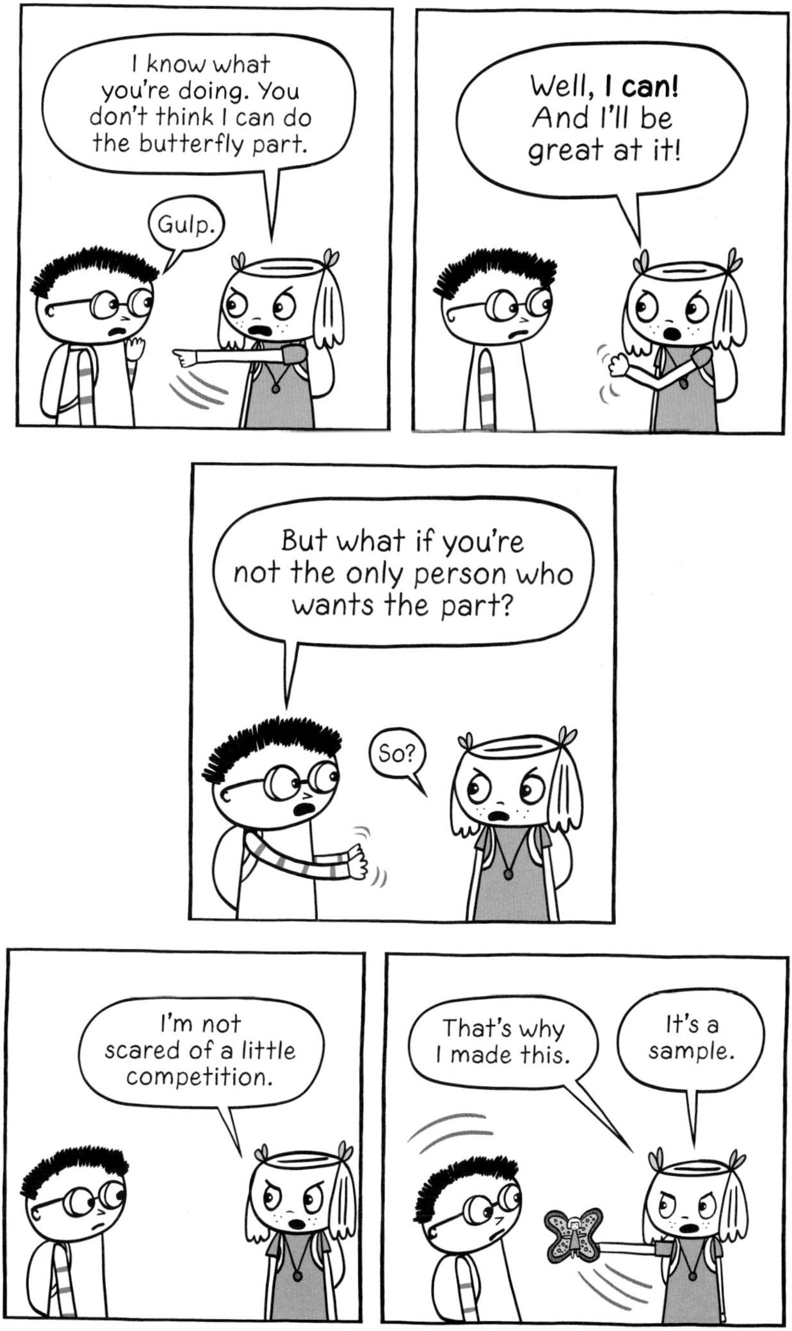
I know what you're doing. You don't think I can do the butterfly part.
Gulp.
Well, **I can!** And I'll be great at it!
But what if you're not the only person who wants the part?
So?
I'm not scared of a little competition.
That's why I made this.
It's a sample.

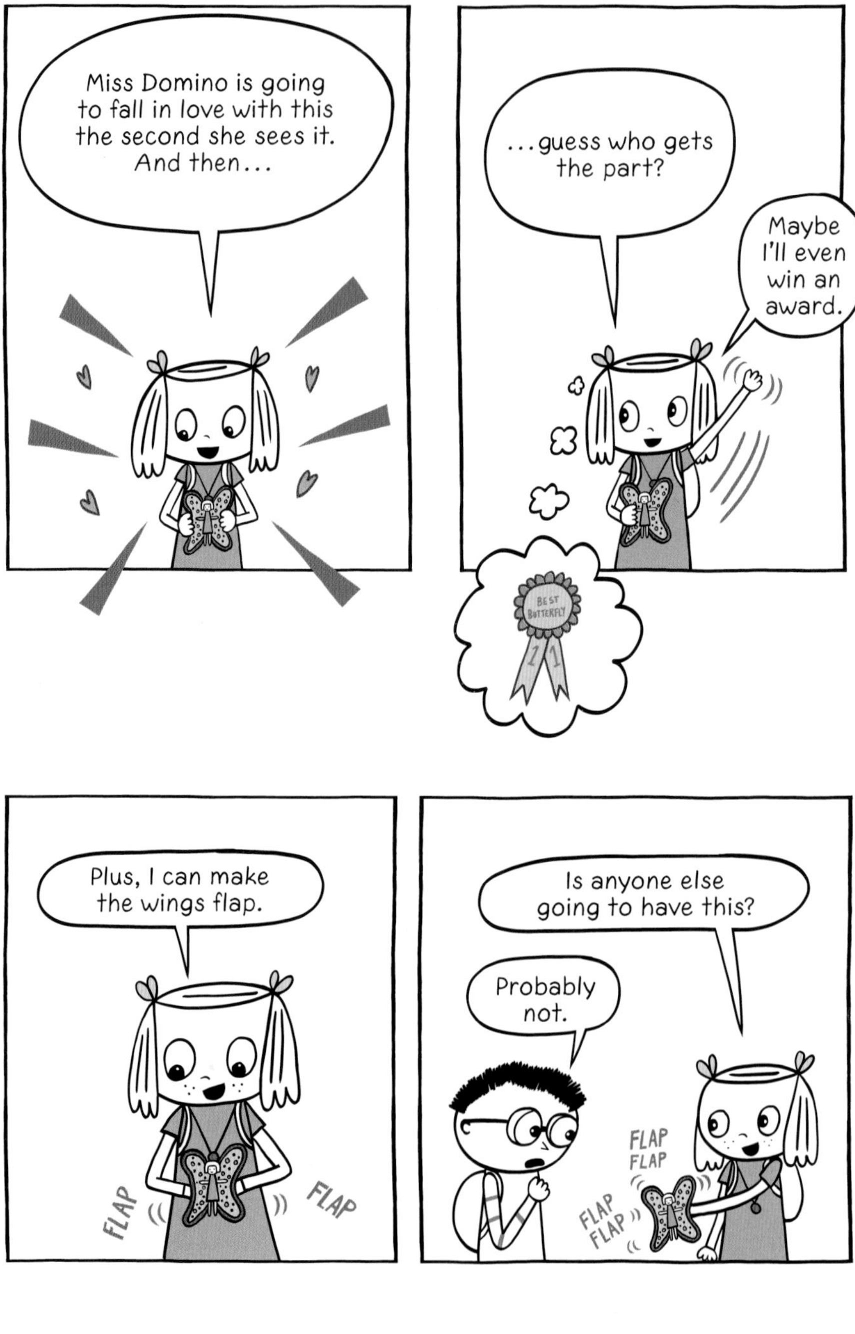
Miss Domino is going to fall in love with this the second she sees it. And then...
...guess who gets the part?
Maybe I'll even win an award.
BEST BUTTERFLY
Plus, I can make the wings flap.
FLAP
FLAP
Is anyone else going to have this?
Probably not.
FLAP FLAP
FLAP FLAP

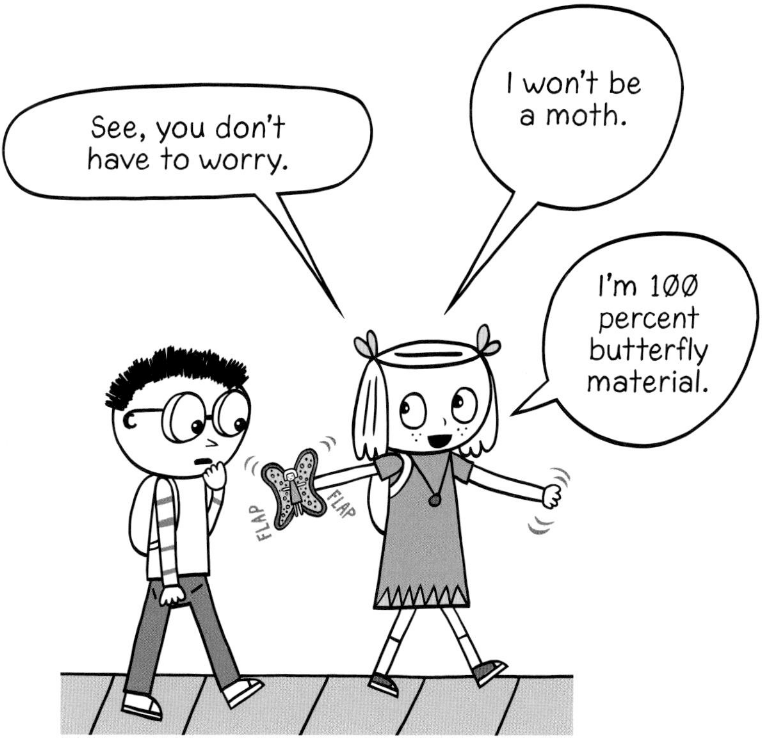
See, you don't have to worry.
I won't be a moth.
I'm 100 percent butterfly material.
FLAP
FLAP

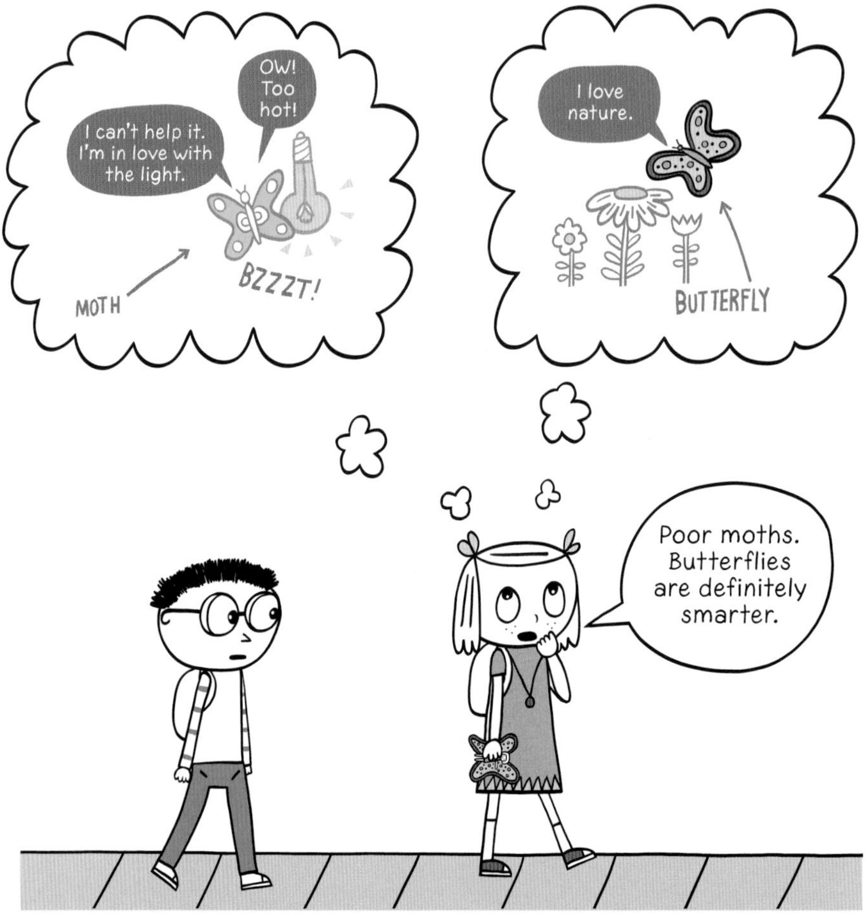
I can't help it. I'm in love with the light.
OW! Too hot!
BZZZT!
MOTH
I love nature.
BUTTERFLY
Poor moths. Butterflies are definitely smarter.

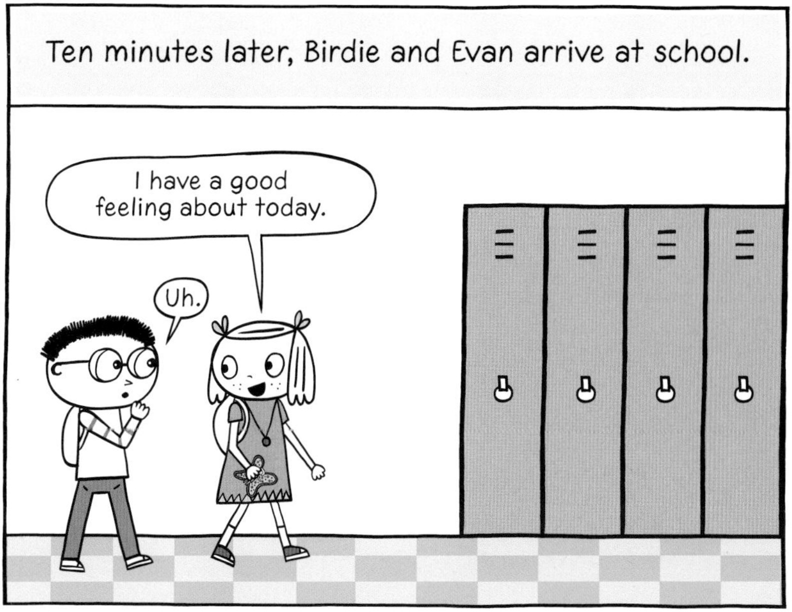
Ten minutes later, Birdie and Evan arrive at school.
I have a good feeling about today.
Uh.

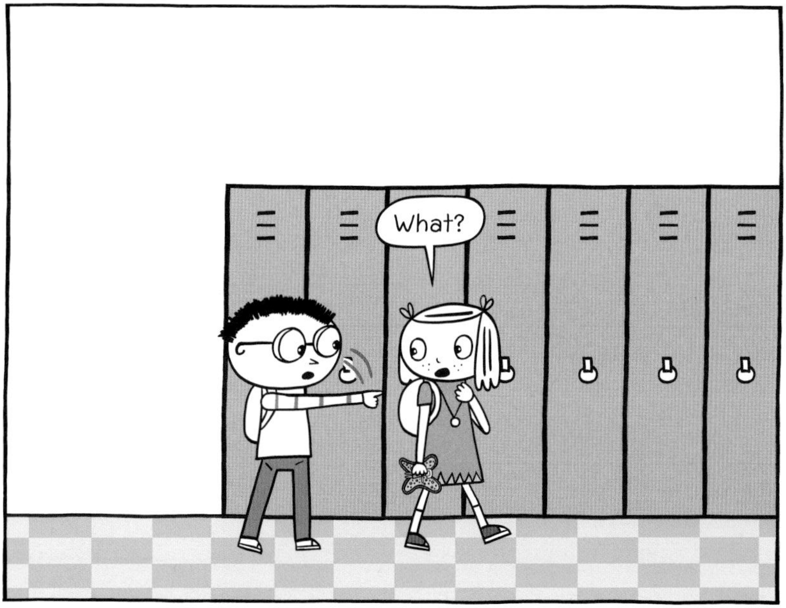
What?

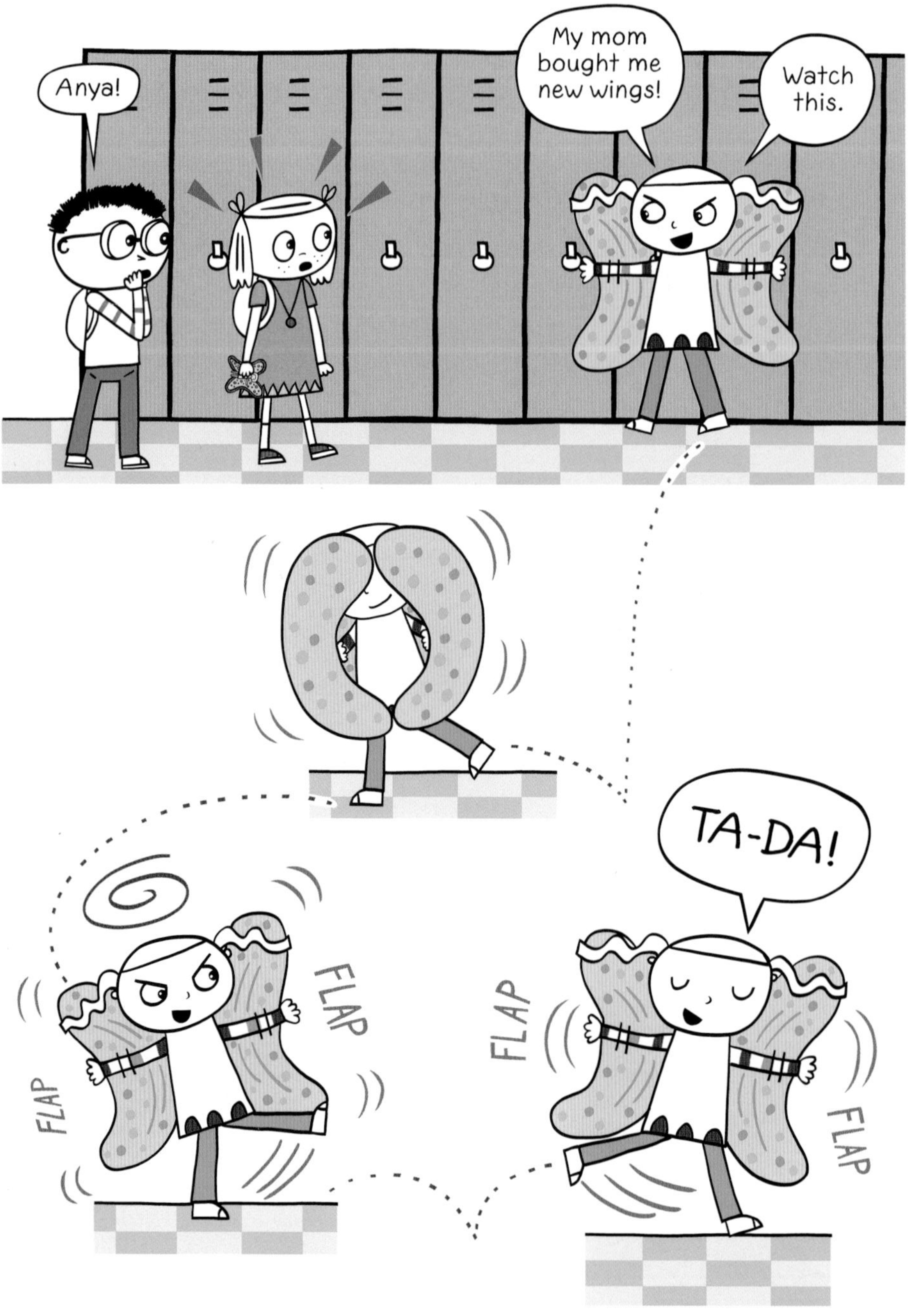
Anya!
My mom bought me new wings!
Watch this.
FLAP
FLAP
TA-DA!
FLAP
FLAP

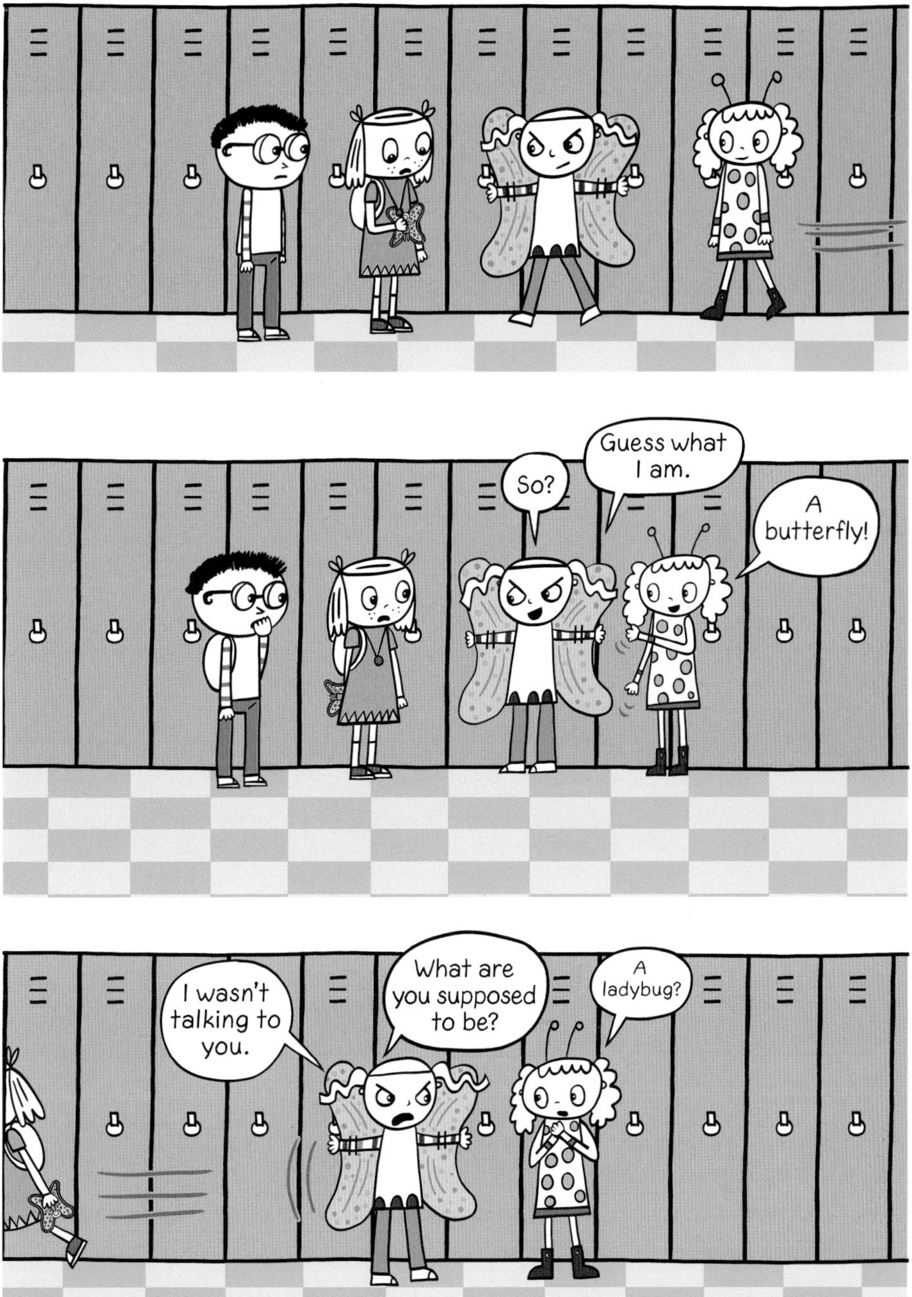
So?
Guess what I am.
A butterfly!
I wasn't talking to you.
What are you supposed to be?
A ladybug?

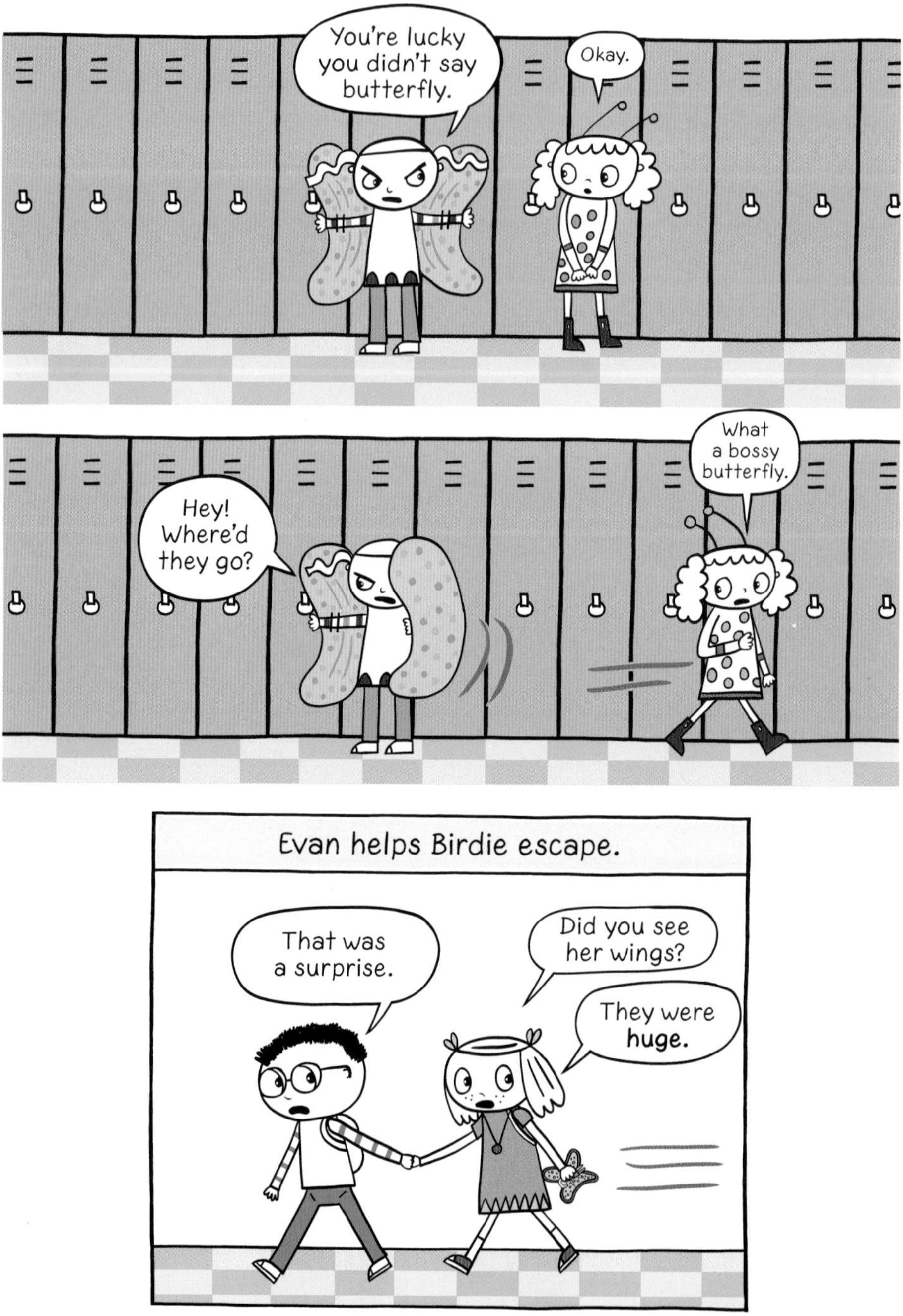
You're lucky you didn't say butterfly.
Okay.
Hey! Where'd they go?
What a bossy butterfly.
Evan helps Birdie escape.
That was a surprise.
Did you see her wings?
They were **huge.**

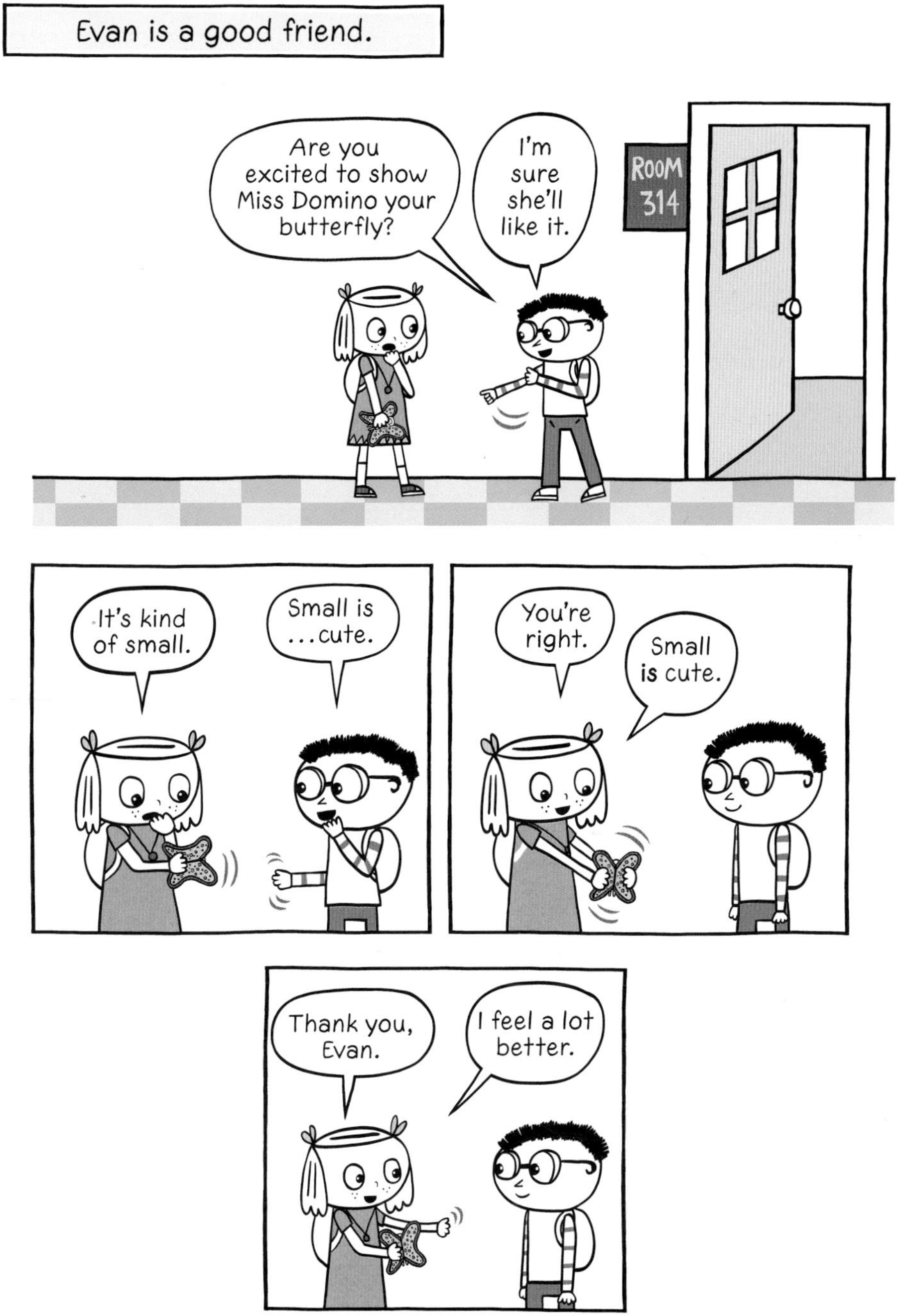
Evan is a good friend.
Are you excited to show Miss Domino your butterfly?
I'm sure she'll like it.
ROOM 314
It's kind of small.
Small is . . . cute.
You're right.
Small **is** cute.
Thank you, Evan.
I feel a lot better.

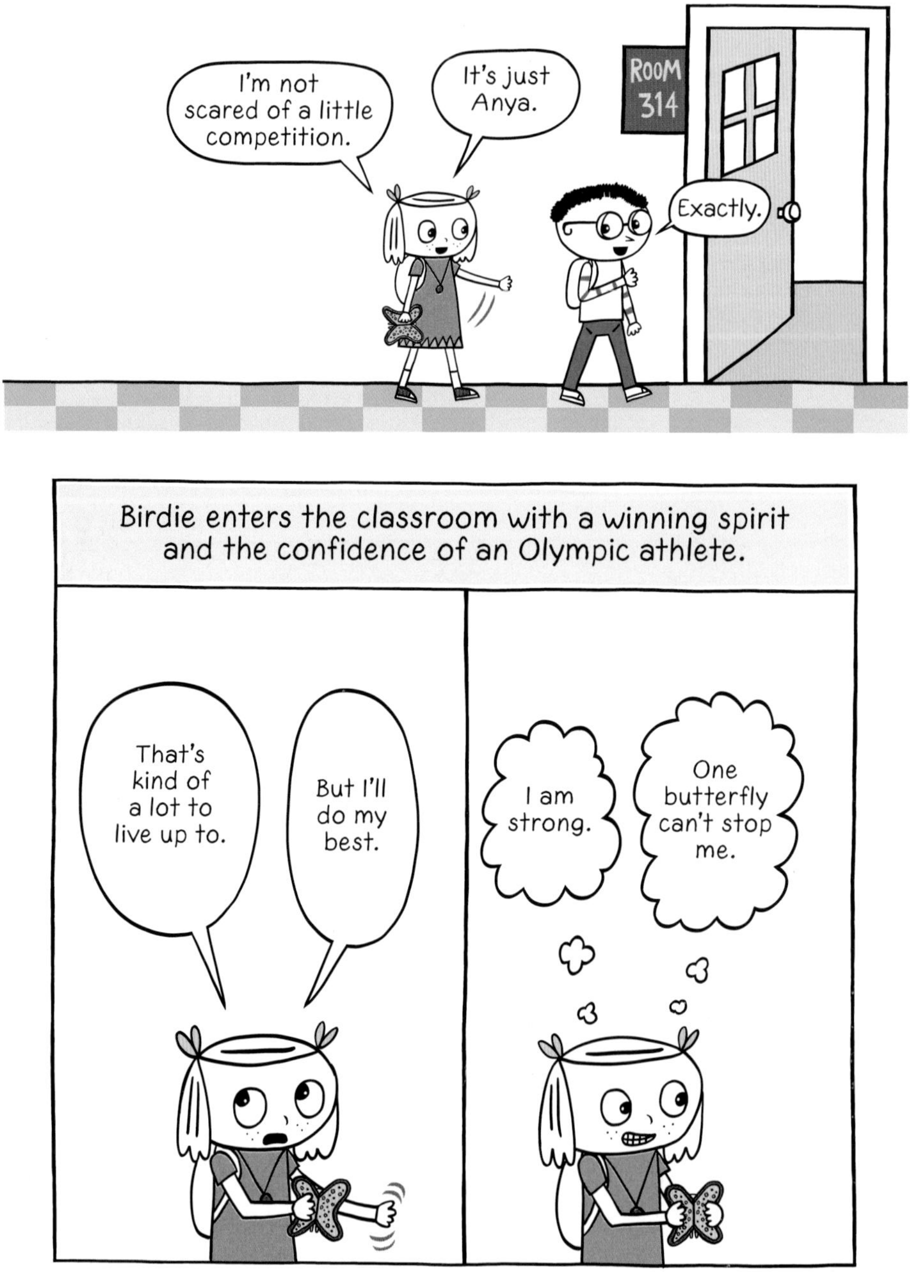
ROOM 314
I'm not scared of a little competition.
It's just Anya.
Exactly.
Birdie enters the classroom with a winning spirit and the confidence of an Olympic athlete.
That's kind of a lot to live up to.
But I'll do my best.
I am strong.
One butterfly can't stop me.

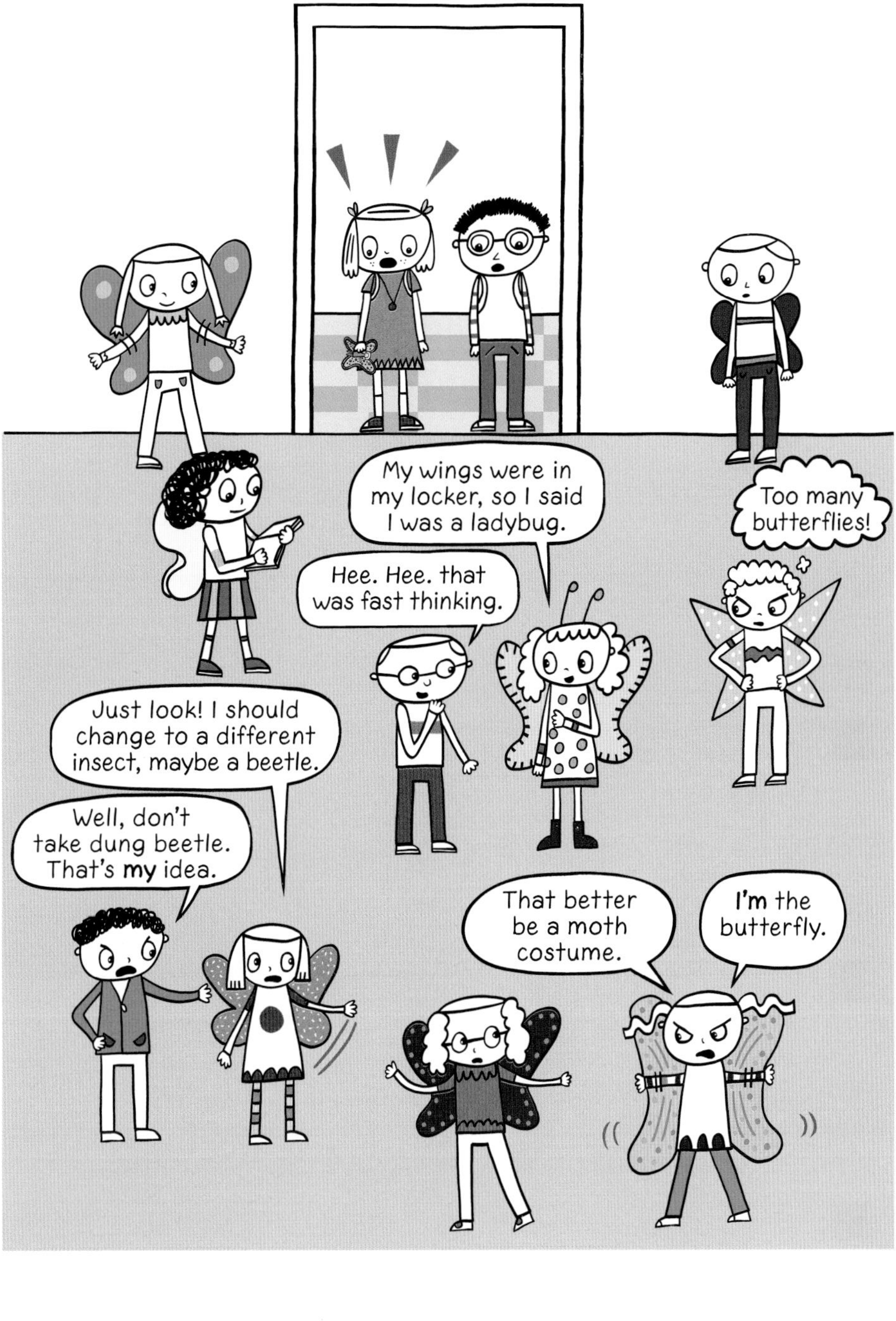
My wings were in my locker, so I said I was a ladybug.
Hee. Hee. that was fast thinking.
Too many butterflies!
Just look! I should change to a different insect, maybe a beetle.
Well, don't take dung beetle. That's **my** idea.
That better be a moth costume.
I'm the butterfly.

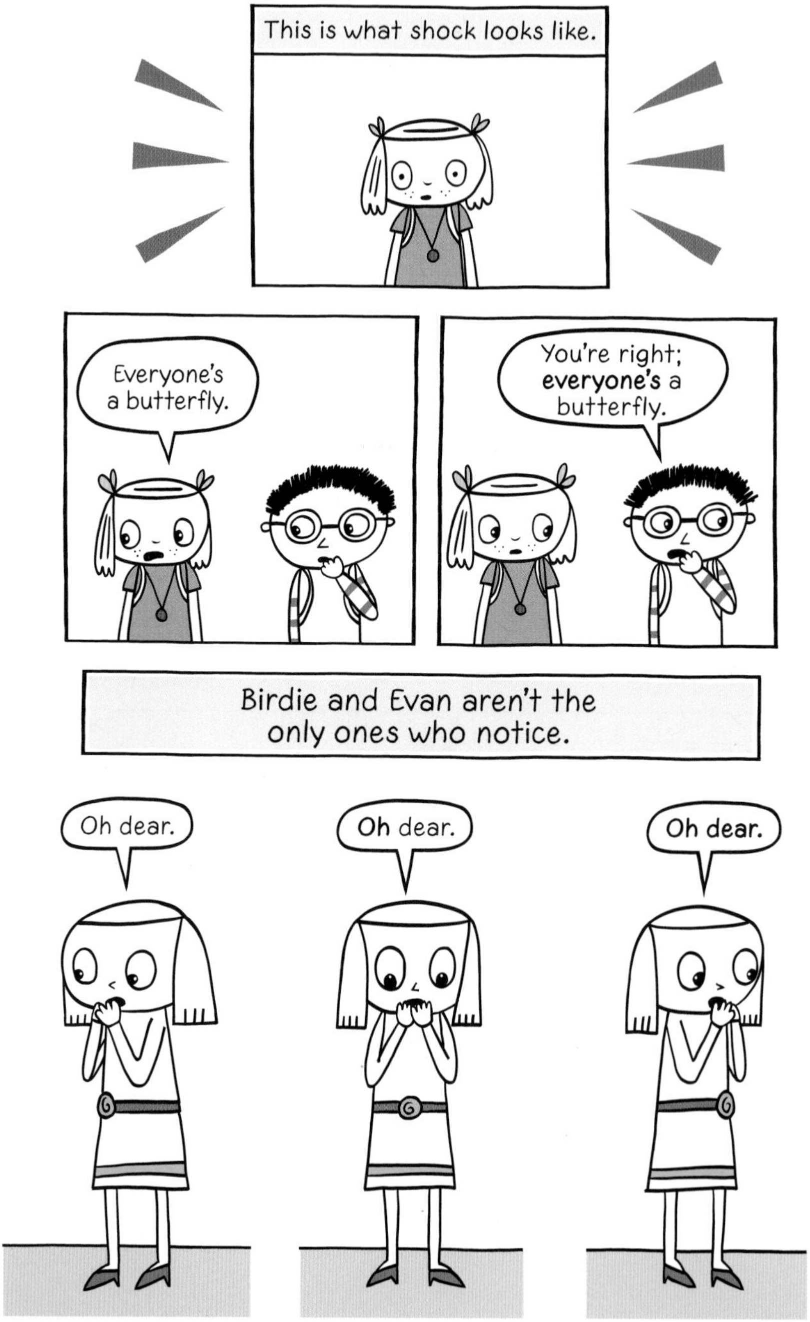
This is what shock looks like.
Everyone's a butterfly.
You're right; **everyone's** a butterfly.
Birdie and Evan aren't the only ones who notice.
Oh dear.
Oh dear.
Oh dear.

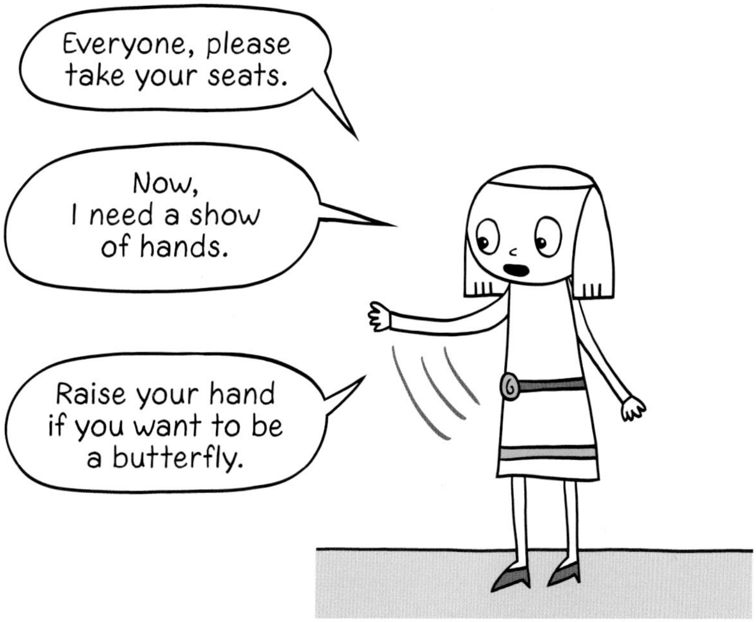
Everyone, please take your seats.
Now, I need a show of hands.
Raise your hand if you want to be a butterfly.

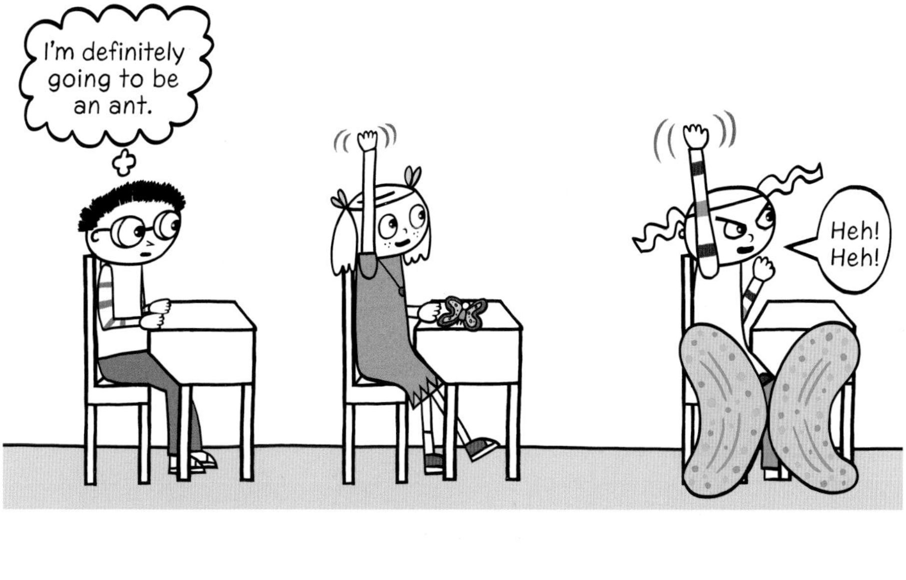
I'm definitely going to be an ant.
Heh! Heh!

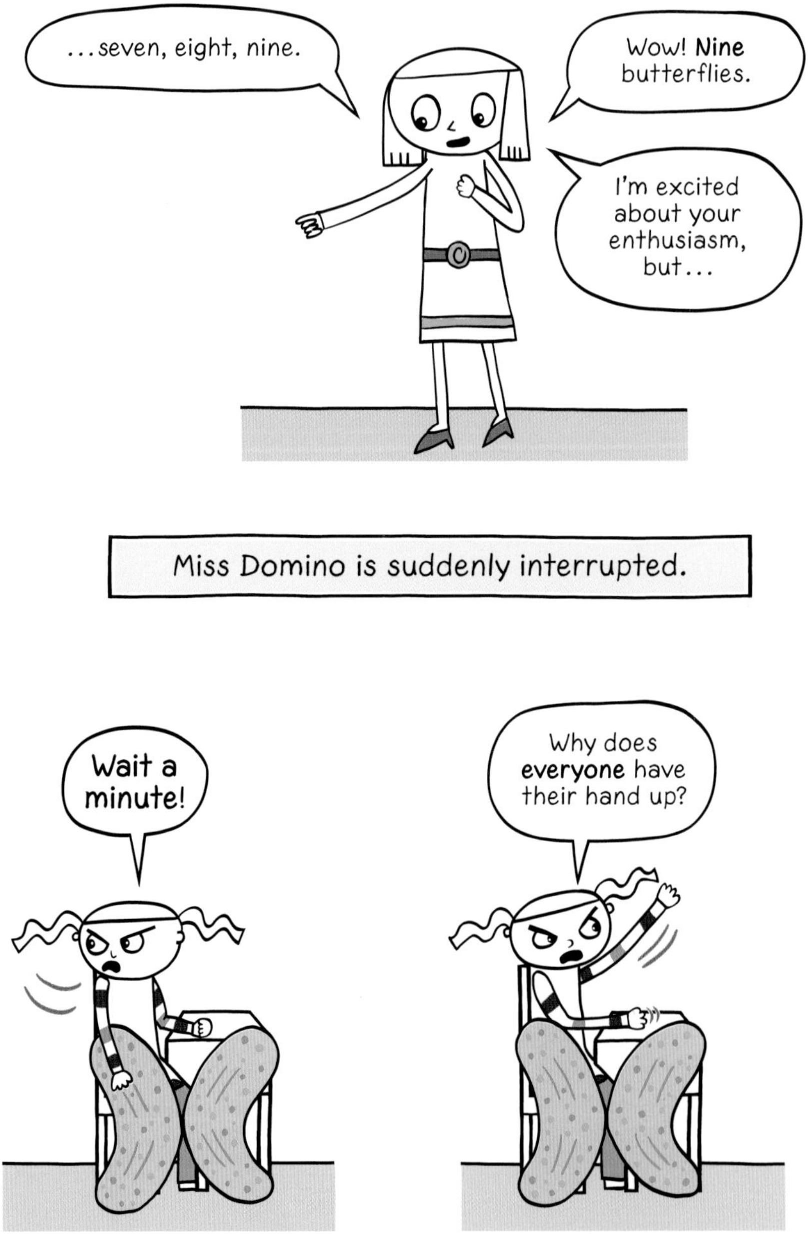
...seven, eight, nine.
Wow! **Nine** butterflies.
I'm excited about your enthusiasm, but...
Miss Domino is suddenly interrupted.
Wait a minute!
Why does **everyone** have their hand up?

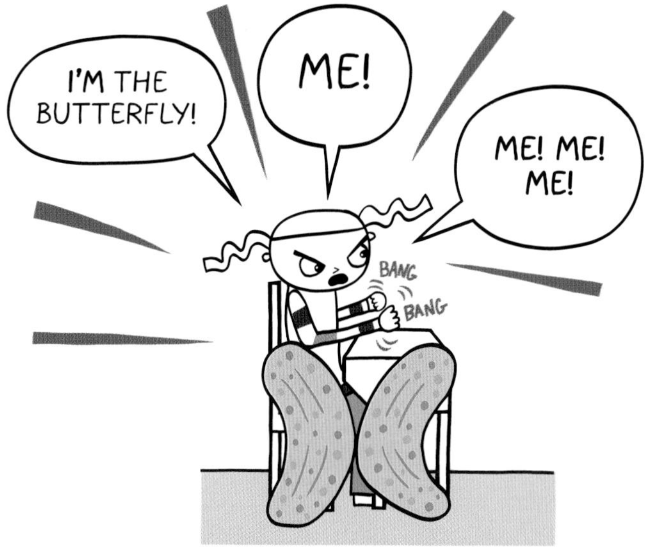
I'M THE BUTTERFLY!
ME!
ME! ME! ME!
BANG
BANG

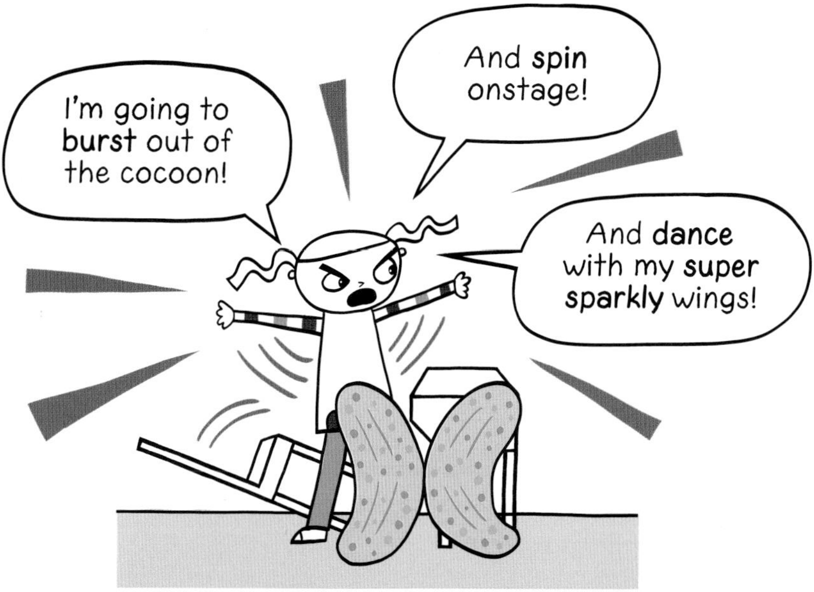
I'm going to **burst** out of the cocoon!
And **spin** onstage!
And **dance** with my **super sparkly** wings!

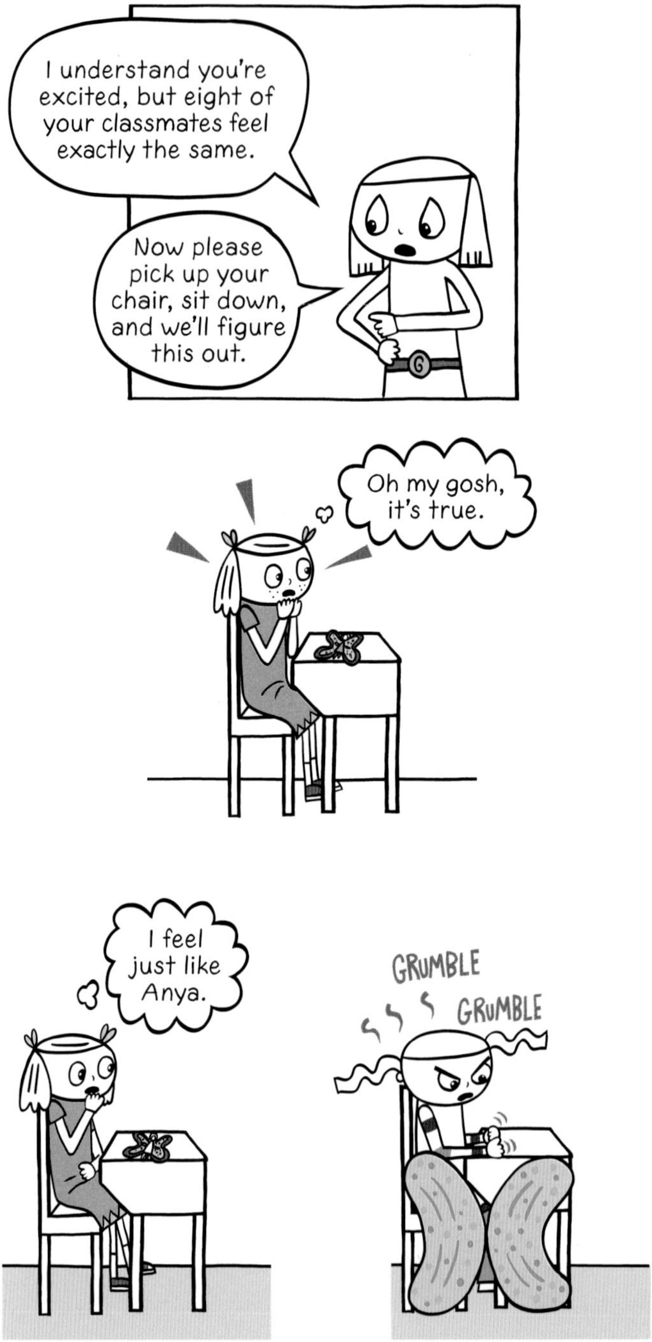
I understand you're excited, but eight of your classmates feel exactly the same.
Now please pick up your chair, sit down, and we'll figure this out.
Oh my gosh, it's true.
I feel just like Anya.
GRUMBLE
GRUMBLE

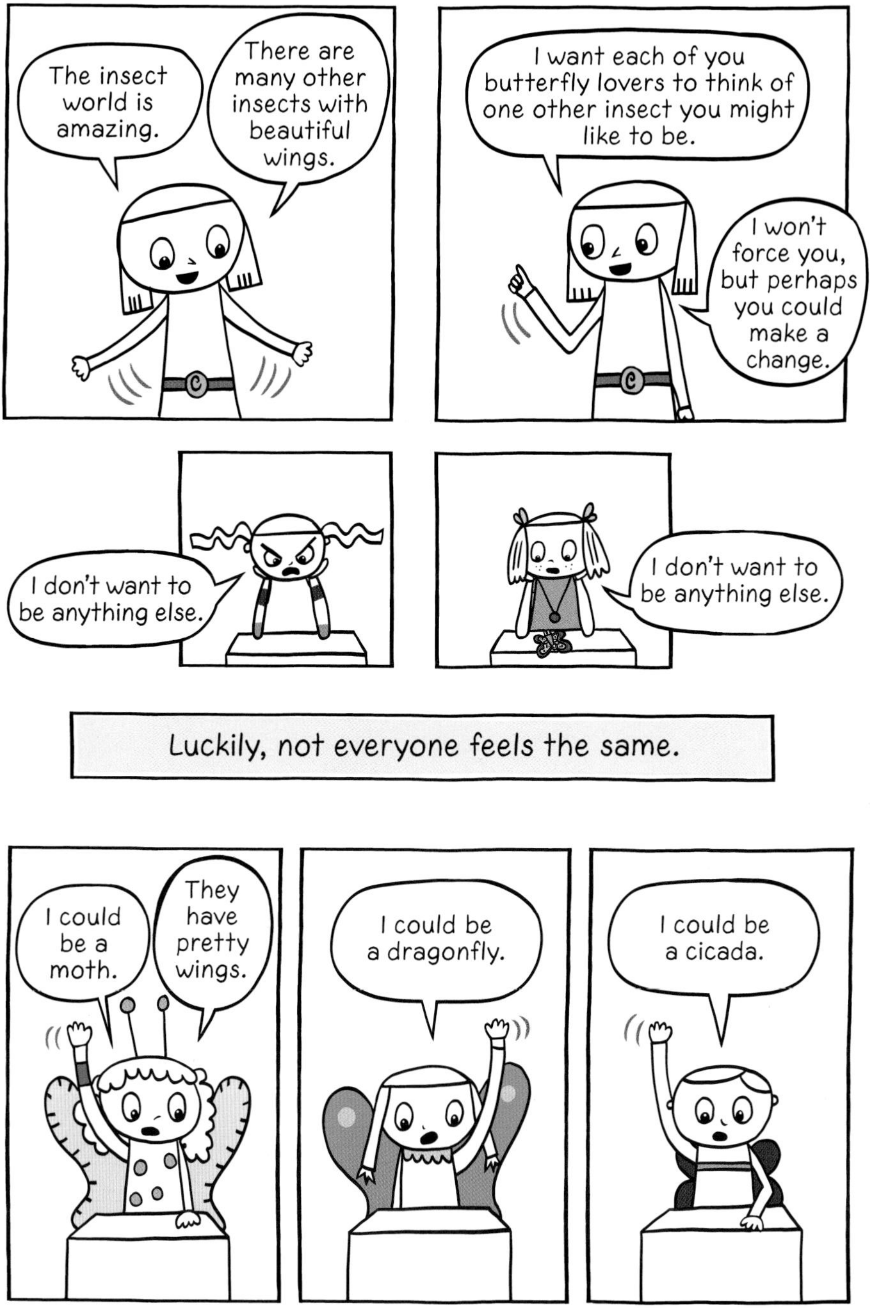
The insect world is amazing.
There are many other insects with beautiful wings.
I want each of you butterfly lovers to think of one other insect you might like to be.
I won't force you, but perhaps you could make a change.
I don't want to be anything else.
I don't want to be anything else.
Luckily, not everyone feels the same.
I could be a moth.
They have pretty wings.
I could be a dragonfly.
I could be a cicada.

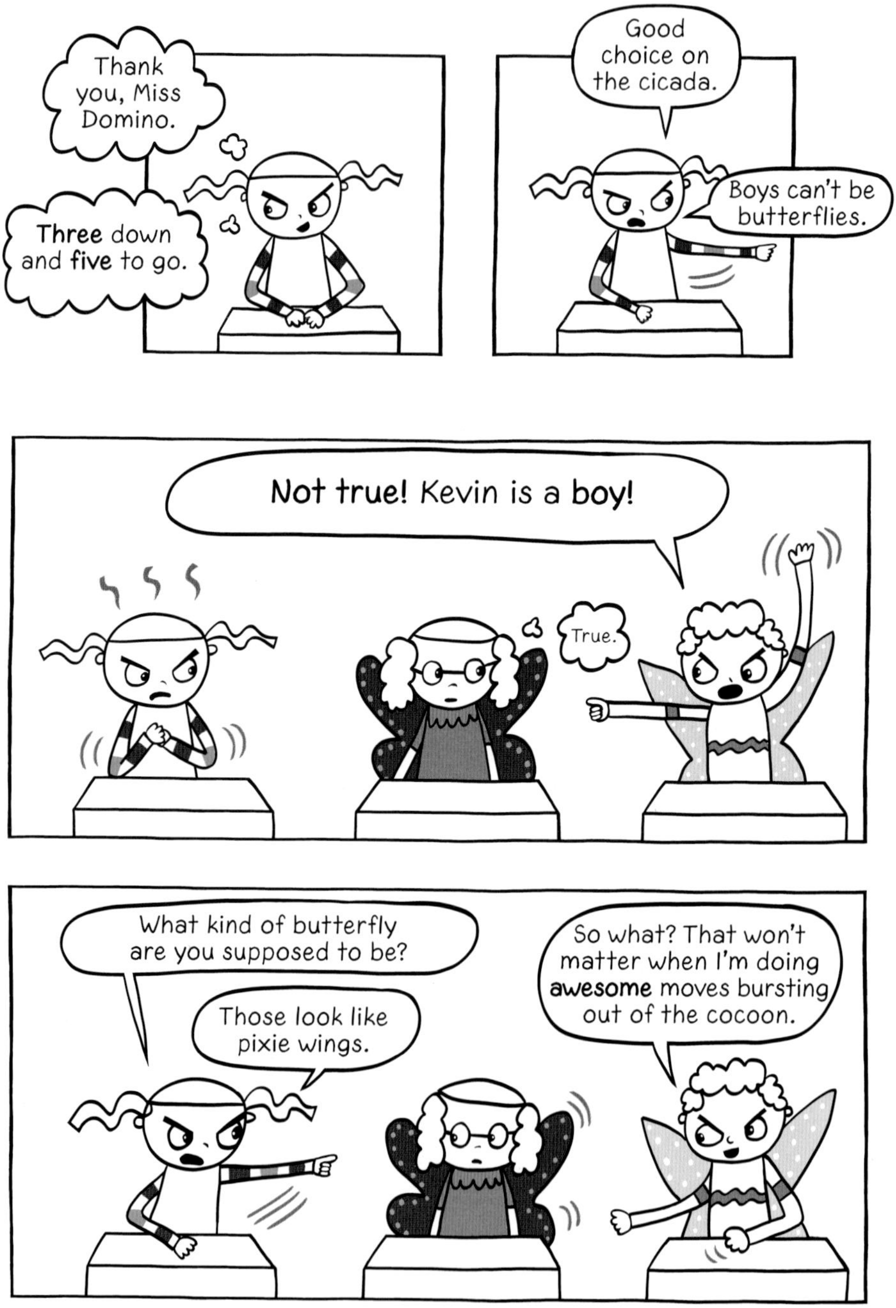
Thank you, Miss Domino.
Three down and five to go.
Good choice on the cicada.
Boys can't be butterflies.
Not true! Kevin is a boy!
True.
What kind of butterfly are you supposed to be?
Those look like pixie wings.
So what? That won't matter when I'm doing awesome moves bursting out of the cocoon.

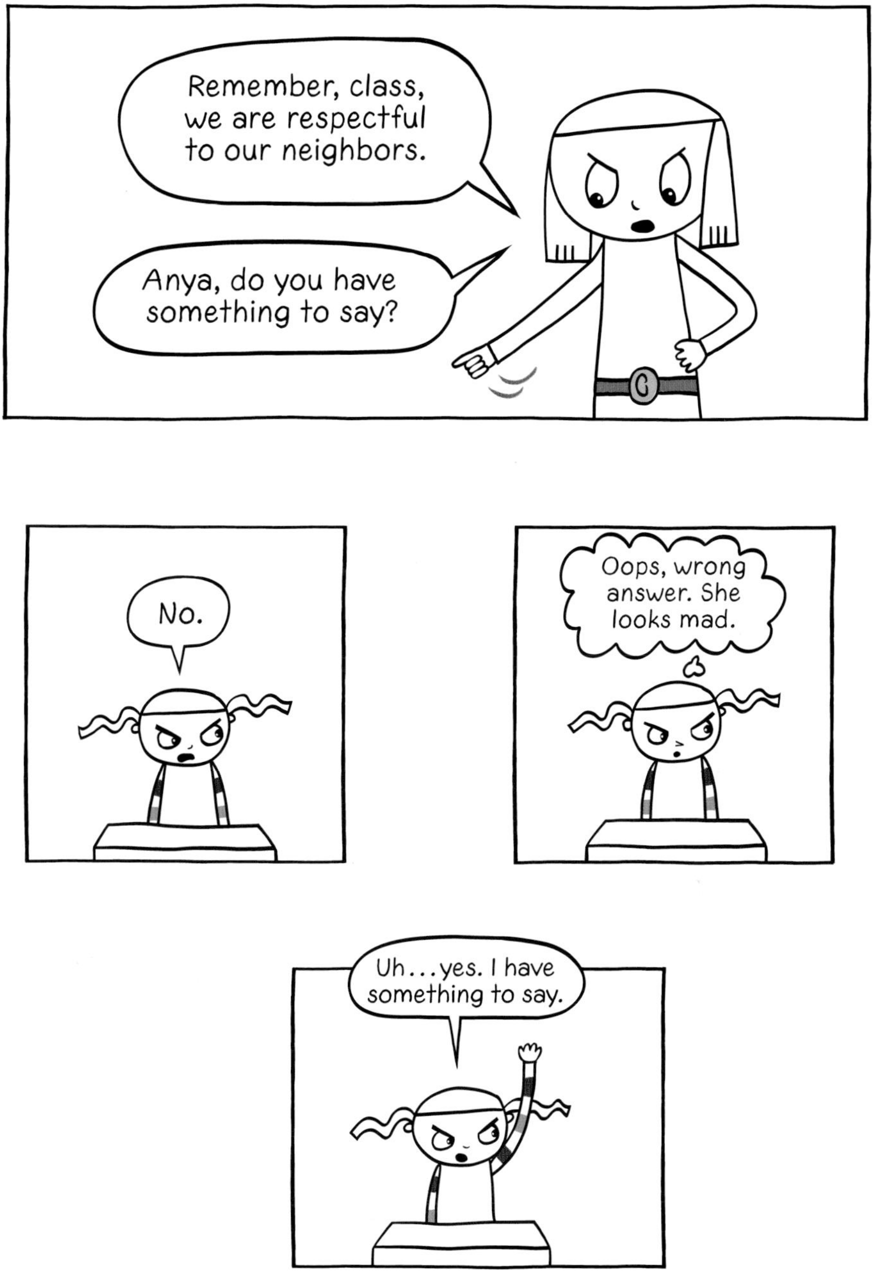
Remember, class, we are respectful to our neighbors.
Anya, do you have something to say?
No.
Oops, wrong answer. She looks mad.
Uh...yes. I have something to say.

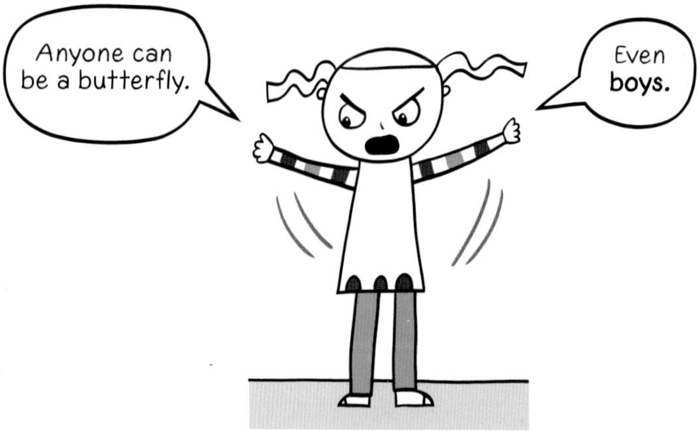
Anyone can be a butterfly.
Even **boys.**

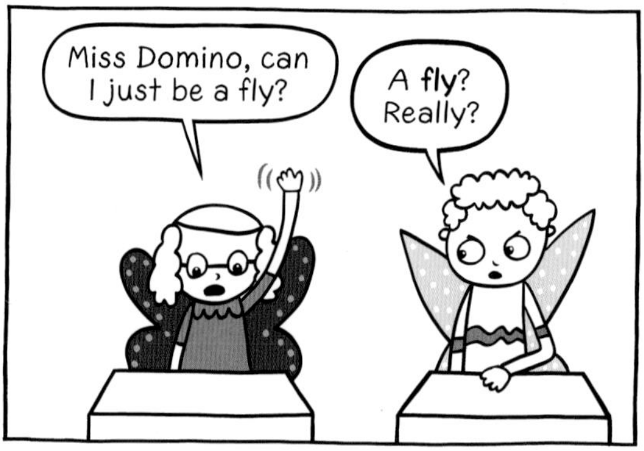
Miss Domino, can I just be a fly?
A **fly**? Really?

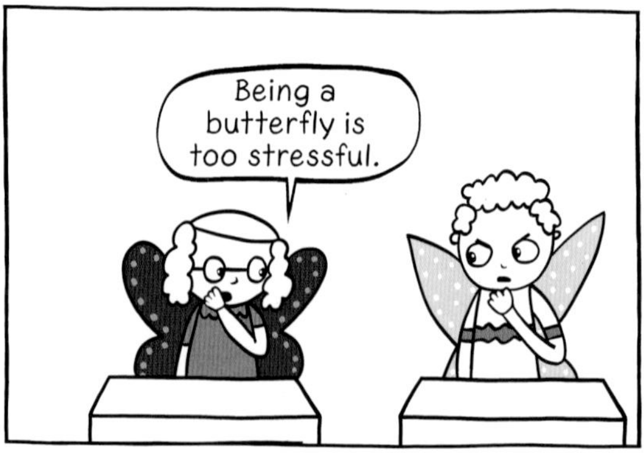
Being a butterfly is too stressful.

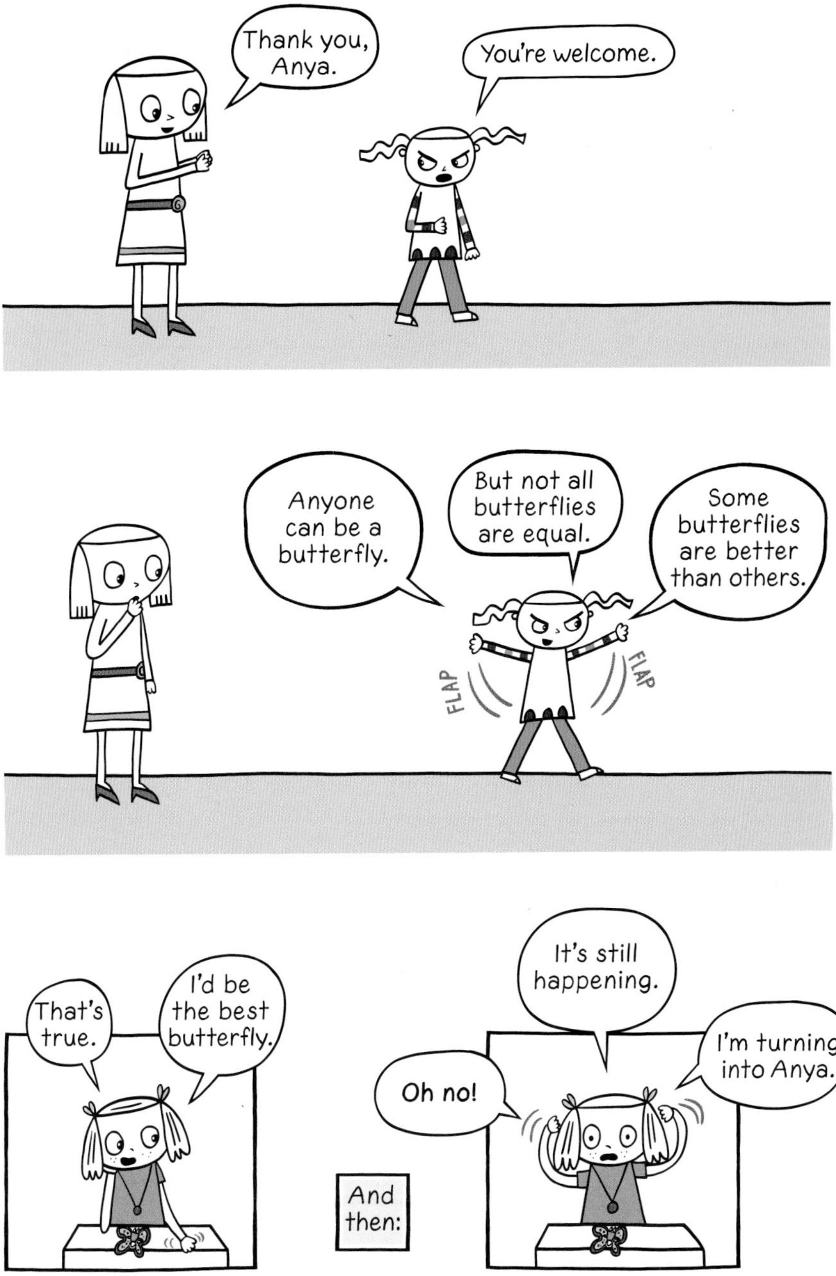
Thank you, Anya.
You're welcome.
Anyone can be a butterfly.
But not all butterflies are equal.
Some butterflies are better than others.
FLAP
FLAP
That's true.
I'd be the best butterfly.
And then:
It's still happening.
Oh no!
I'm turning into Anya.

Birdie's thoughts are interrupted
by a new announcement.

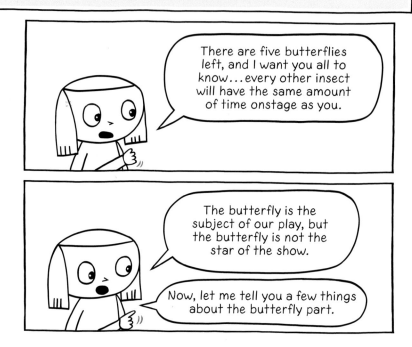

There are five butterflies left, and I want you all to know... every other insect will have the same amount of time onstage as you.

The butterfly is the subject of our play, but the butterfly is not the star of the show.

Now, let me tell you a few things about the butterfly part.

Birdie stops listening.

No matter what.

I don't care.

I still want to be the butterfly.

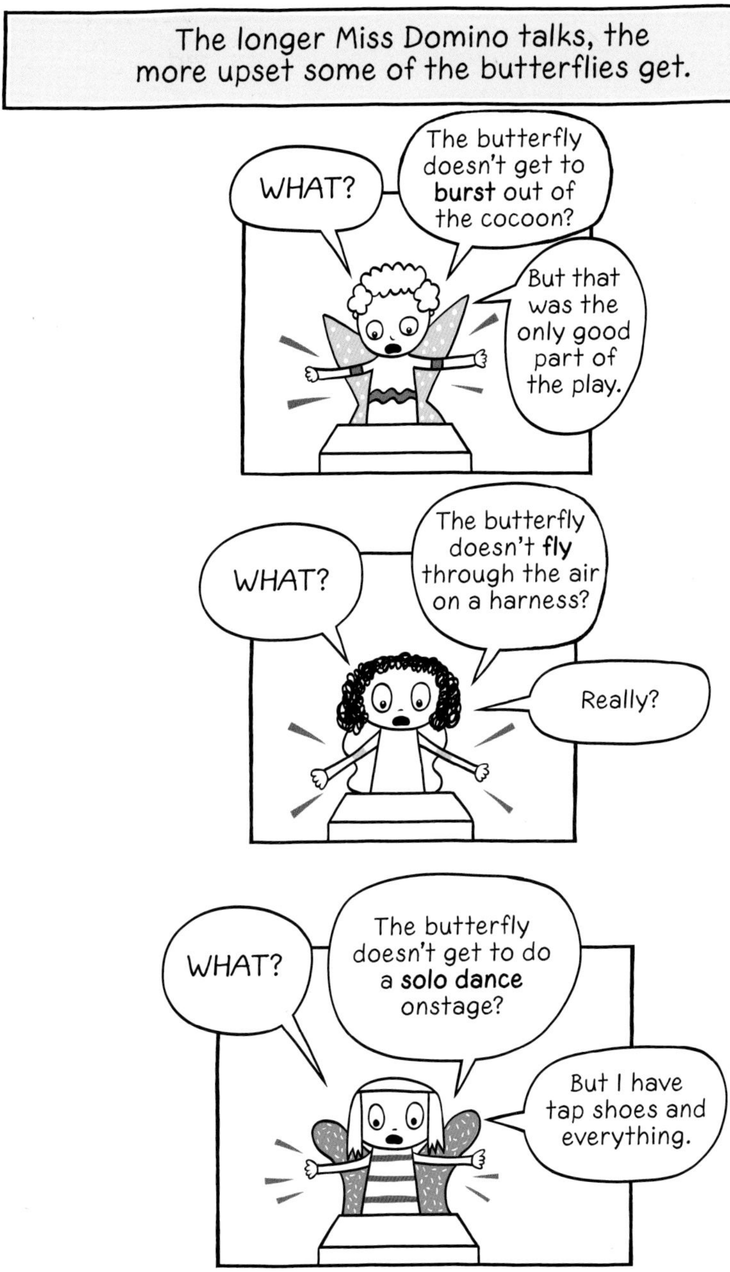
The longer Miss Domino talks, the more upset some of the butterflies get.
WHAT?
The butterfly doesn't get to **burst** out of the cocoon?
But that was the only good part of the play.
WHAT?
The butterfly doesn't **fly** through the air on a harness?
Really?
WHAT?
The butterfly doesn't get to do a **solo dance** onstage?
But I have tap shoes and everything.

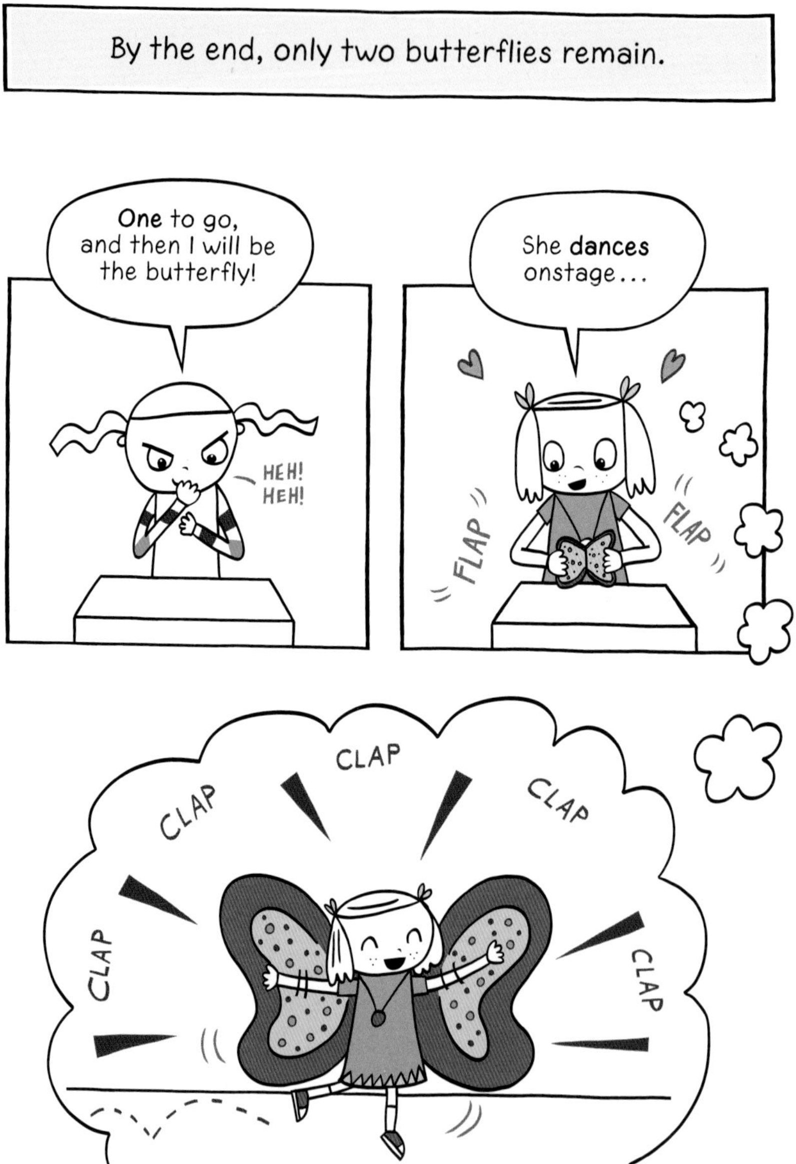
By the end, only two butterflies remain.
One to go, and then I will be the butterfly!
HEH! HEH!
She dances onstage...
FLAP
FLAP
CLAP
CLAP
CLAP
CLAP
CLAP
CLAP

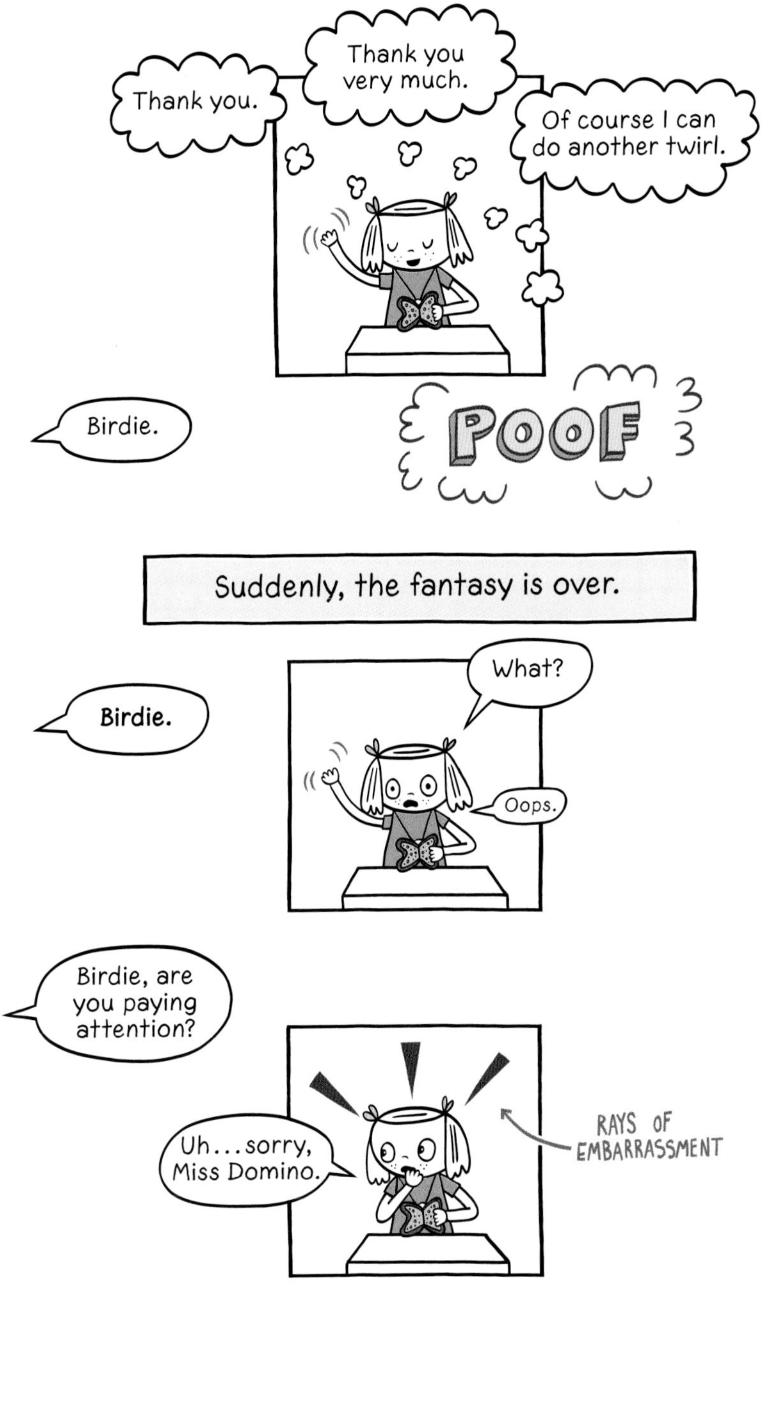
Thank you.
Thank you very much.
Of course I can do another twirl.
Birdie.
POOF
Suddenly, the fantasy is over.
Birdie.
What?
Oops.
Birdie, are you paying attention?
Uh...sorry, Miss Domino.
RAYS OF EMBARRASSMENT

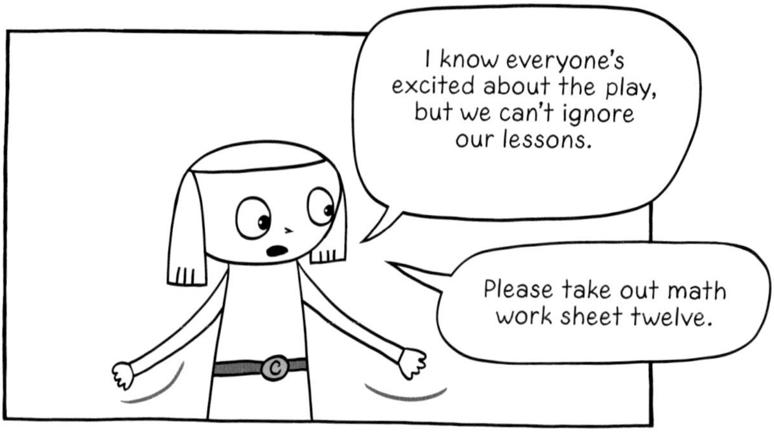
I know everyone's excited about the play, but we can't ignore our lessons.
Please take out math work sheet twelve.

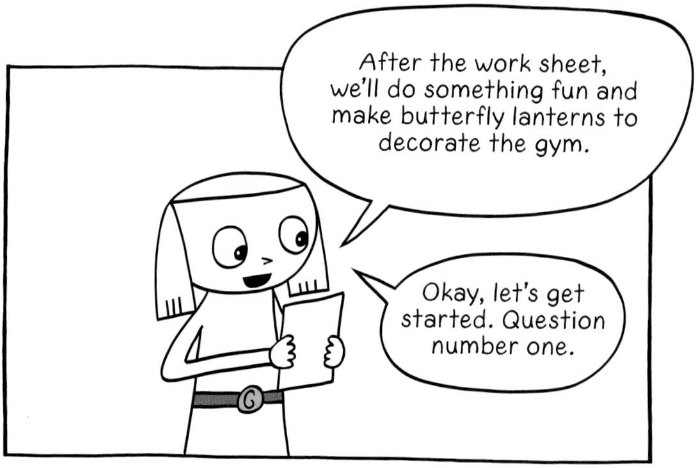
After the work sheet, we'll do something fun and make butterfly lanterns to decorate the gym.
Okay, let's get started. Question number one.

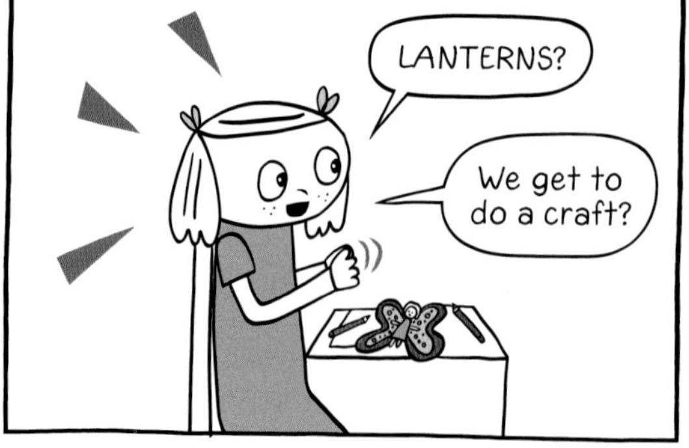
LANTERNS?
We get to do a craft?

Birdie can't wait to share the good news.

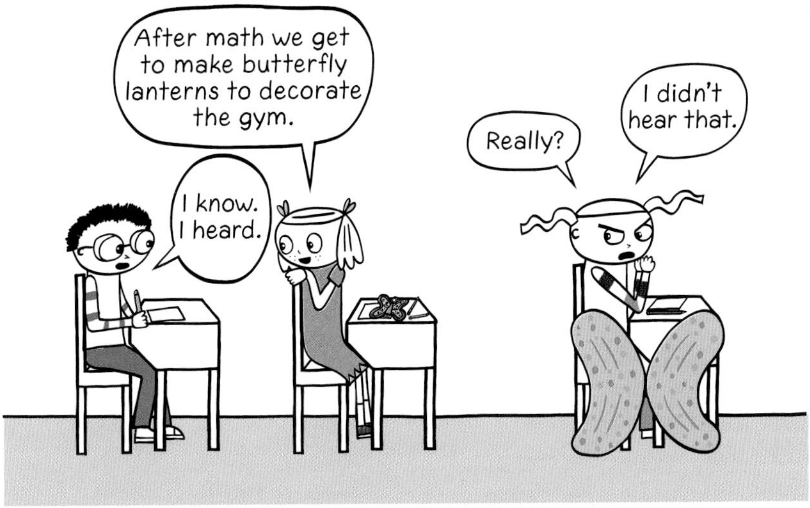
After math we get to make butterfly lanterns to decorate the gym.
I know. I heard.
Really?
I didn't hear that.

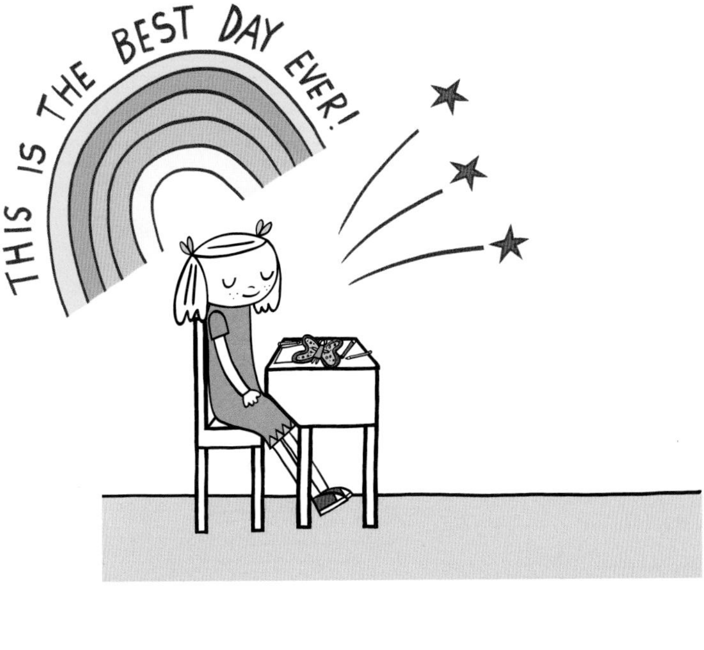
THIS IS THE BEST DAY EVER!

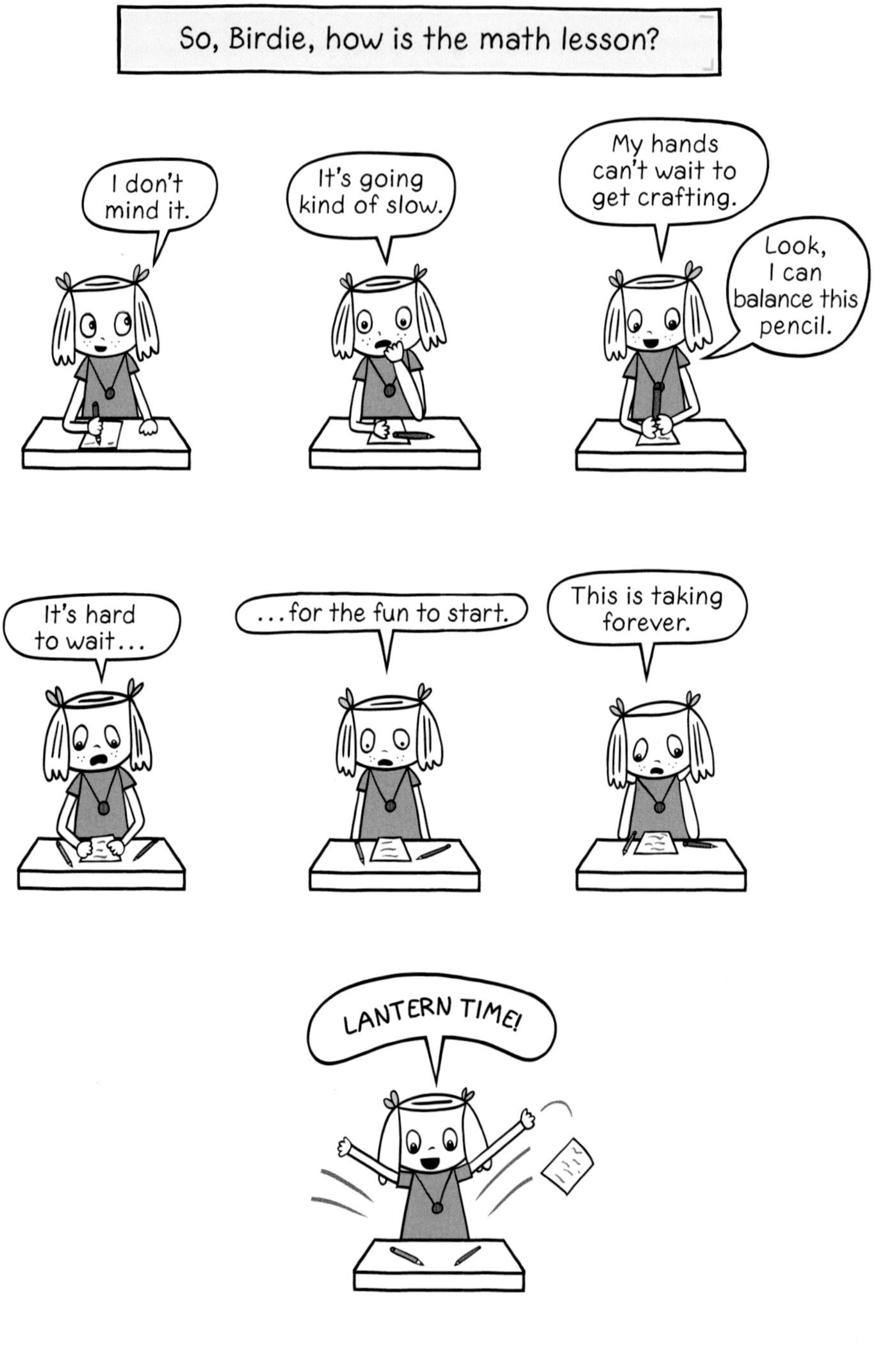

So, Birdie, how is the math lesson?
I don't mind it.
It's going kind of slow.
My hands can't wait to get crafting.
Look, I can balance this pencil.
It's hard to wait...
...for the fun to start.
This is taking forever.
LANTERN TIME!

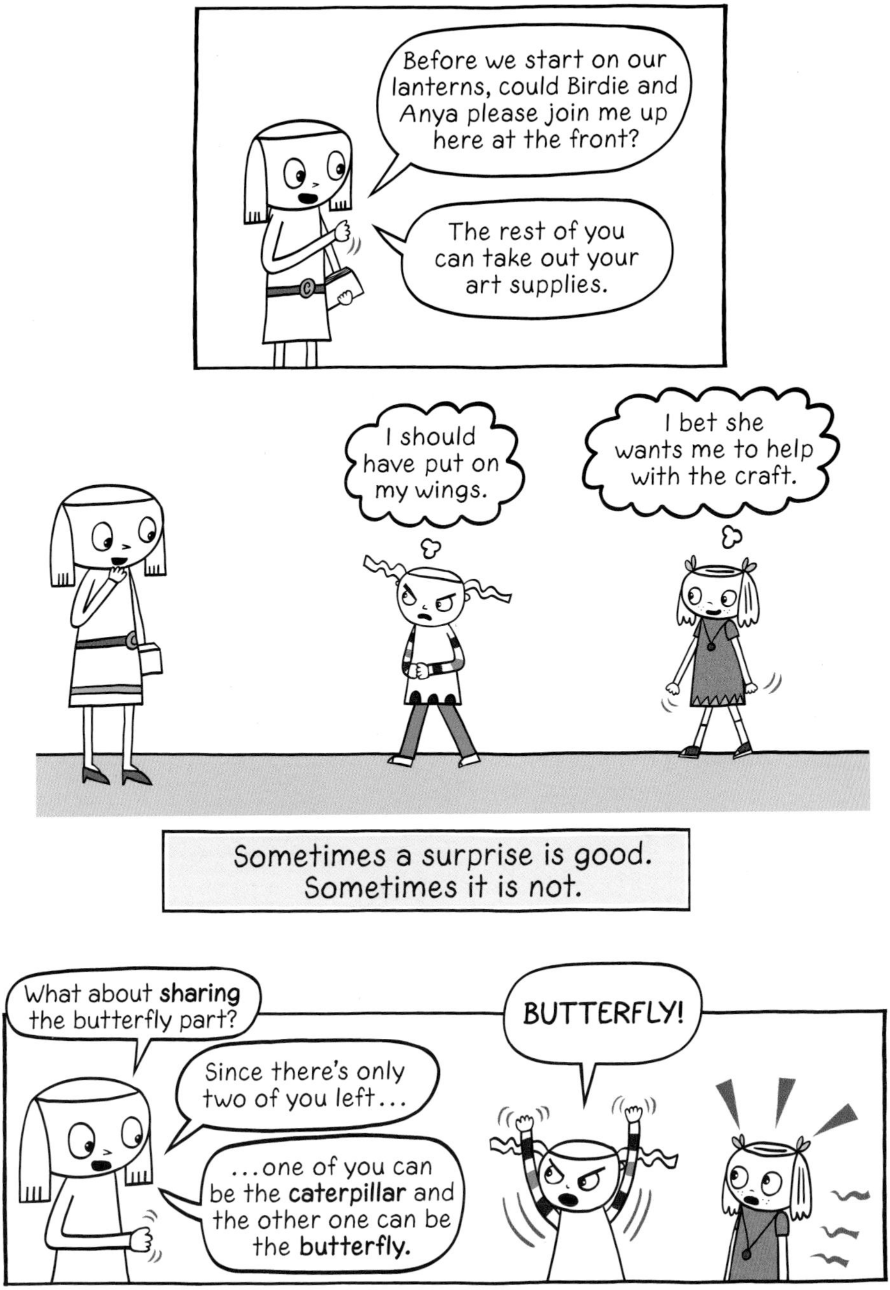
Before we start on our lanterns, could Birdie and Anya please join me up here at the front?
The rest of you can take out your art supplies.
I should have put on my wings.
I bet she wants me to help with the craft.
Sometimes a surprise is good. Sometimes it is not.
What about **sharing** the butterfly part?
Since there's only two of you left...
...one of you can be the **caterpillar** and the other one can be the **butterfly.**
BUTTERFLY!

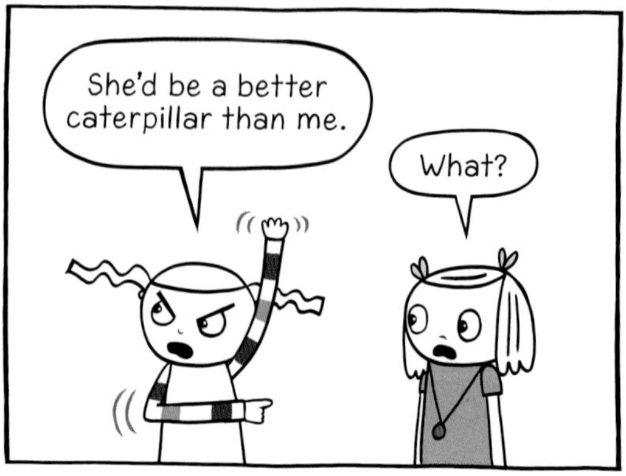
She'd be a better caterpillar than me.
What?

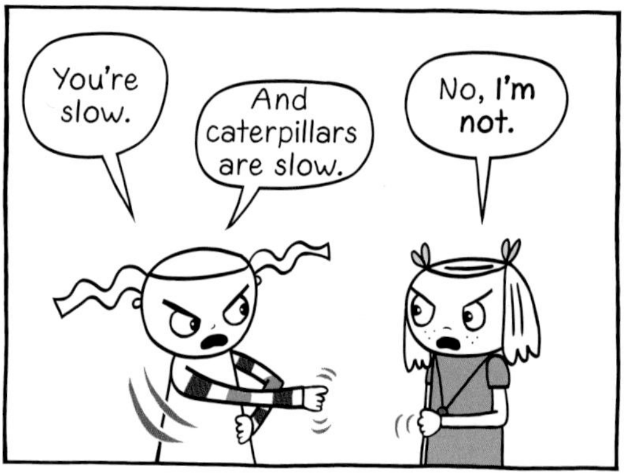
You're slow.
And caterpillars are slow.
No, **I'm not.**

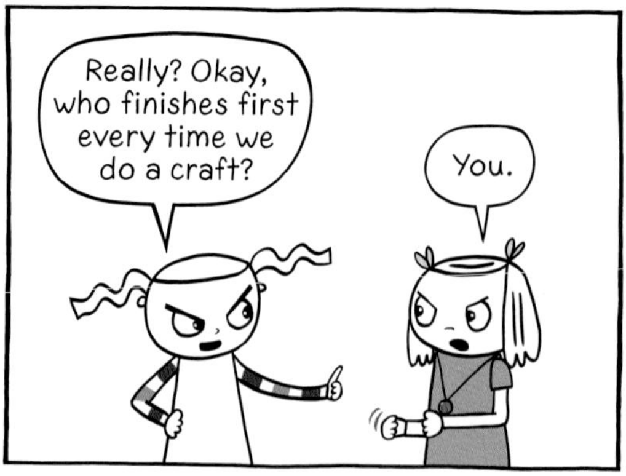
Really? Okay, who finishes first every time we do a craft?
You.

And who takes forever and always finishes last?
Me.
Art isn't a race.
But I always win.
FLAP
FLAP

Miss Domino, I already have the wings.
But... so do I.
Anya, I like your enthusiasm, but you and Birdie will have to decide this together.
The play is tomorrow, so I'll need your answers this afternoon.
Remember, you can't get a butterfly unless you start with a caterpillar.

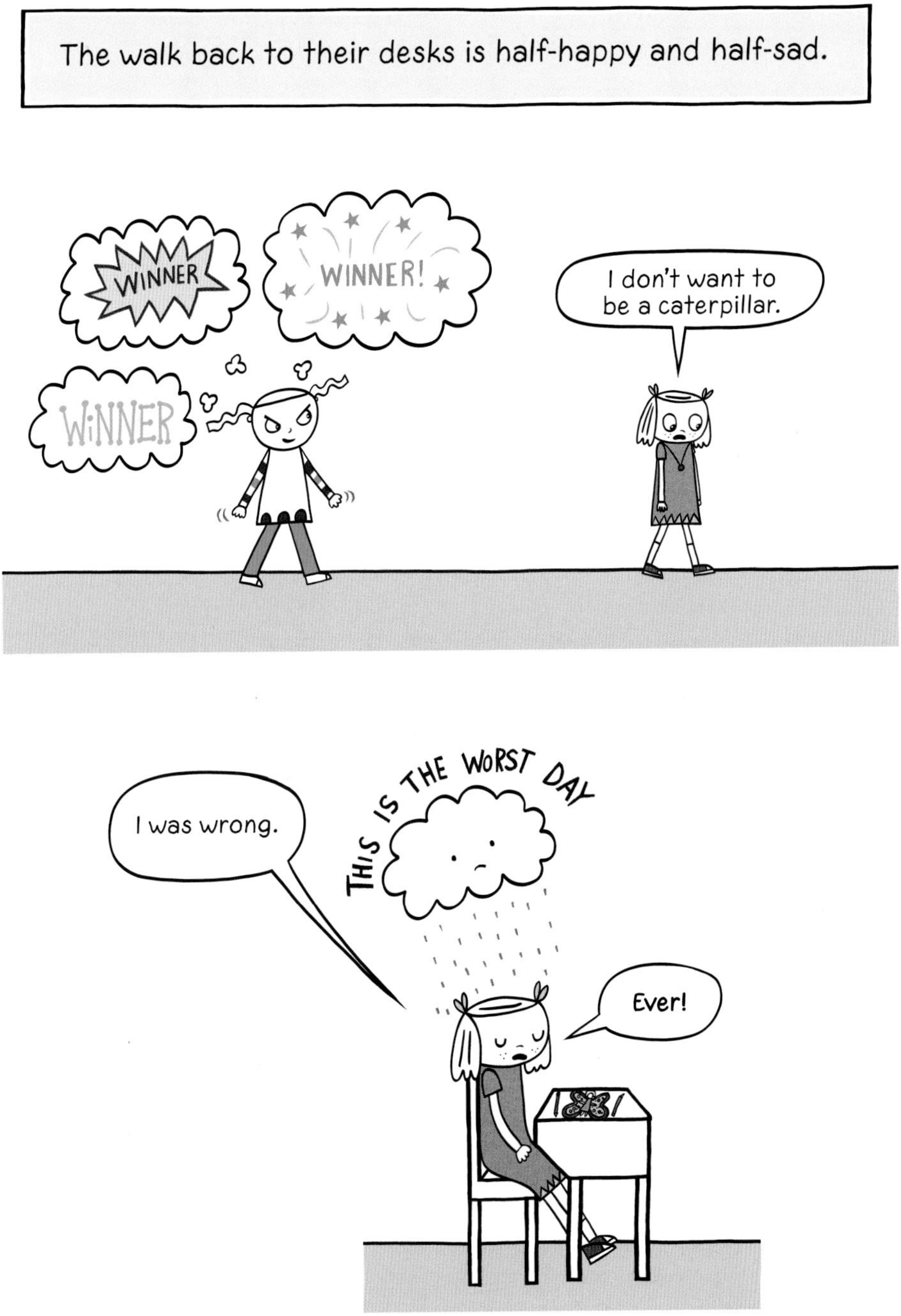
The walk back to their desks is half-happy and half-sad.
WINNER
WINNER!
WINNER
I don't want to be a caterpillar.
I was wrong.
THIS IS THE WORST DAY
Ever!

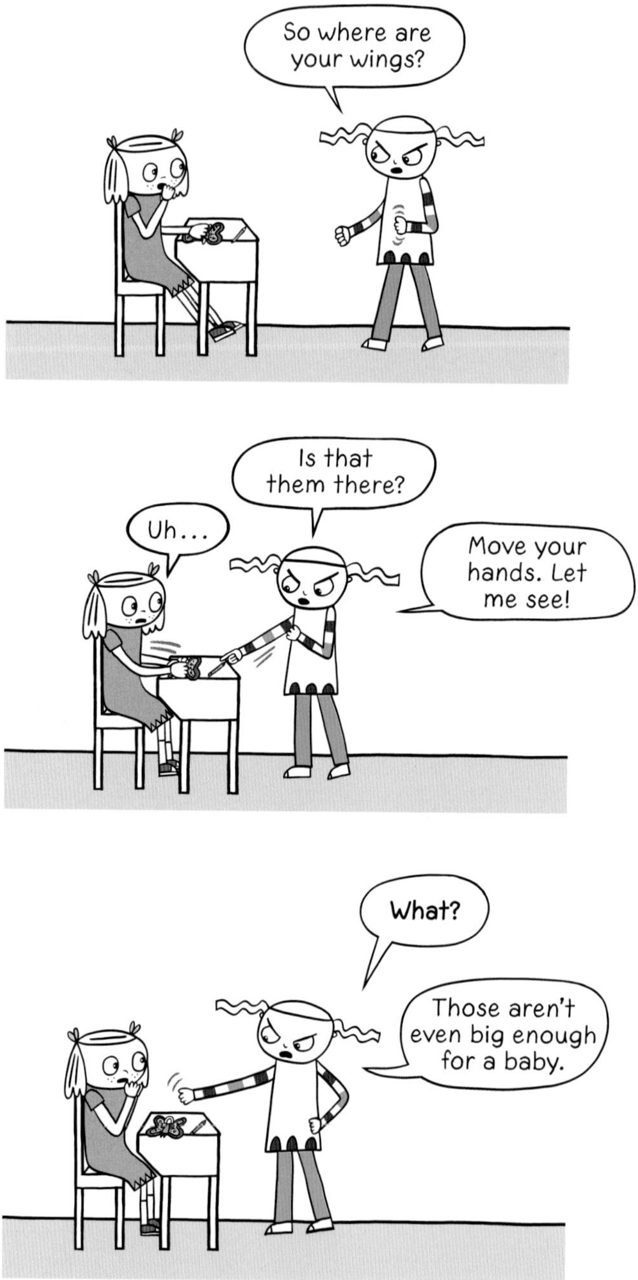
So where are your wings?
Is that them there?
Uh...
Move your hands. Let me see!
What?
Those aren't even big enough for a baby.

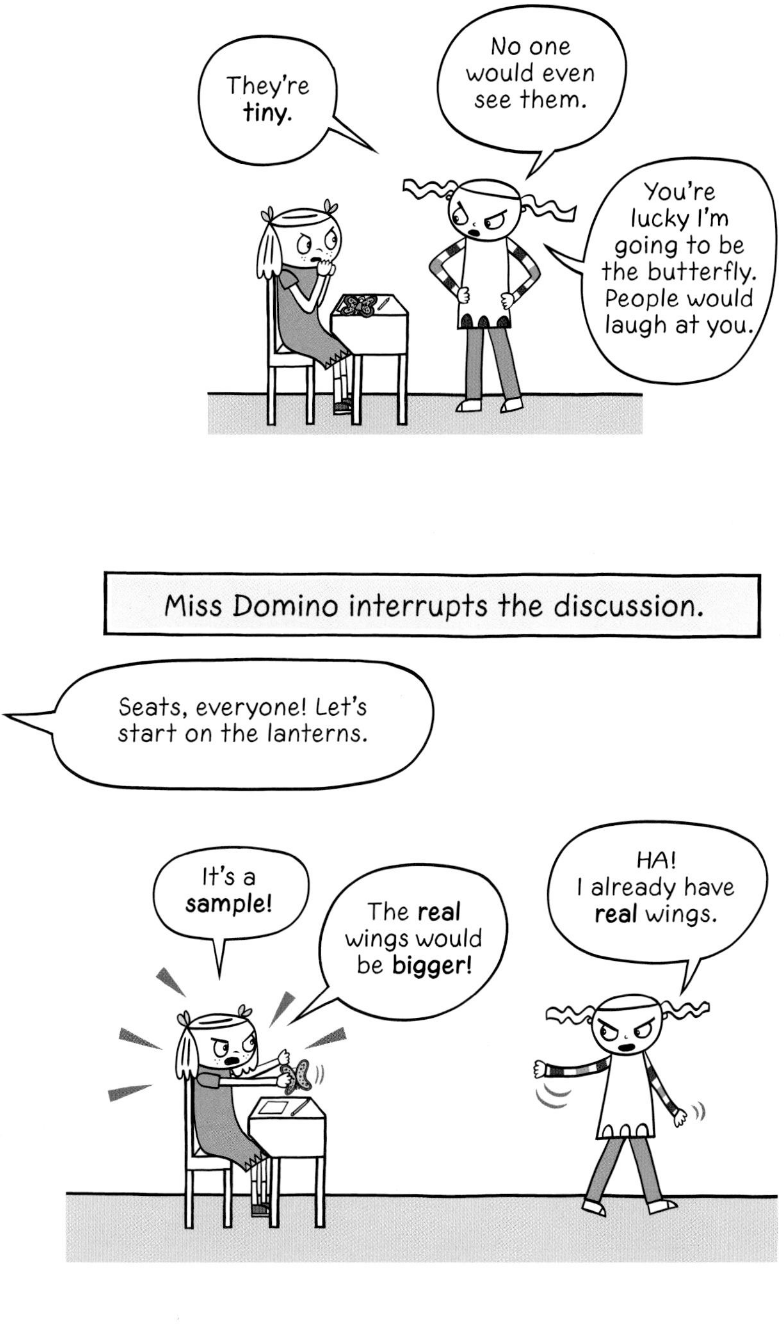
They're **tiny.**
No one would even see them.
You're lucky I'm going to be the butterfly. People would laugh at you.
Miss Domino interrupts the discussion.
Seats, everyone! Let's start on the lanterns.
It's a **sample!**
The **real** wings would be **bigger!**
HA! I already have **real** wings.

Grrr!
I know something that can help.
You do?
Of course. It's right in front of you.
Crafts?
The lantern!
It's working.
I'm feeling better already.
FOLD
FOLD

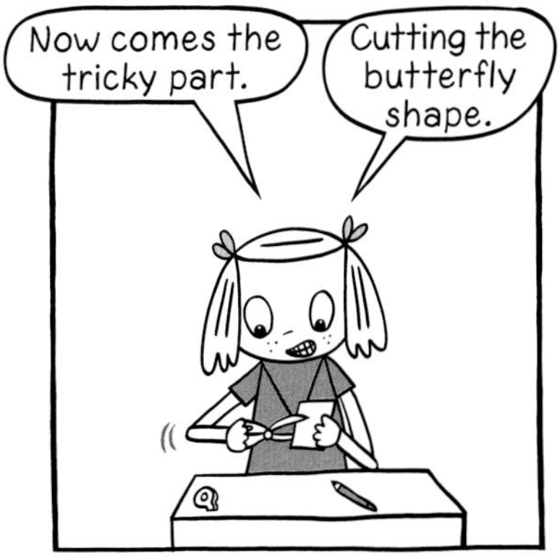
Now comes the tricky part.
Cutting the butterfly shape.

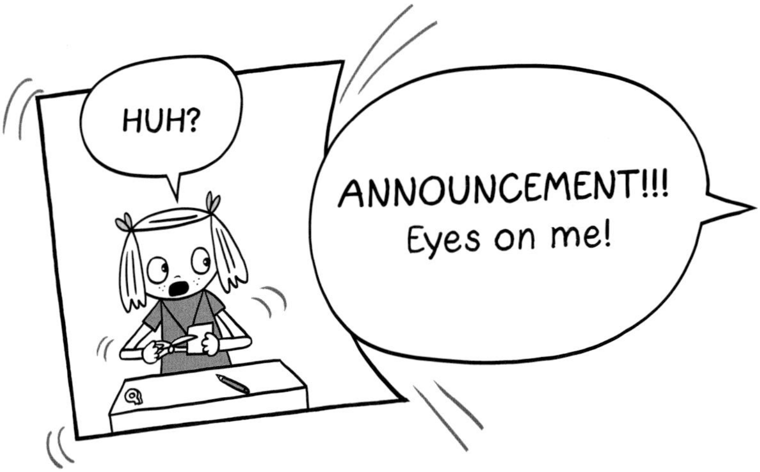
HUH?
ANNOUNCEMENT!!!
Eyes on me!

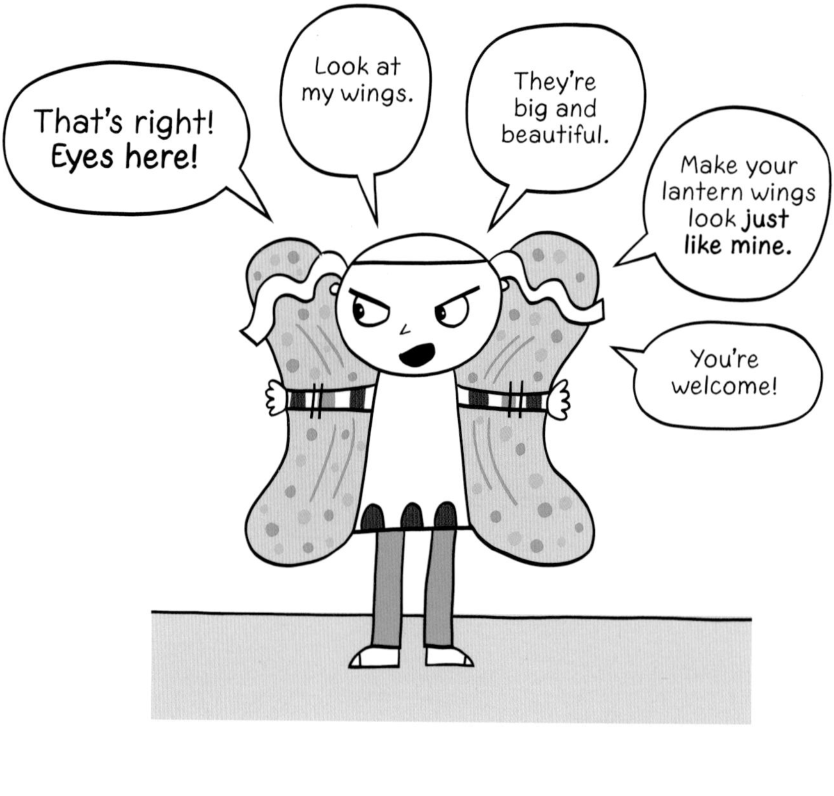
That's right! **Eyes here!**
Look at my wings.
They're big and beautiful.
Make your lantern wings look **just like mine.**
You're welcome!

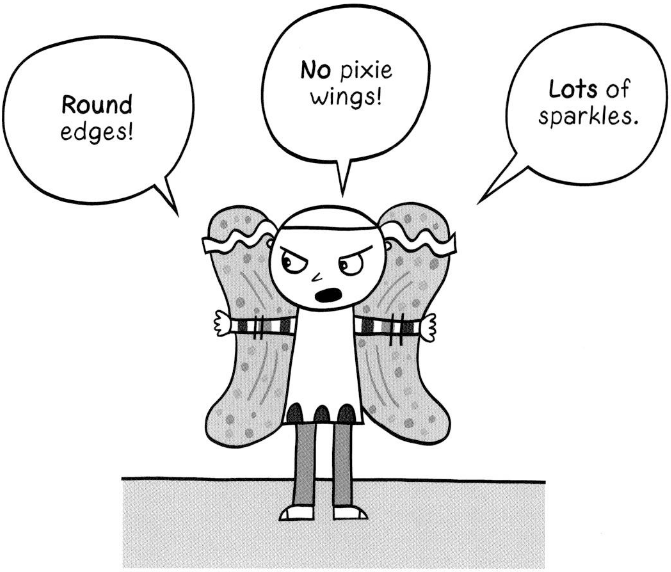
Round edges!
No pixie wings!
Lots of sparkles.

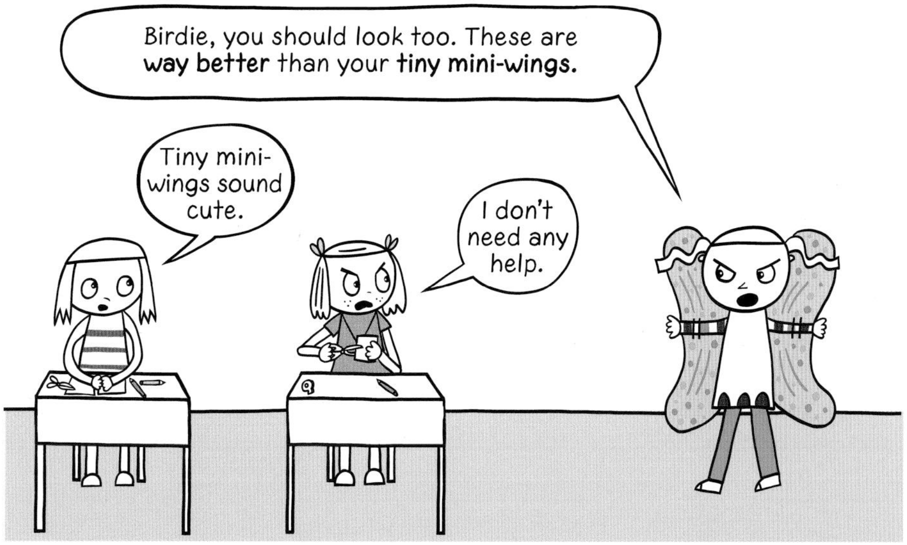
Birdie, you should look too. These are **way better** than your **tiny mini-wings.**
Tiny mini-wings sound cute.
I don't need any help.

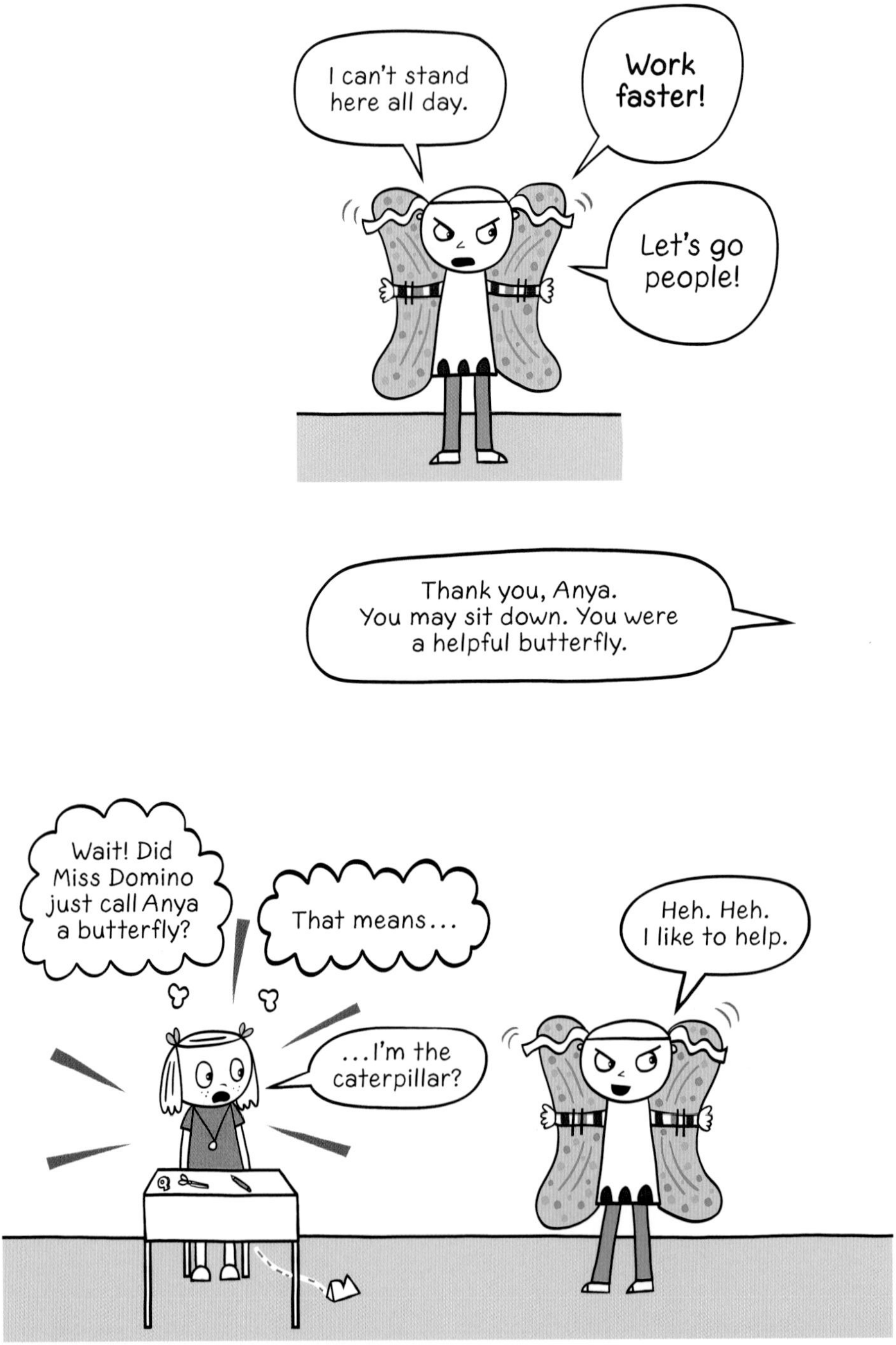
I can't stand here all day.
Work faster!
Let's go people!
Thank you, Anya. You may sit down. You were a helpful butterfly.
Wait! Did Miss Domino just call Anya a butterfly?
That means...
...I'm the caterpillar?
Heh. Heh. I like to help.

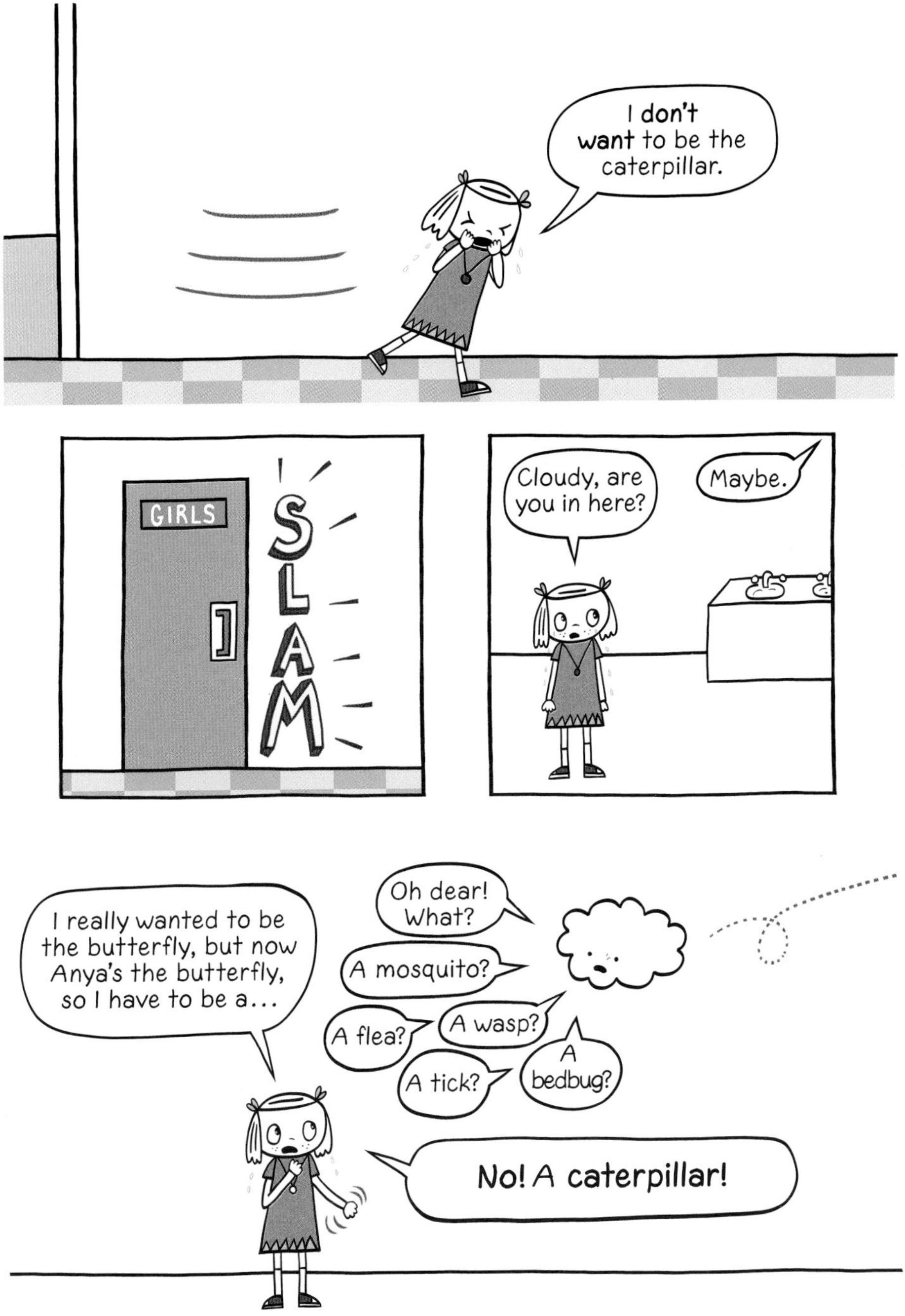
I **don't want** to be the caterpillar.
GIRLS
SLAM
Cloudy, are you in here?
Maybe.
I really wanted to be the butterfly, but now Anya's the butterfly, so I have to be a...
Oh dear! What?
A mosquito?
A flea?
A wasp?
A tick?
A bedbug?
No! A caterpillar!

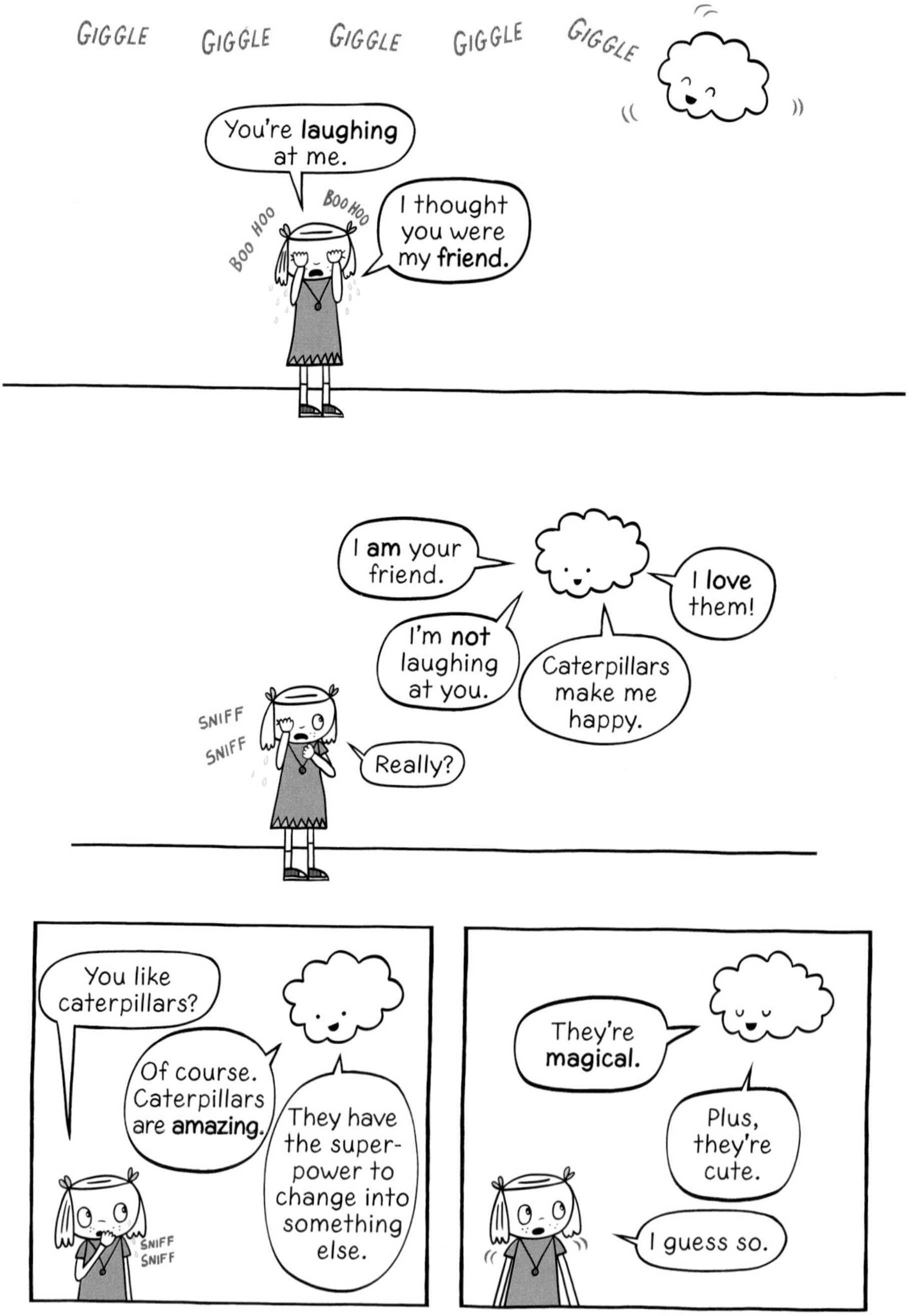
GIGGLE GIGGLE GIGGLE GIGGLE GIGGLE
You're **laughing** at me.
BOO HOO
BOO HOO
I thought you were my **friend.**
I **am** your friend.
I **love** them!
I'm **not** laughing at you.
Caterpillars make me happy.
SNIFF
SNIFF
Really?
You like caterpillars?
Of course. Caterpillars are **amazing.**
They have the superpower to change into something else.
SNIFF
SNIFF
They're **magical.**
Plus, they're cute.
I guess so.

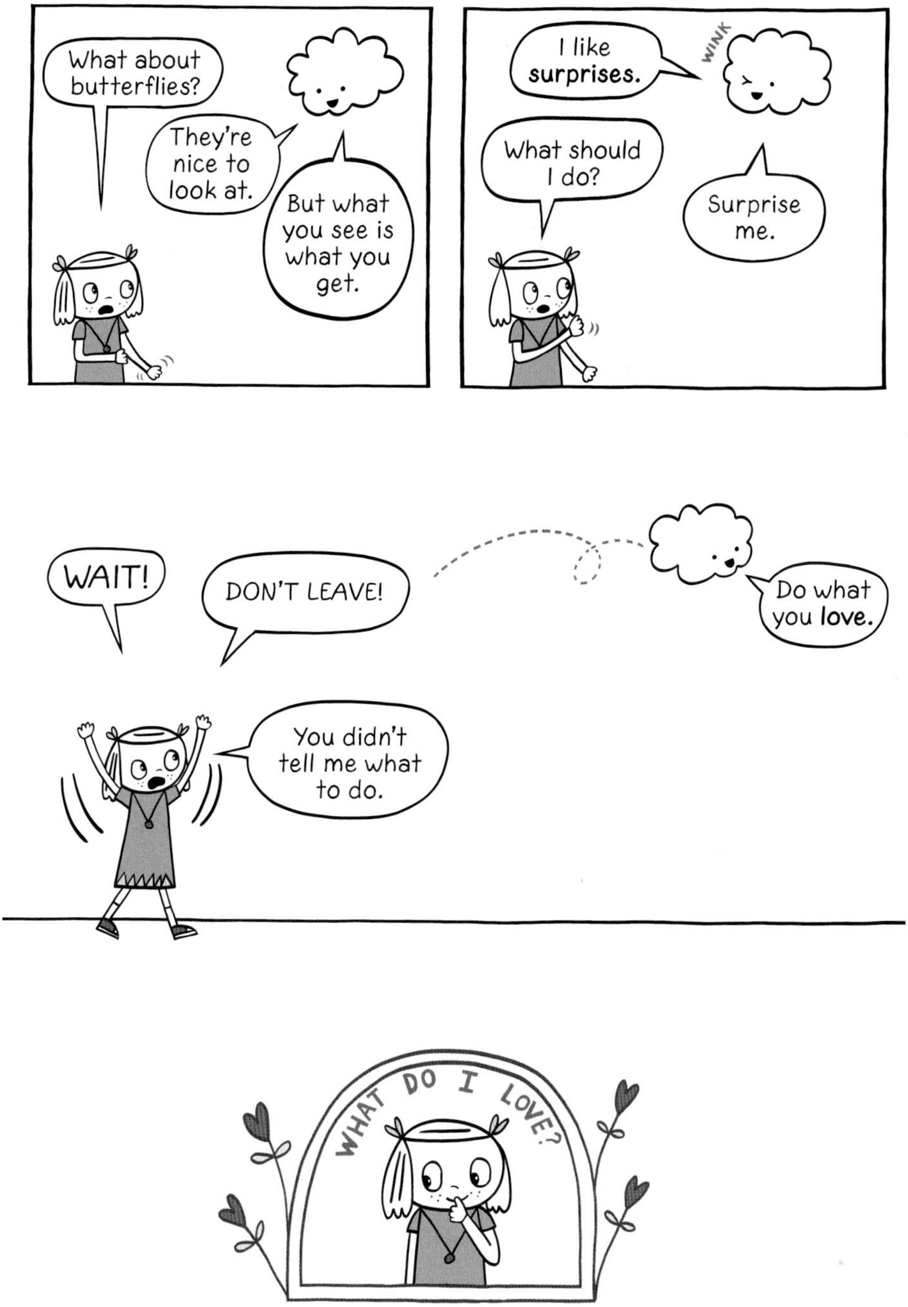
What about butterflies?
They're nice to look at.
But what you see is what you get.
I like **surprises.**
WINK
What should I do?
Surprise me.
WAIT!
DON'T LEAVE!
Do what you **love.**
You didn't tell me what to do.
WHAT DO I LOVE?

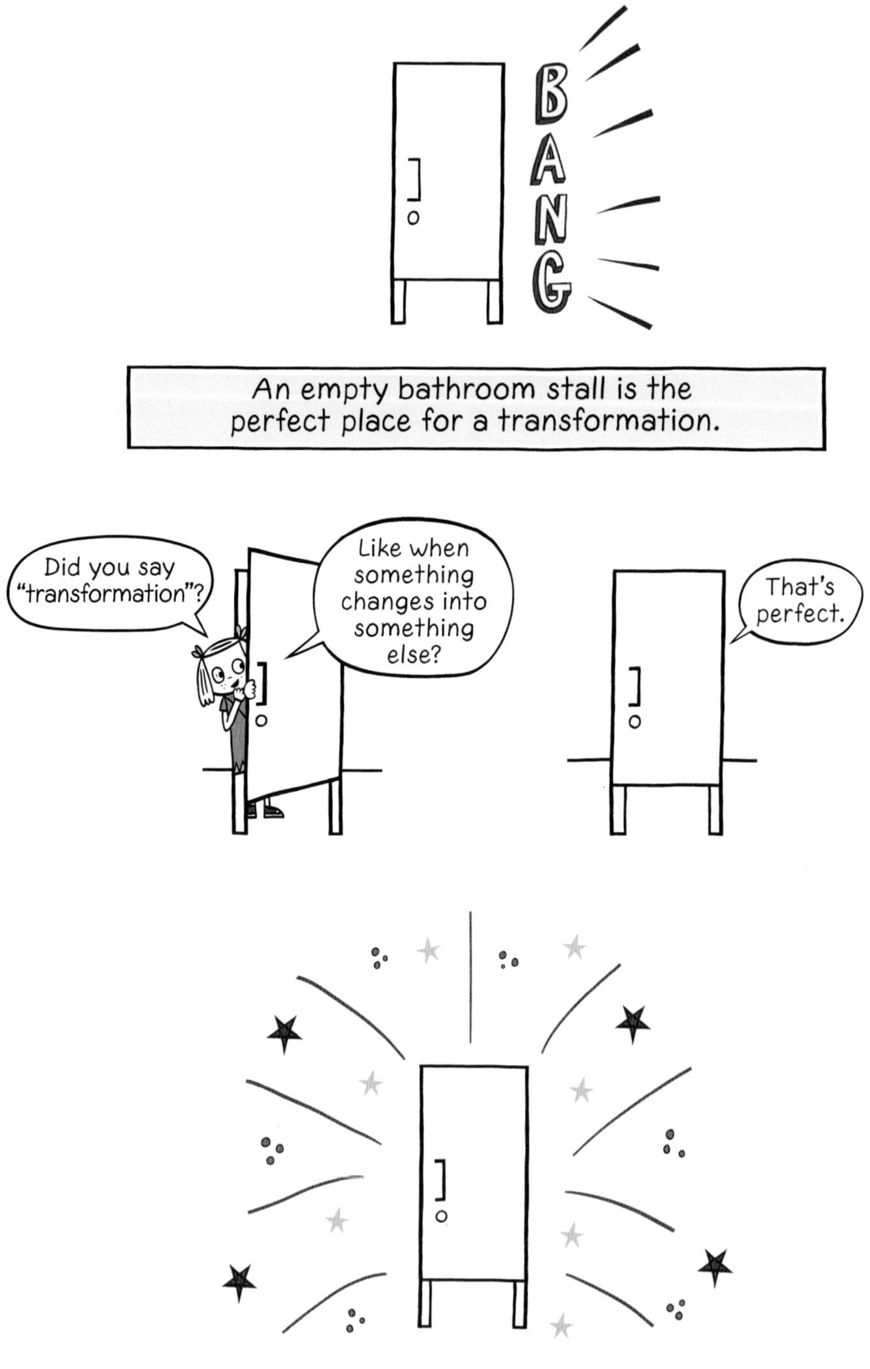
BANG
An empty bathroom stall is the perfect place for a transformation.
Did you say "transformation"?
Like when something changes into something else?
That's perfect.

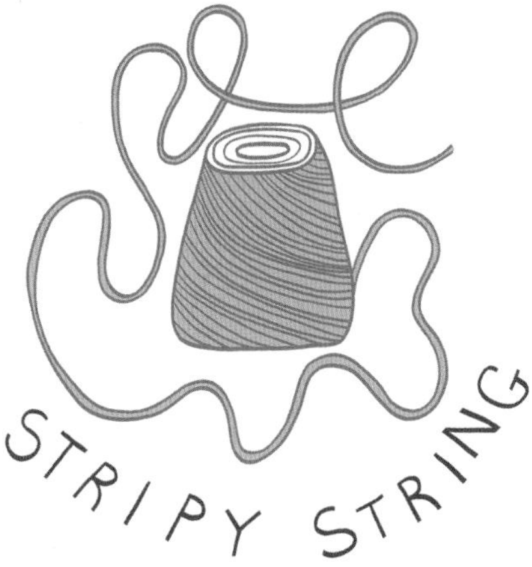
STRIPY STRING

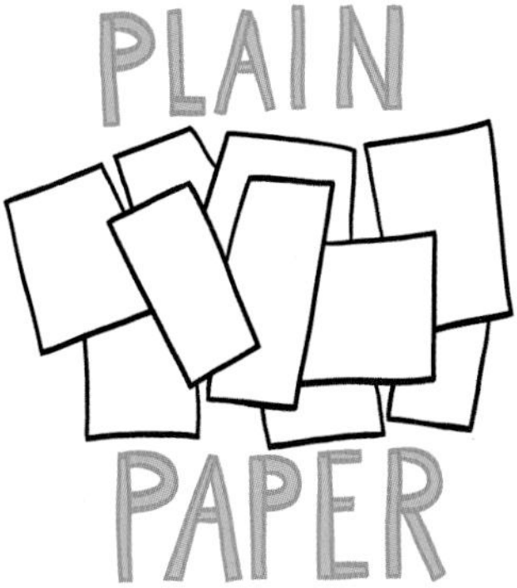
PLAIN
PAPER

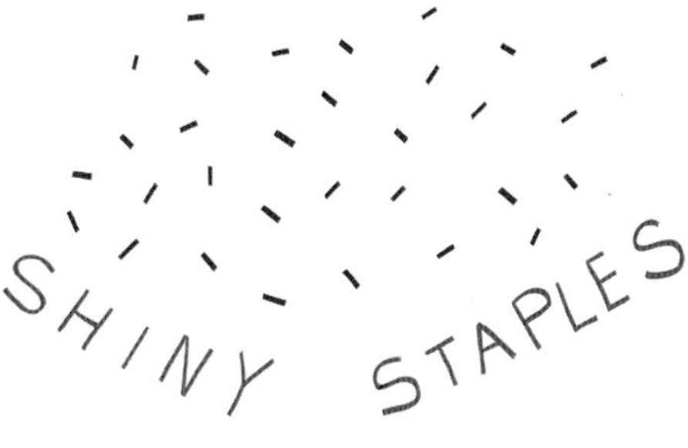
SHINY STAPLES

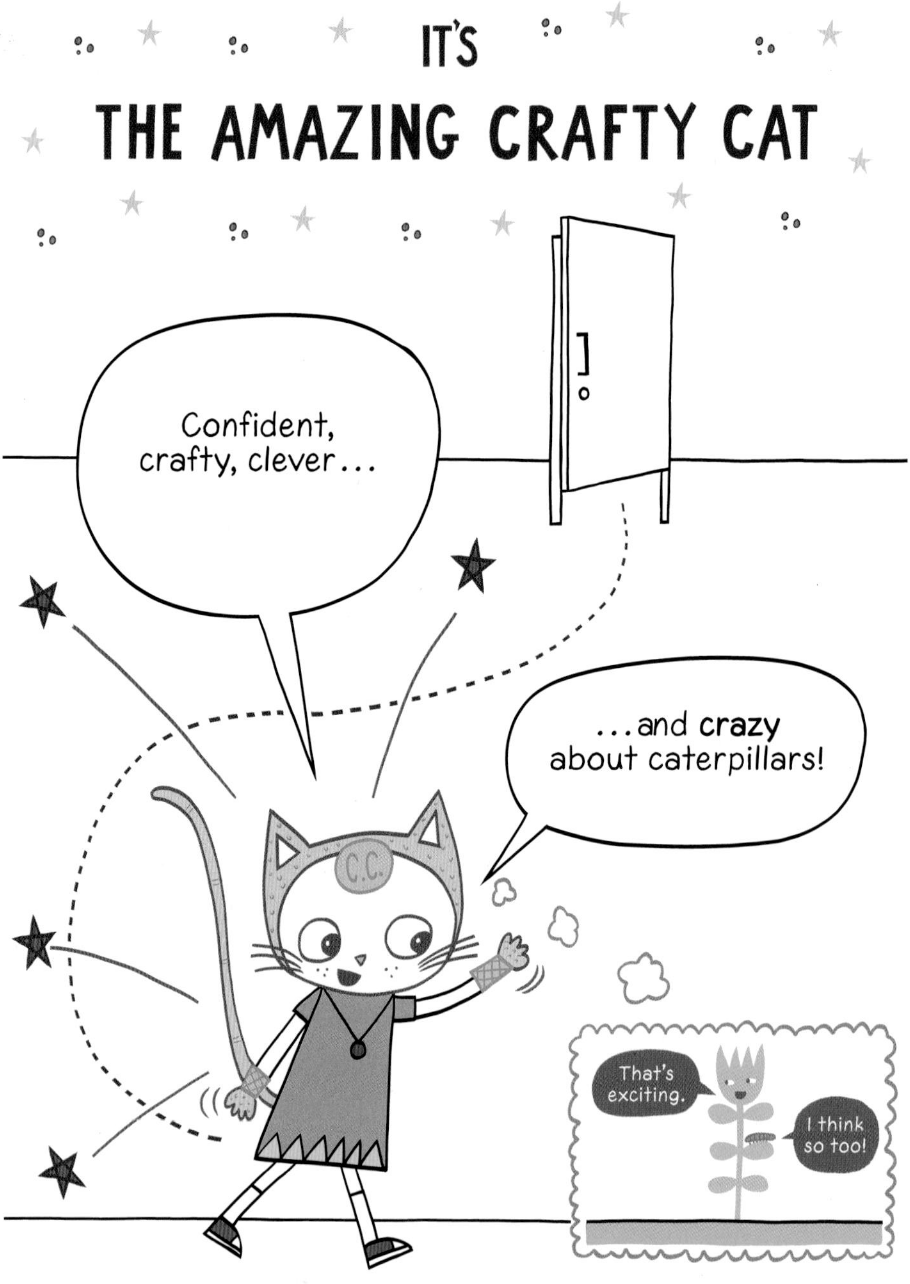
IT'S
THE AMAZING CRAFTY CAT
Confident, crafty, clever...
...and **crazy** about caterpillars!
C.C.
That's exciting.
I think so too!

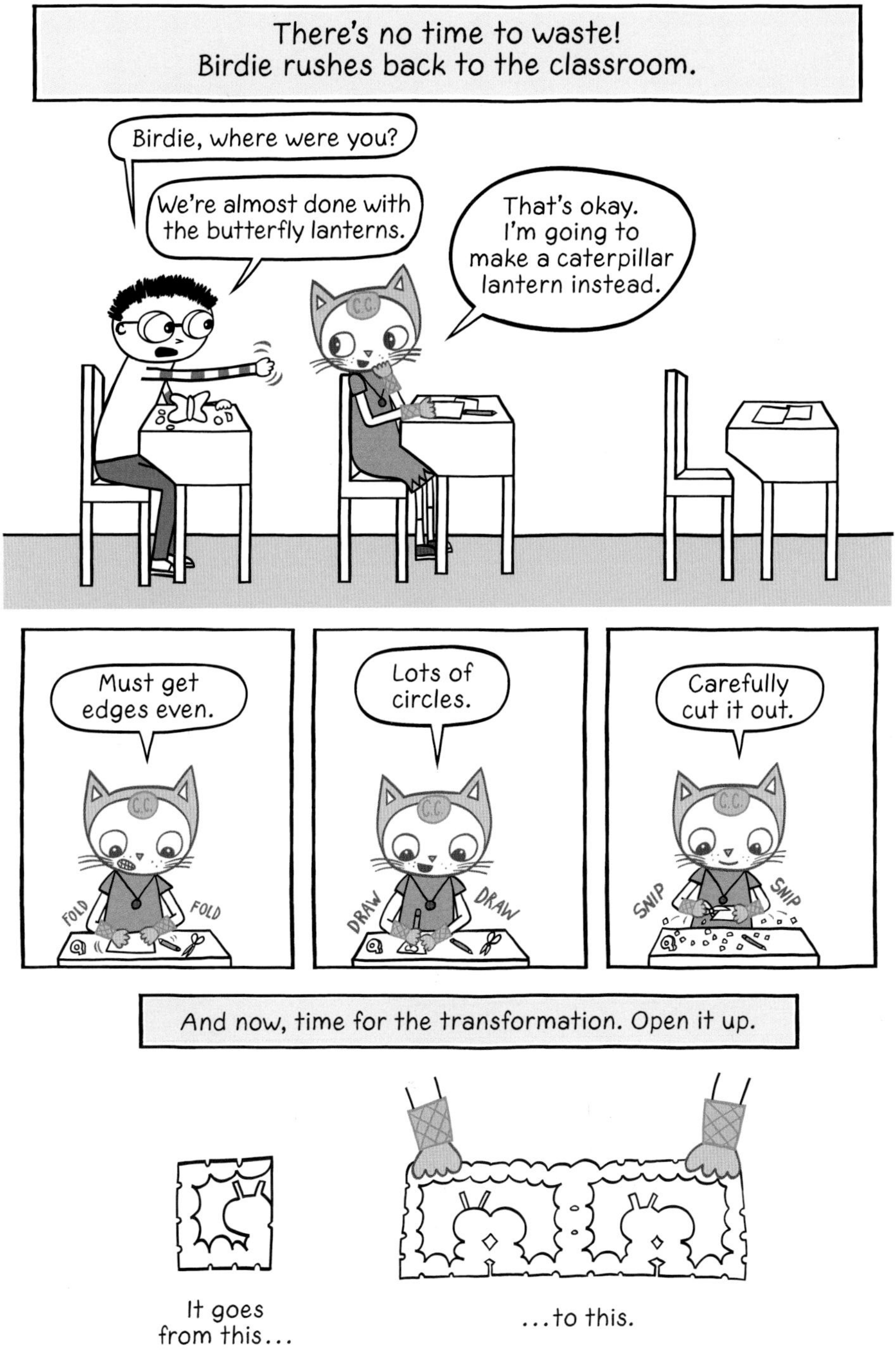
There's no time to waste!
Birdie rushes back to the classroom.
Birdie, where were you?
We're almost done with the butterfly lanterns.
That's okay. I'm going to make a caterpillar lantern instead.
Must get edges even.
FOLD
FOLD
Lots of circles.
DRAW
DRAW
Carefully cut it out.
SNIP
SNIP
And now, time for the transformation. Open it up.
It goes from this...
...to this.

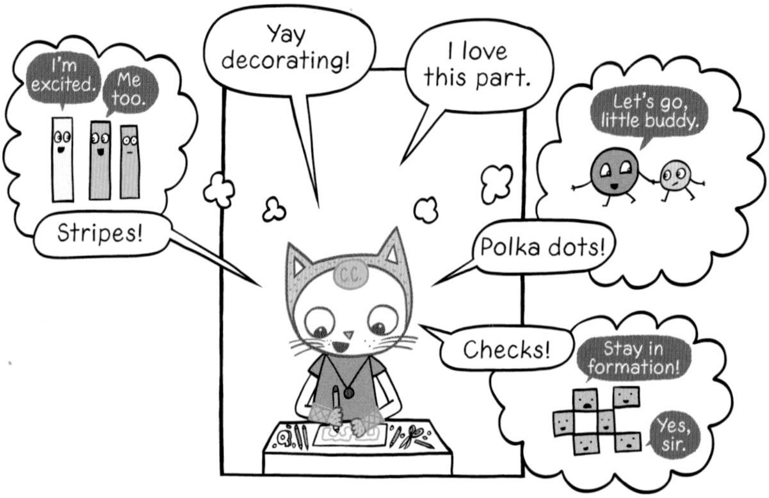
I'm excited.
Me too.
Stripes!
Yay decorating!
I love this part.
Let's go, little buddy.
Polka dots!
Checks!
Stay in formation!
Yes, sir.

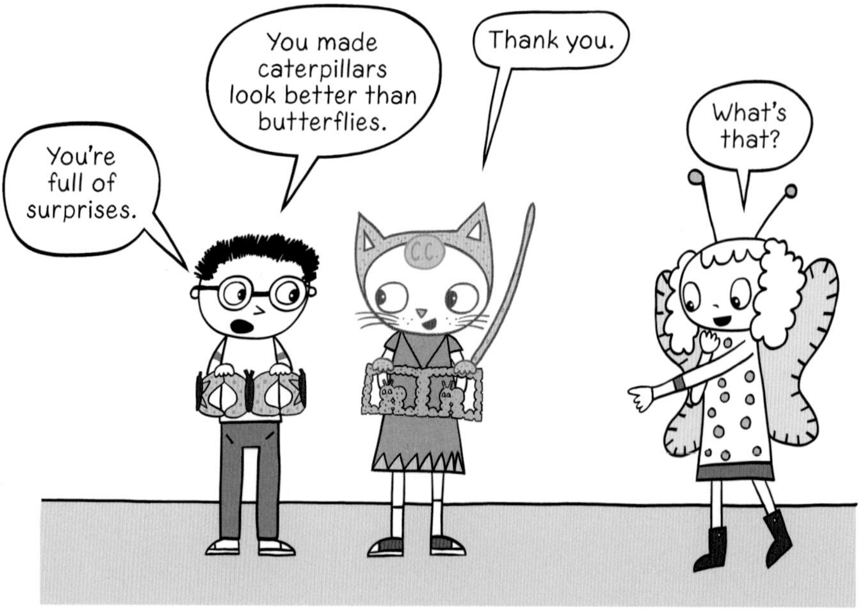
You're full of surprises.
You made caterpillars look better than butterflies.
Thank you.
What's that?

The caterpillar lantern is a creative success.

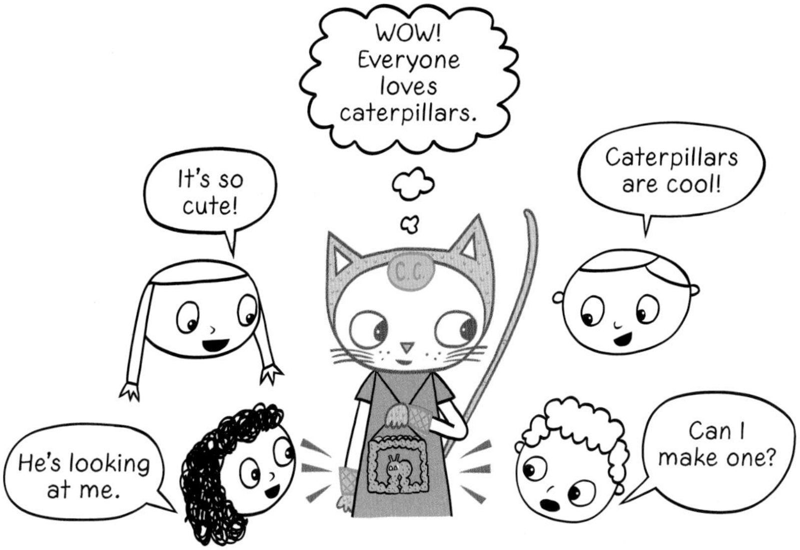
WOW! Everyone loves caterpillars.
It's so cute!
Caterpillars are cool!
He's looking at me.
Can I make one?

But Crafty Cat is wrong—not everyone is a fan.

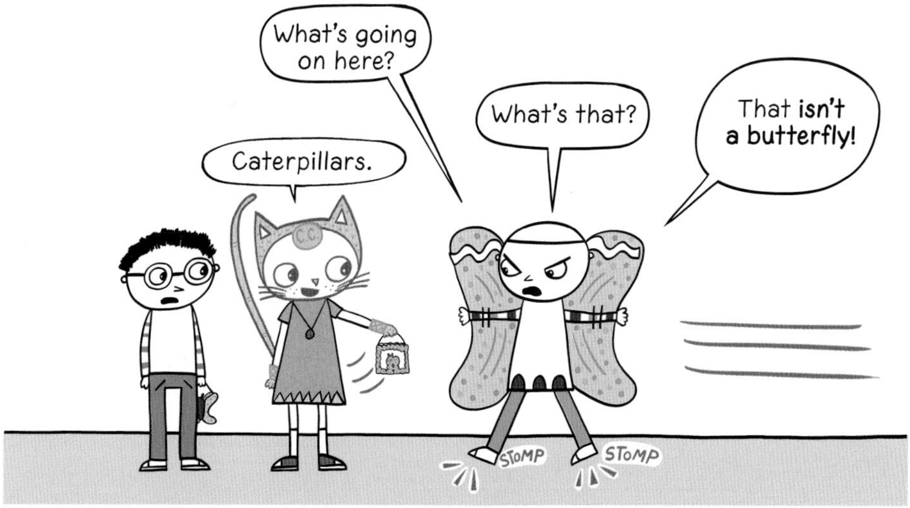
What's going on here?
Caterpillars.
What's that?
That **isn't a butterfly!**
STOMP
STOMP

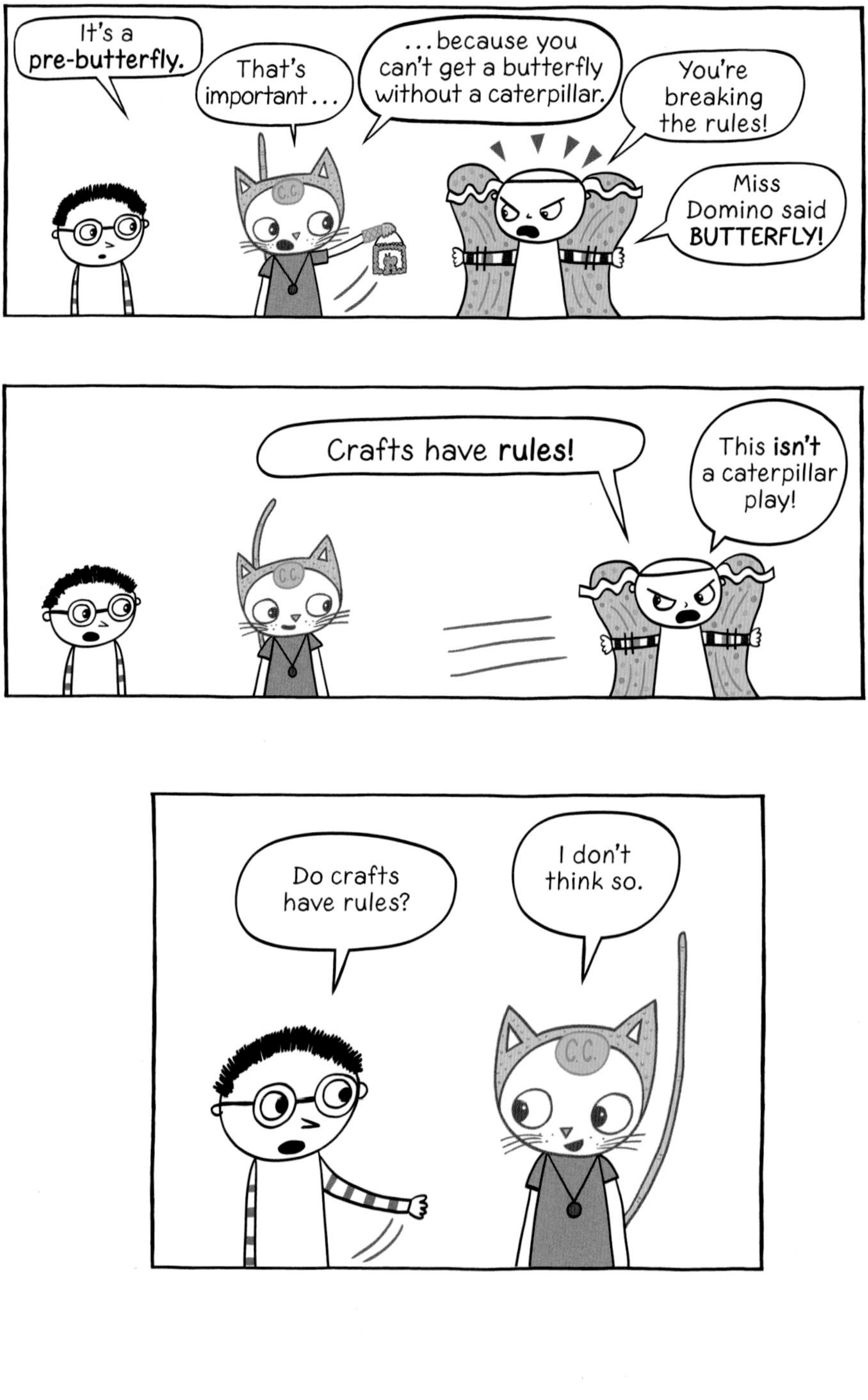

It's a **pre-butterfly.**
That's important...
...because you can't get a butterfly without a caterpillar.
You're breaking the rules!
Miss Domino said **BUTTERFLY!**
Crafts have **rules!**
This **isn't** a caterpillar play!
Do crafts have rules?
I don't think so.

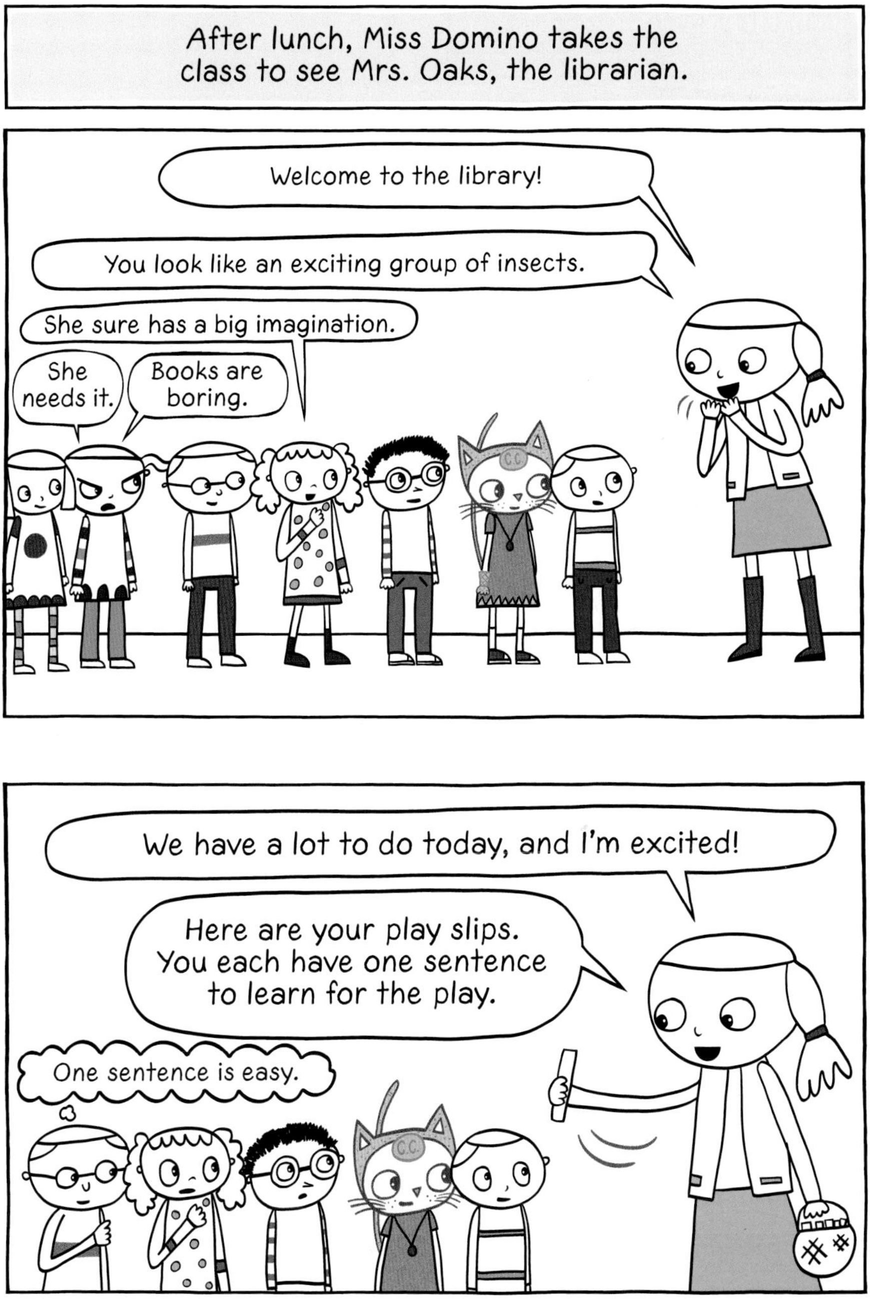
After lunch, Miss Domino takes the class to see Mrs. Oaks, the librarian.
Welcome to the library!
You look like an exciting group of insects.
She sure has a big imagination.
She needs it.
Books are boring.
We have a lot to do today, and I'm excited!
Here are your play slips. You each have one sentence to learn for the play.
One sentence is easy.

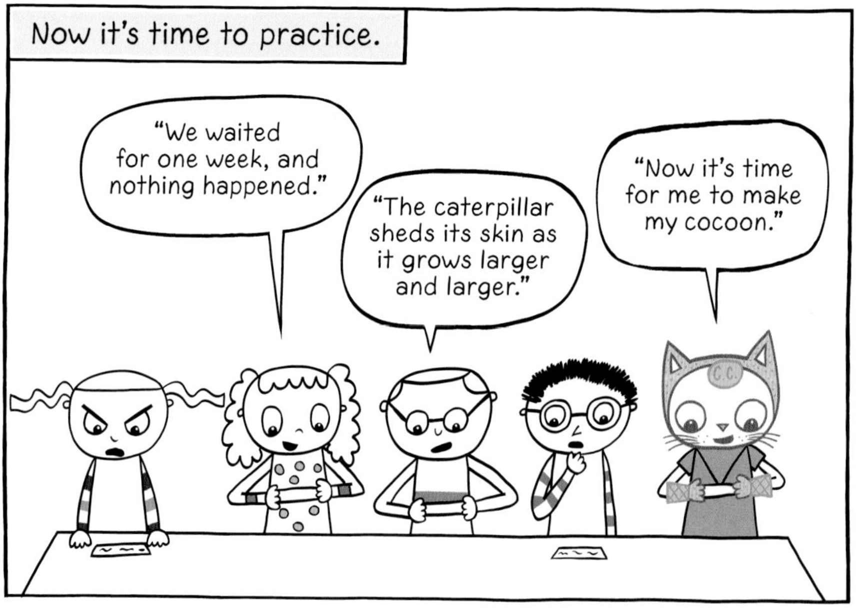
Now it's time to practice.
"We waited for one week, and nothing happened."
"The caterpillar sheds its skin as it grows larger and larger."
"Now it's time for me to make my cocoon."

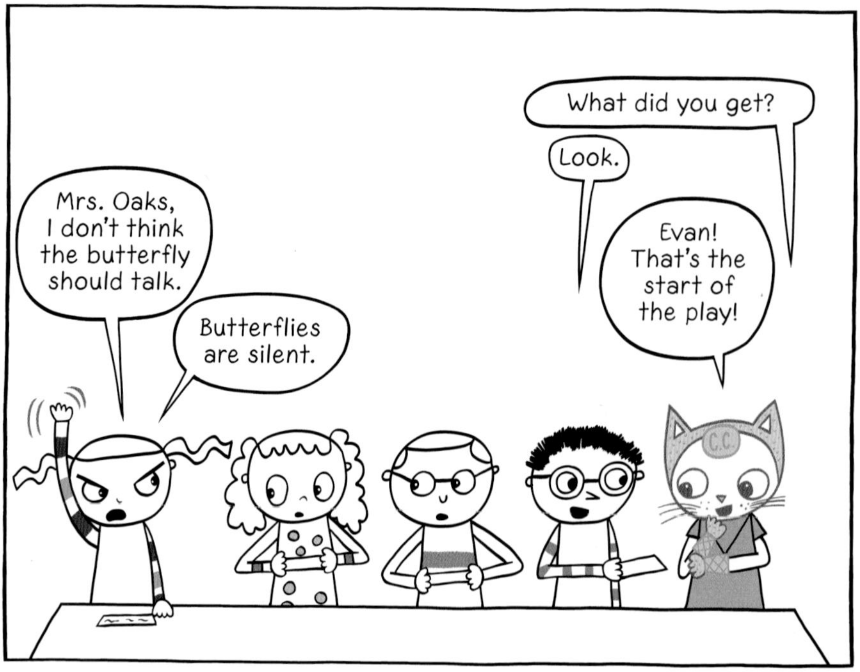
Mrs. Oaks, I don't think the butterfly should talk.
Butterflies are silent.
What did you get?
Look.
Evan! That's the start of the play!

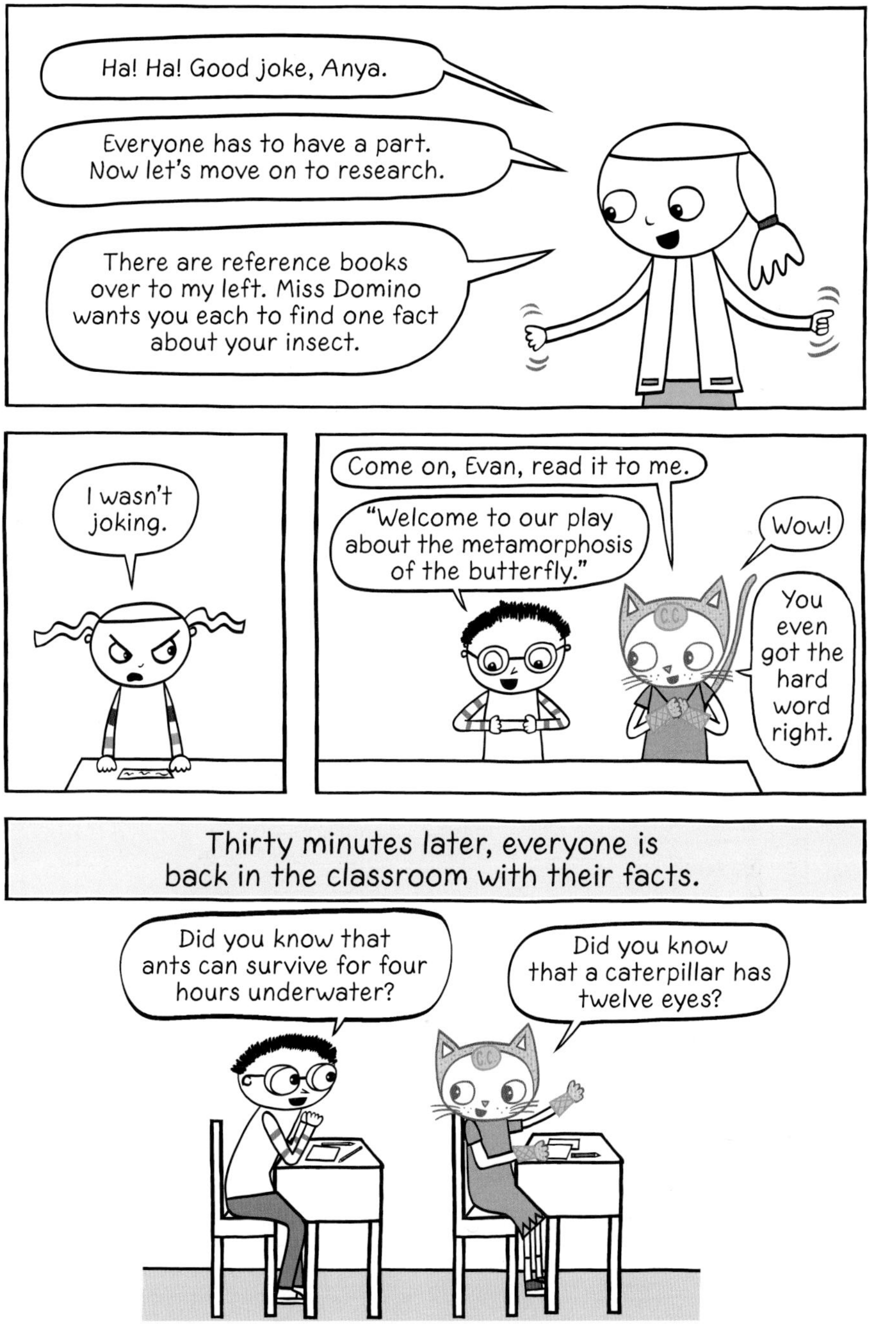
Ha! Ha! Good joke, Anya.
Everyone has to have a part. Now let's move on to research.
There are reference books over to my left. Miss Domino wants you each to find one fact about your insect.
I wasn't joking.
Come on, Evan, read it to me.
"Welcome to our play about the metamorphosis of the butterfly."
Wow!
You even got the hard word right.
Thirty minutes later, everyone is back in the classroom with their facts.
Did you know that ants can survive for four hours underwater?
Did you know that a caterpillar has twelve eyes?

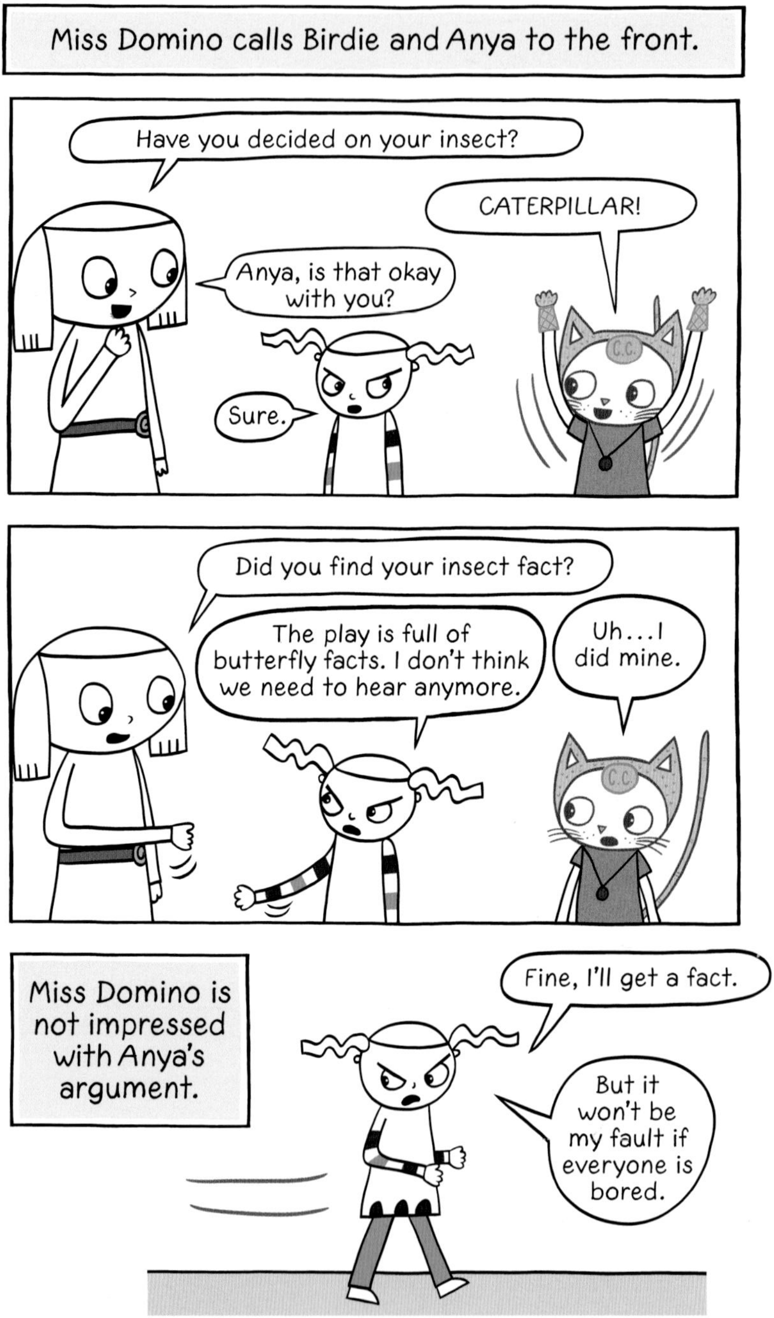
Miss Domino calls Birdie and Anya to the front.
Have you decided on your insect?
CATERPILLAR!
Anya, is that okay with you?
Sure.
Did you find your insect fact?
The play is full of butterfly facts. I don't think we need to hear anymore.
Uh...I did mine.
Miss Domino is not impressed with Anya's argument.
Fine, I'll get a fact.
But it won't be my fault if everyone is bored.

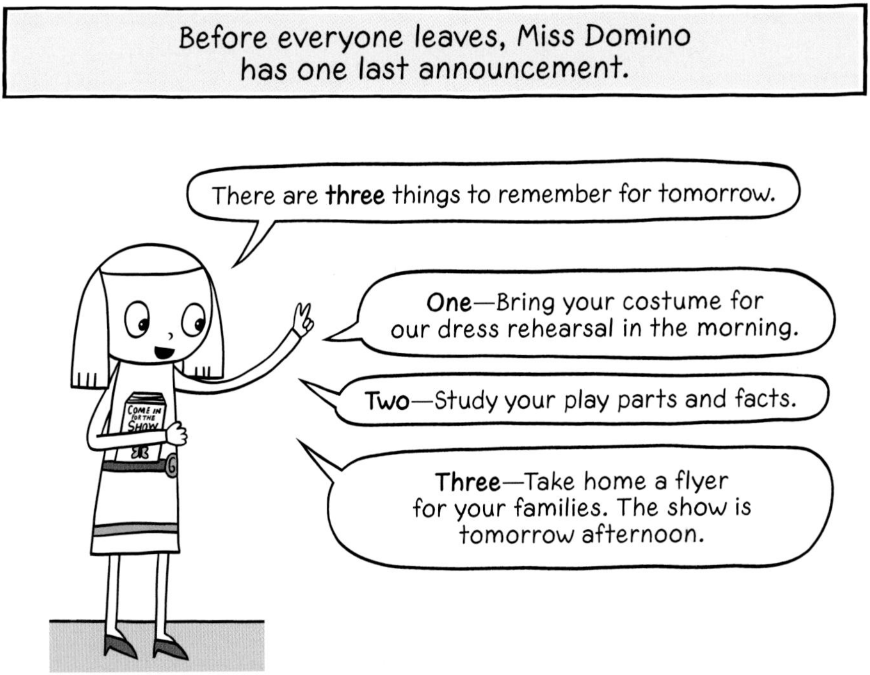
Before everyone leaves, Miss Domino has one last announcement.
There are **three** things to remember for tomorrow.
One—Bring your costume for our dress rehearsal in the morning.
Two—Study your play parts and facts.
Three—Take home a flyer for your families. The show is tomorrow afternoon.
COME IN FOR THE SHOW

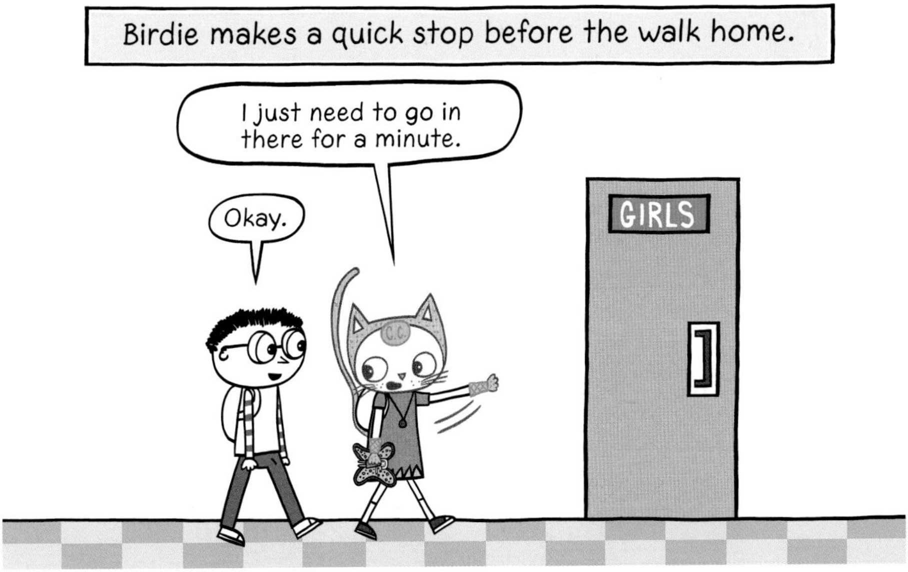
Birdie makes a quick stop before the walk home.
I just need to go in there for a minute.
Okay.
GIRLS

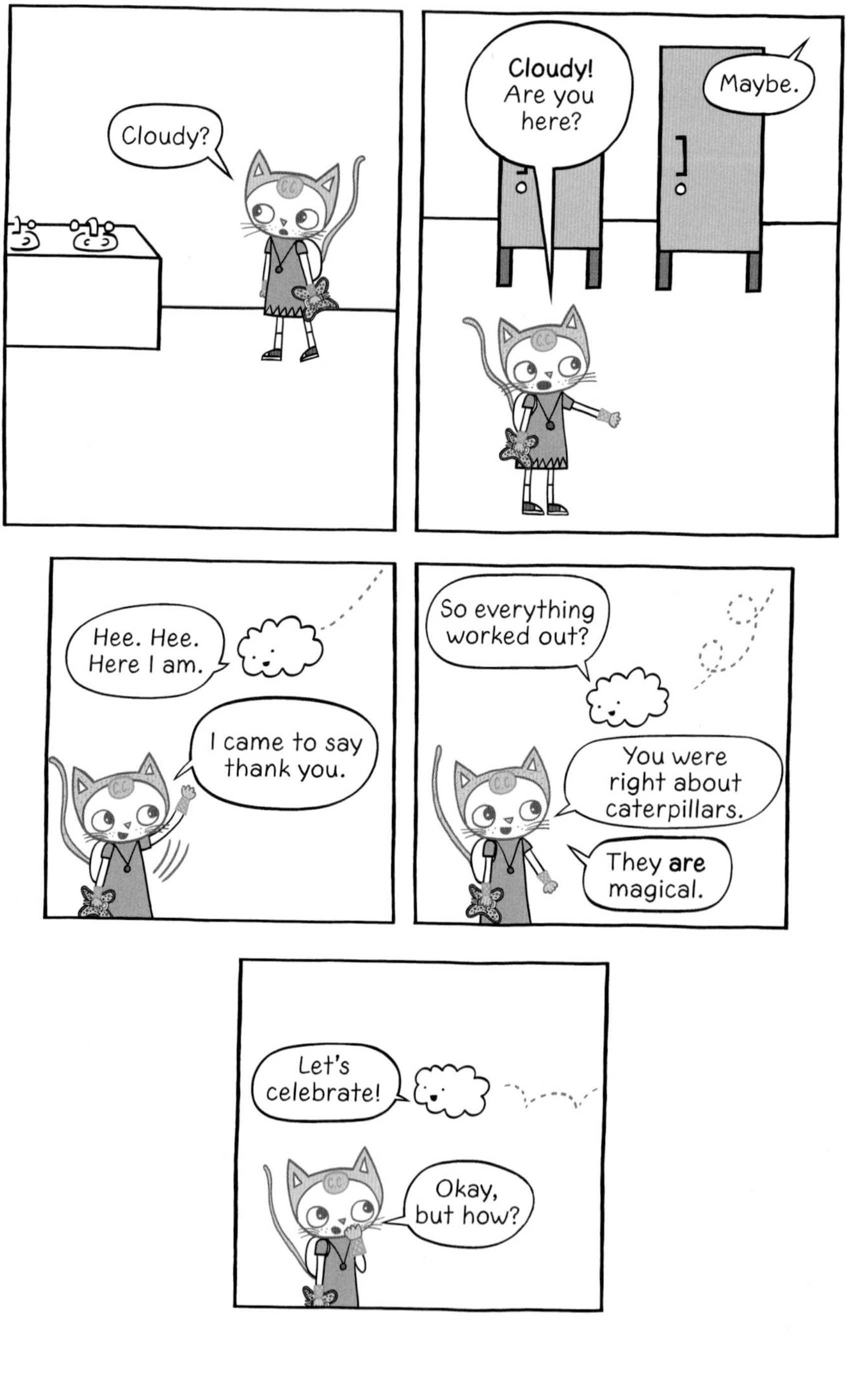
Cloudy?
Cloudy! Are you here?
Maybe.
Hee. Hee. Here I am.
I came to say thank you.
So everything worked out?
You were right about caterpillars.
They **are** magical.
Let's celebrate!
Okay, but how?

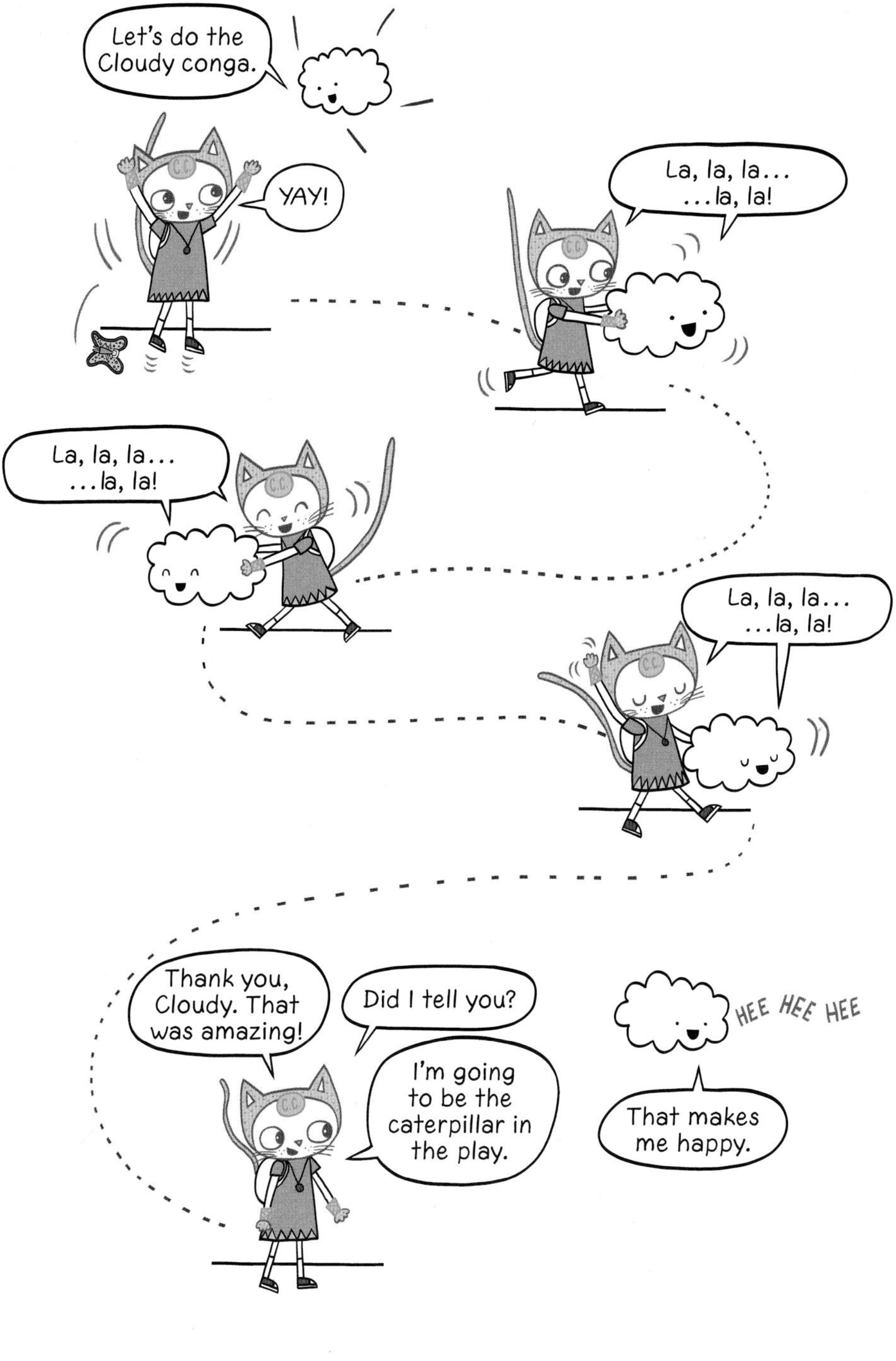
Let's do the Cloudy conga.
YAY!
La, la, la... ...la, la!
La, la, la... ...la, la!
La, la, la... ...la, la!
Thank you, Cloudy. That was amazing!
Did I tell you?
I'm going to be the caterpillar in the play.
HEE HEE HEE
That makes me happy.

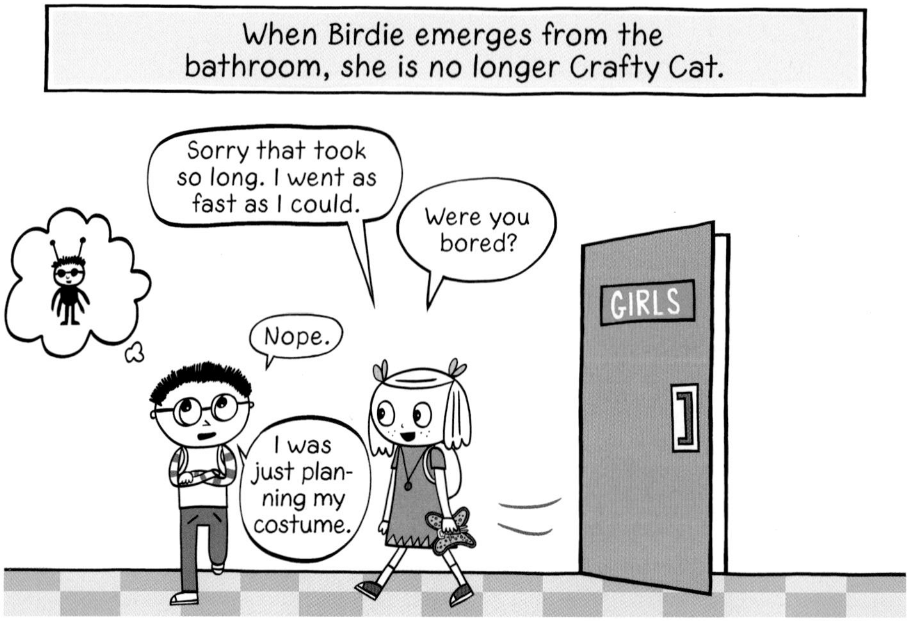
When Birdie emerges from the bathroom, she is no longer Crafty Cat.
Sorry that took so long. I went as fast as I could.
Were you bored?
GIRLS
Nope.
I was just planning my costume.

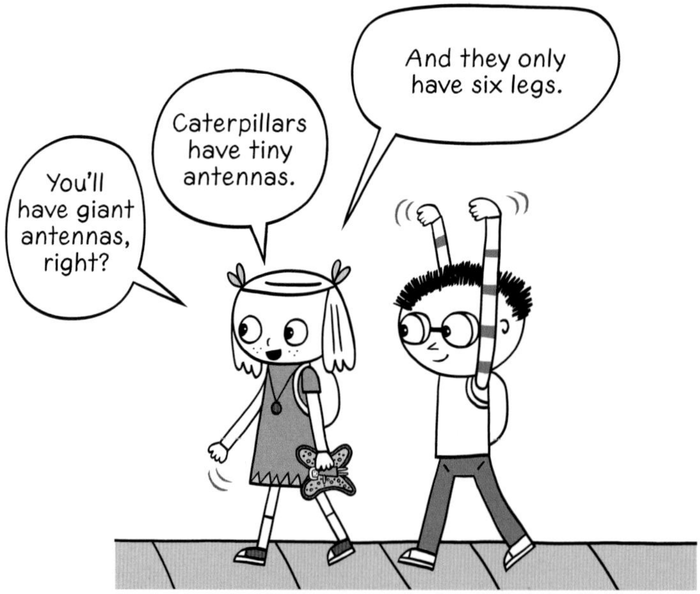
You'll have giant antennas, right?
Caterpillars have tiny antennas.
And they only have six legs.

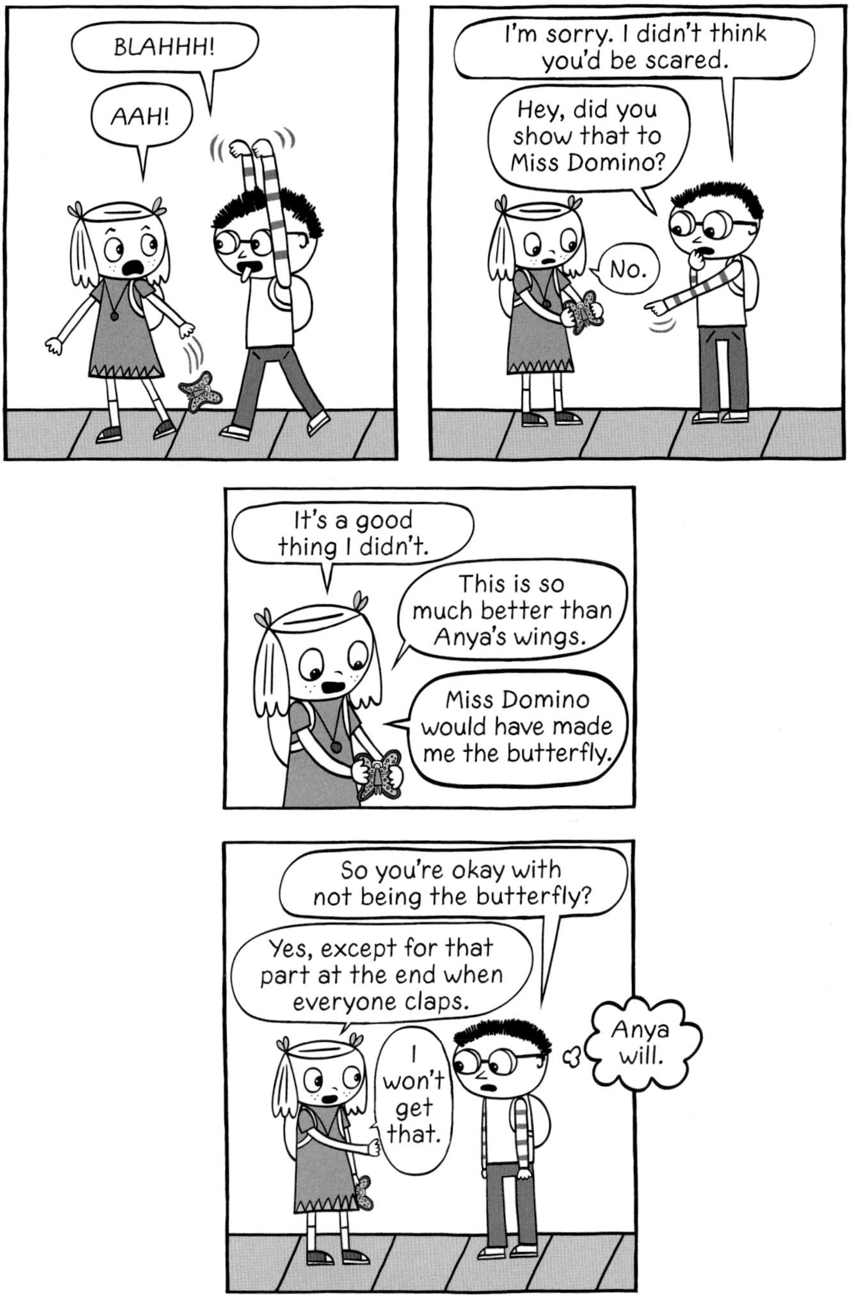
BLAHHH!
AAH!
I'm sorry. I didn't think you'd be scared.
Hey, did you show that to Miss Domino?
No.
It's a good thing I didn't.
This is so much better than Anya's wings.
Miss Domino would have made me the butterfly.
So you're okay with not being the butterfly?
Yes, except for that part at the end when everyone claps.
I won't get that.
Anya will.

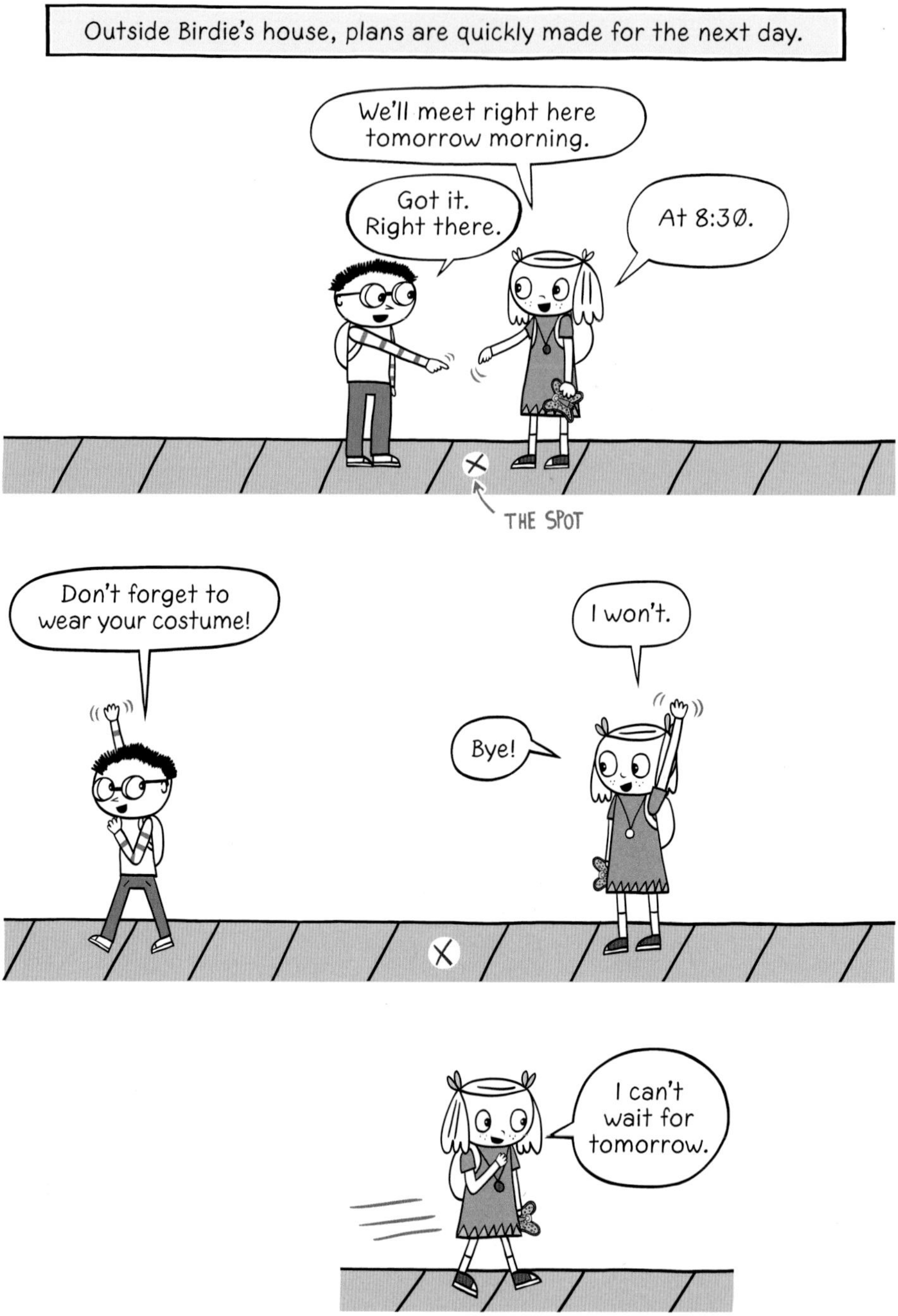
Outside Birdie's house, plans are quickly made for the next day.
We'll meet right here tomorrow morning.
Got it. Right there.
At 8:3Ø.
THE SPOT
Don't forget to wear your costume!
I won't.
Bye!
I can't wait for tomorrow.

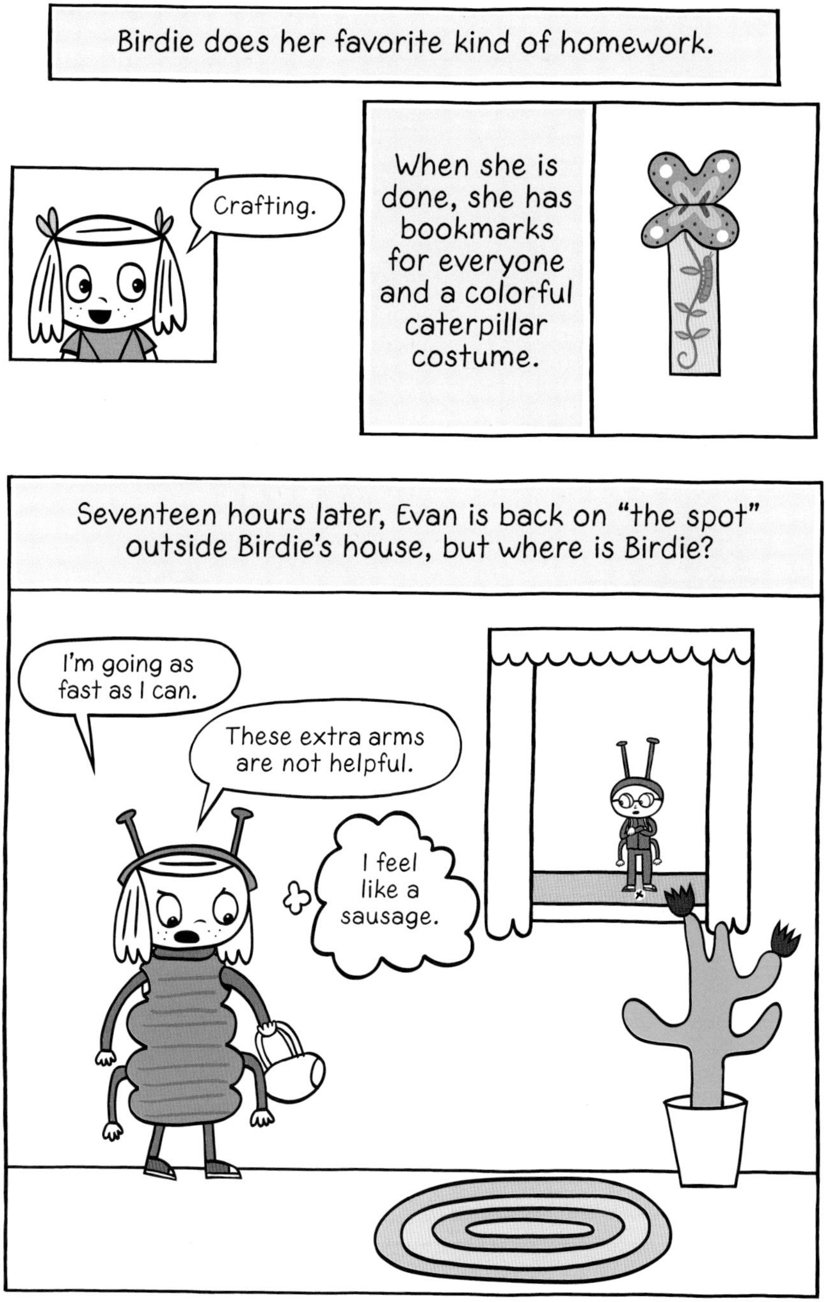
Birdie does her favorite kind of homework.
Crafting.
When she is done, she has bookmarks for everyone and a colorful caterpillar costume.
Seventeen hours later, Evan is back on "the spot" outside Birdie's house, but where is Birdie?
I'm going as fast as I can.
These extra arms are not helpful.
I feel like a sausage.

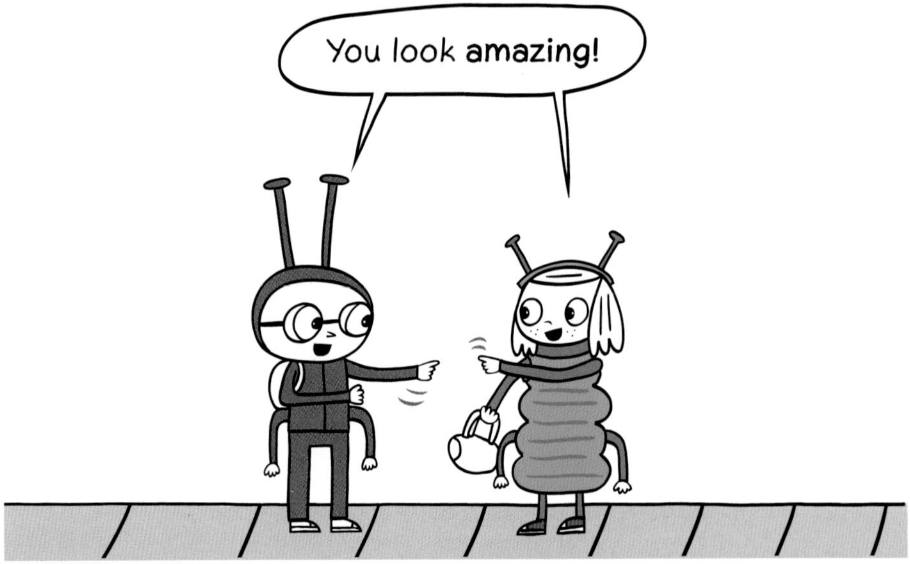
You look amazing!

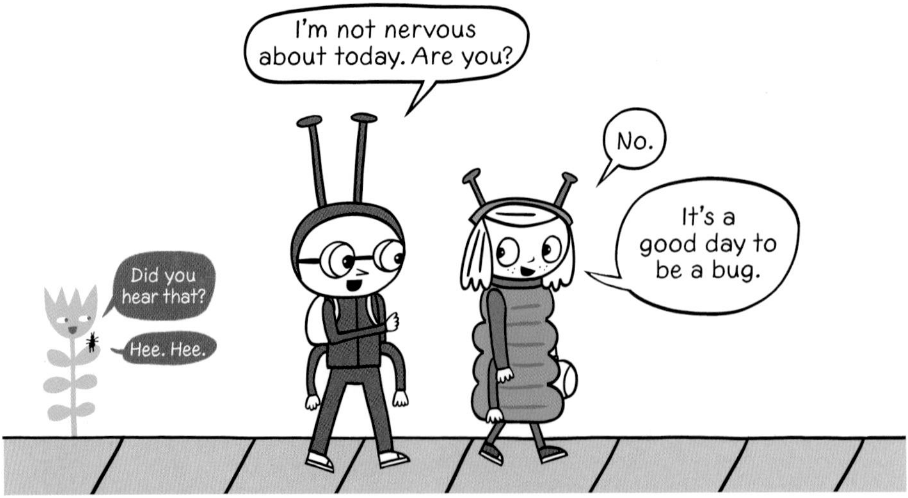
I'm not nervous about today. Are you?
No.
It's a good day to be a bug.
Did you hear that?
Hee. Hee.

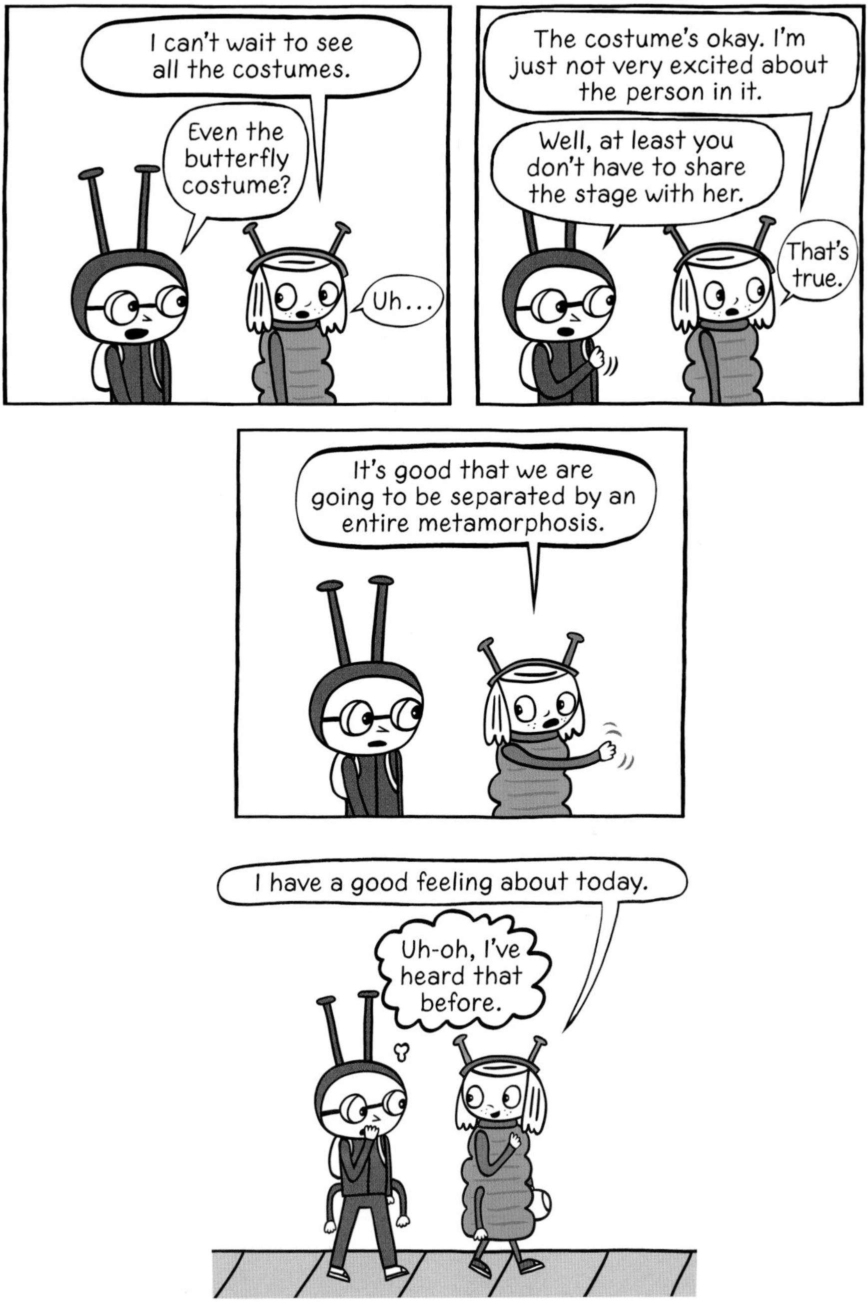
I can't wait to see all the costumes.
Even the butterfly costume?
Uh...
The costume's okay. I'm just not very excited about the person in it.
Well, at least you don't have to share the stage with her.
That's true.
It's good that we are going to be separated by an entire metamorphosis.
I have a good feeling about today.
Uh-oh, I've heard that before.

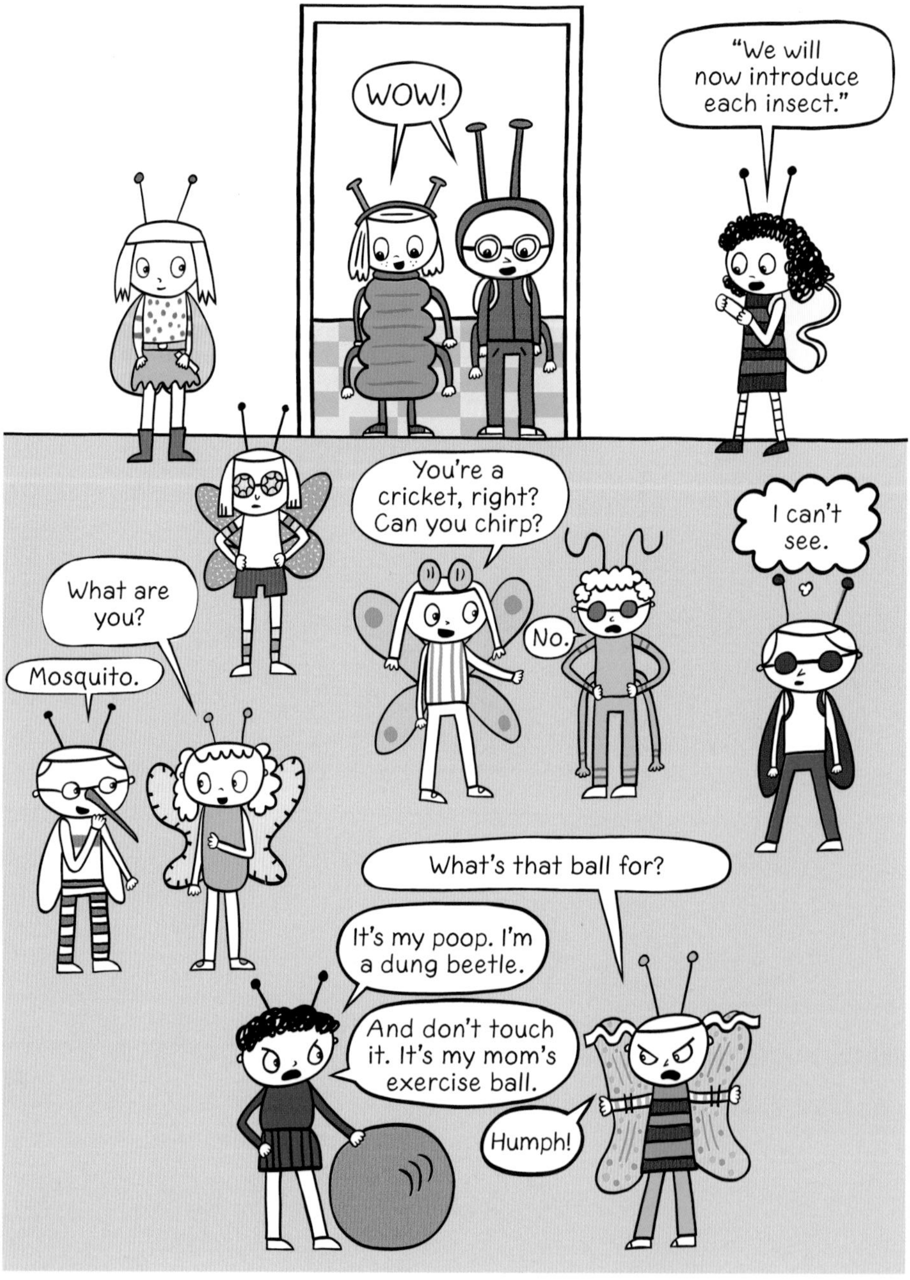
WOW!
"We will now introduce each insect."
You're a cricket, right? Can you chirp?
No.
I can't see.
What are you?
Mosquito.
What's that ball for?
It's my poop. I'm a dung beetle.
And don't touch it. It's my mom's exercise ball.
Humph!

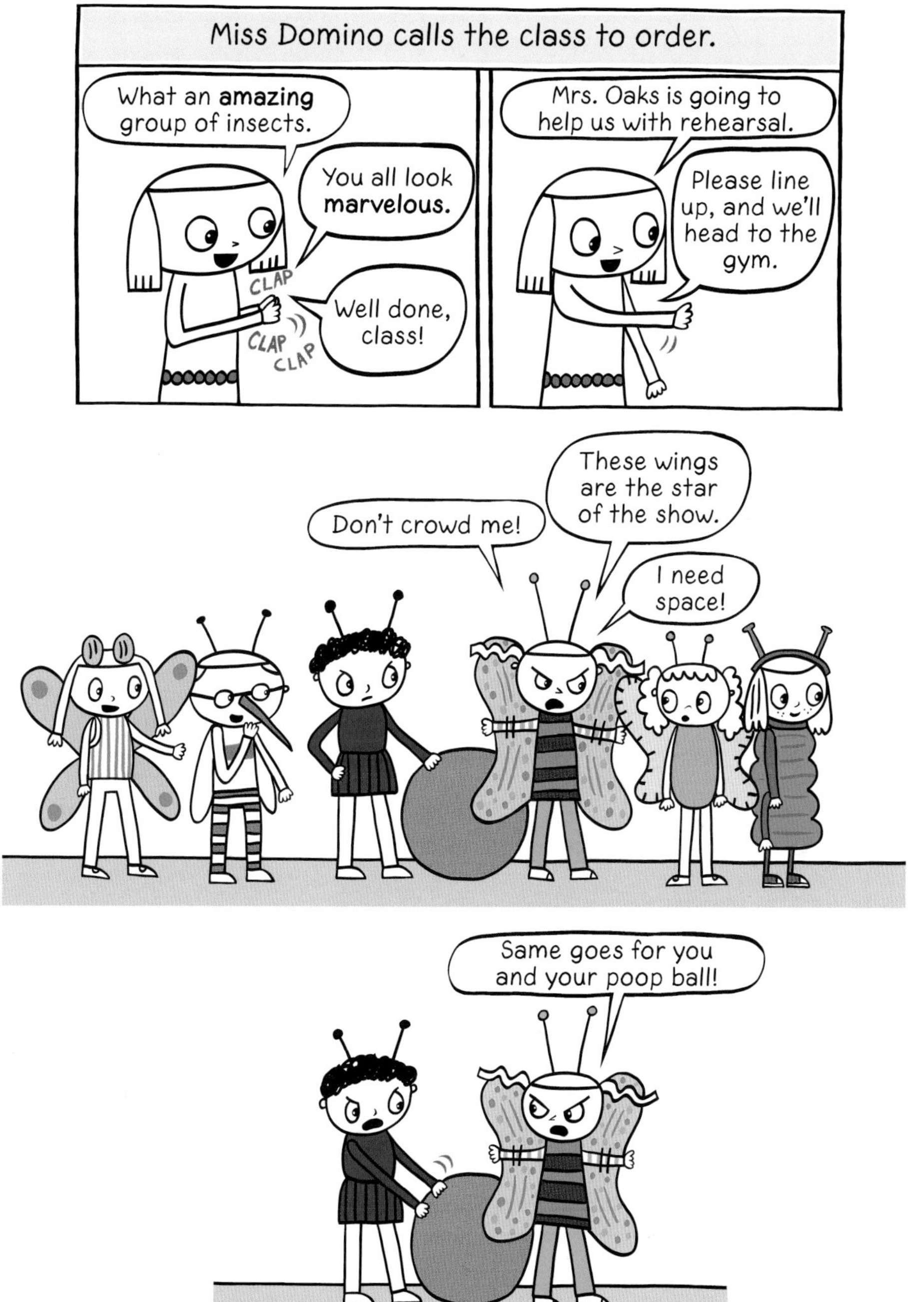
Miss Domino calls the class to order.
What an **amazing** group of insects.
You all look **marvelous.**
CLAP
CLAP
CLAP
Well done, class!
Mrs. Oaks is going to help us with rehearsal.
Please line up, and we'll head to the gym.
Don't crowd me!
These wings are the star of the show.
I need space!
Same goes for you and your poop ball!

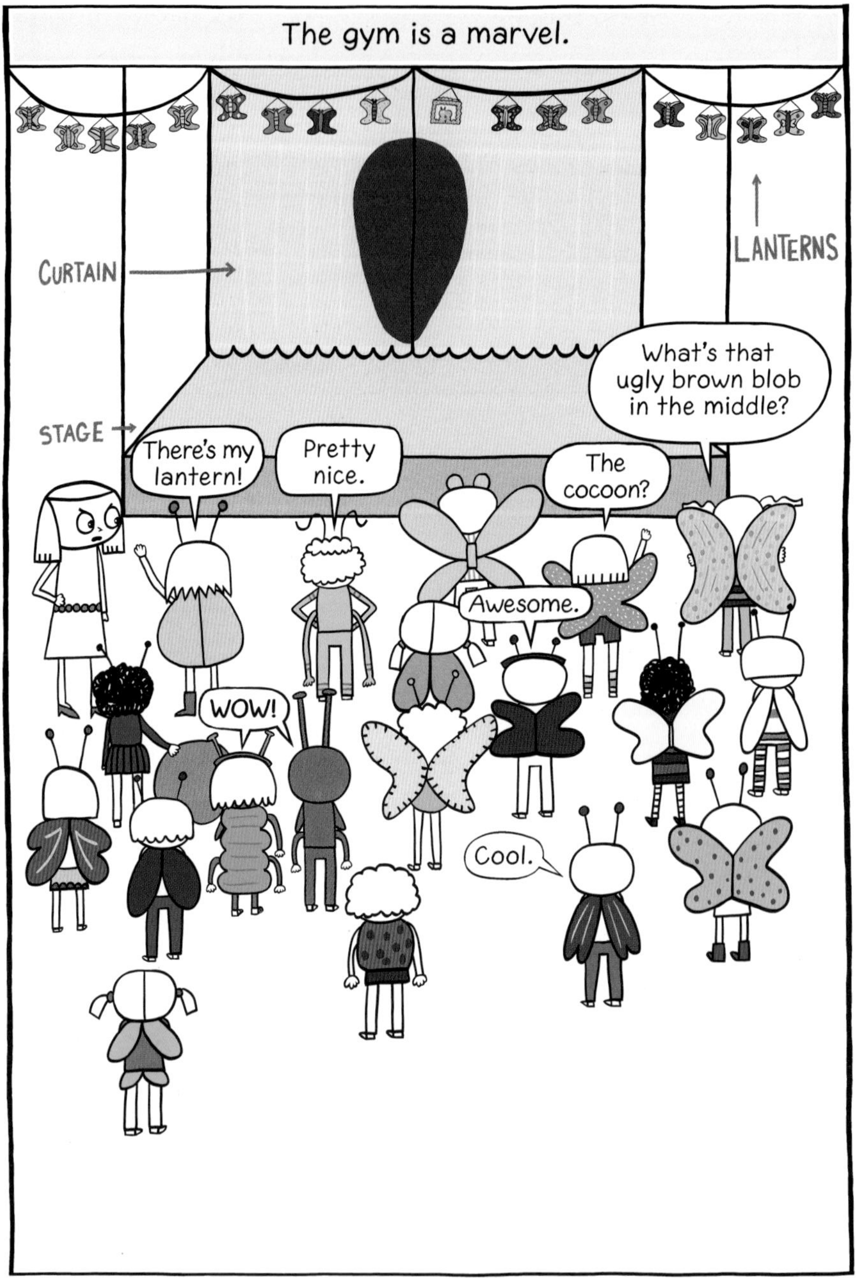
The gym is a marvel.
CURTAIN
LANTERNS
STAGE
What's that ugly brown blob in the middle?
There's my lantern!
Pretty nice.
The cocoon?
Awesome.
WOW!
Cool.

Everyone gathers around the stage to listen to the instructions.

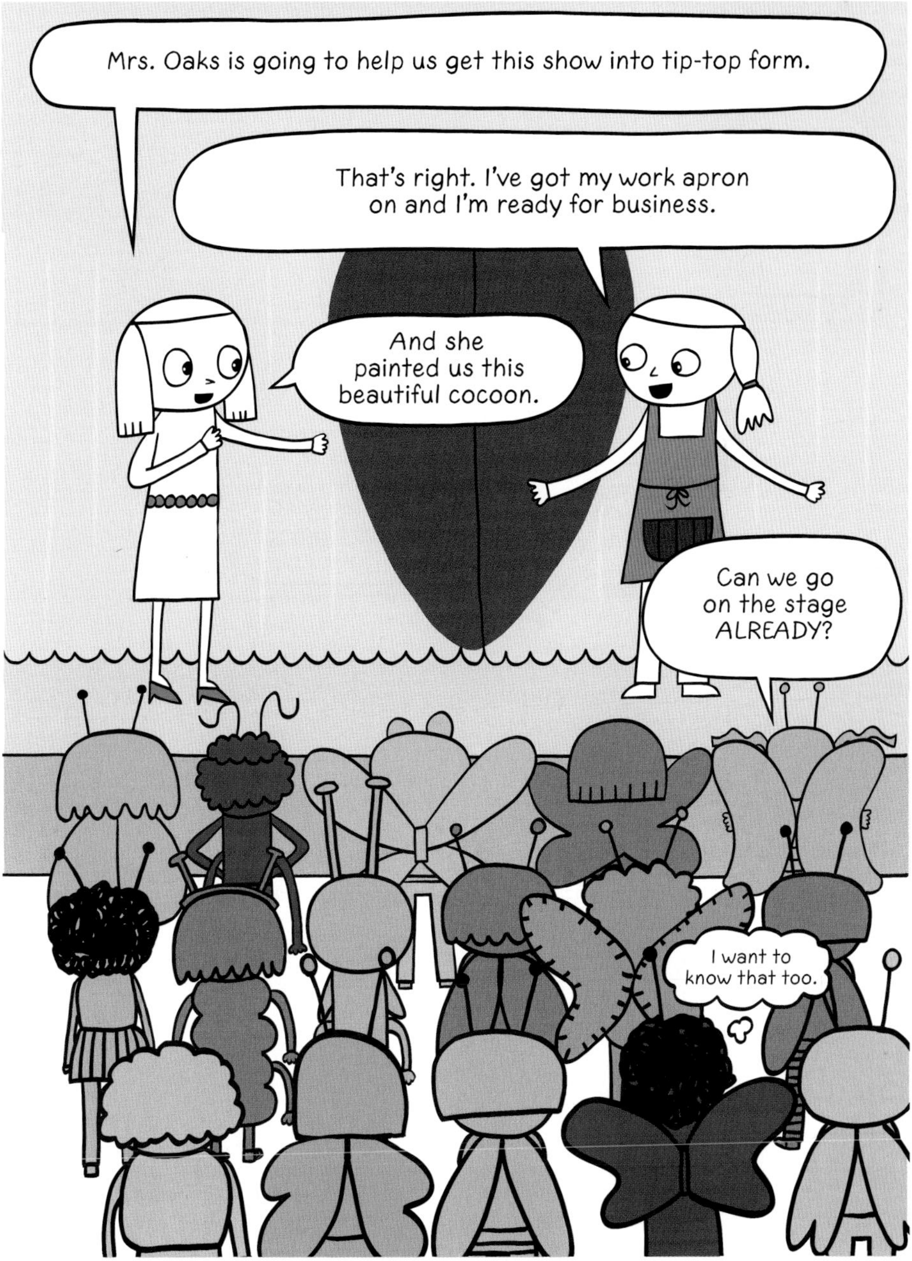
Mrs. Oaks is going to help us get this show into tip-top form.
That's right. I've got my work apron on and I'm ready for business.
And she painted us this beautiful cocoon.
Can we go on the stage ALREADY?
I want to know that too.

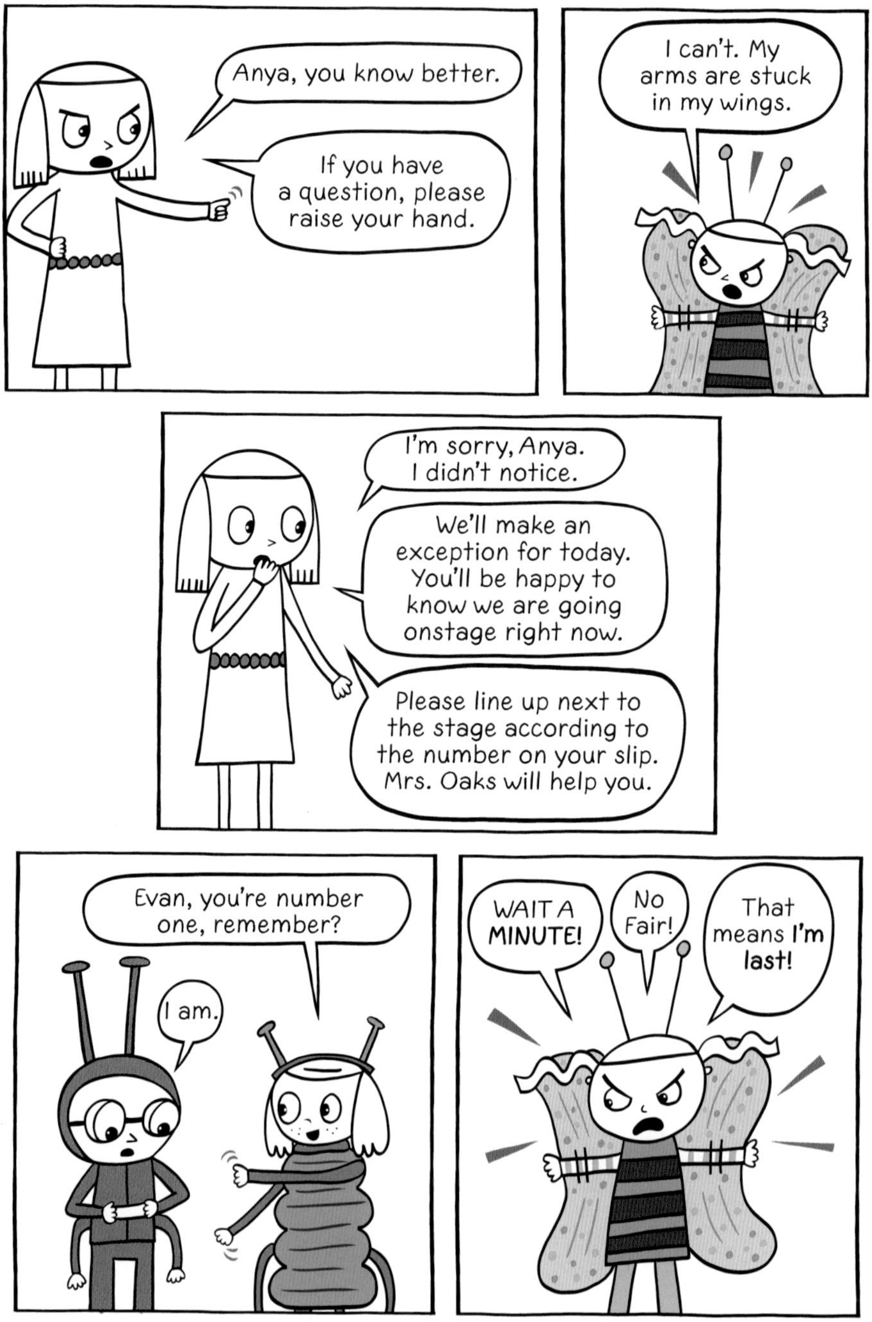
Anya, you know better.
If you have a question, please raise your hand.
I can't. My arms are stuck in my wings.
I'm sorry, Anya. I didn't notice.
We'll make an exception for today. You'll be happy to know we are going onstage right now.
Please line up next to the stage according to the number on your slip. Mrs. Oaks will help you.
Evan, you're number one, remember?
I am.
WAIT A **MINUTE!**
No Fair!
That means **I'm last!**

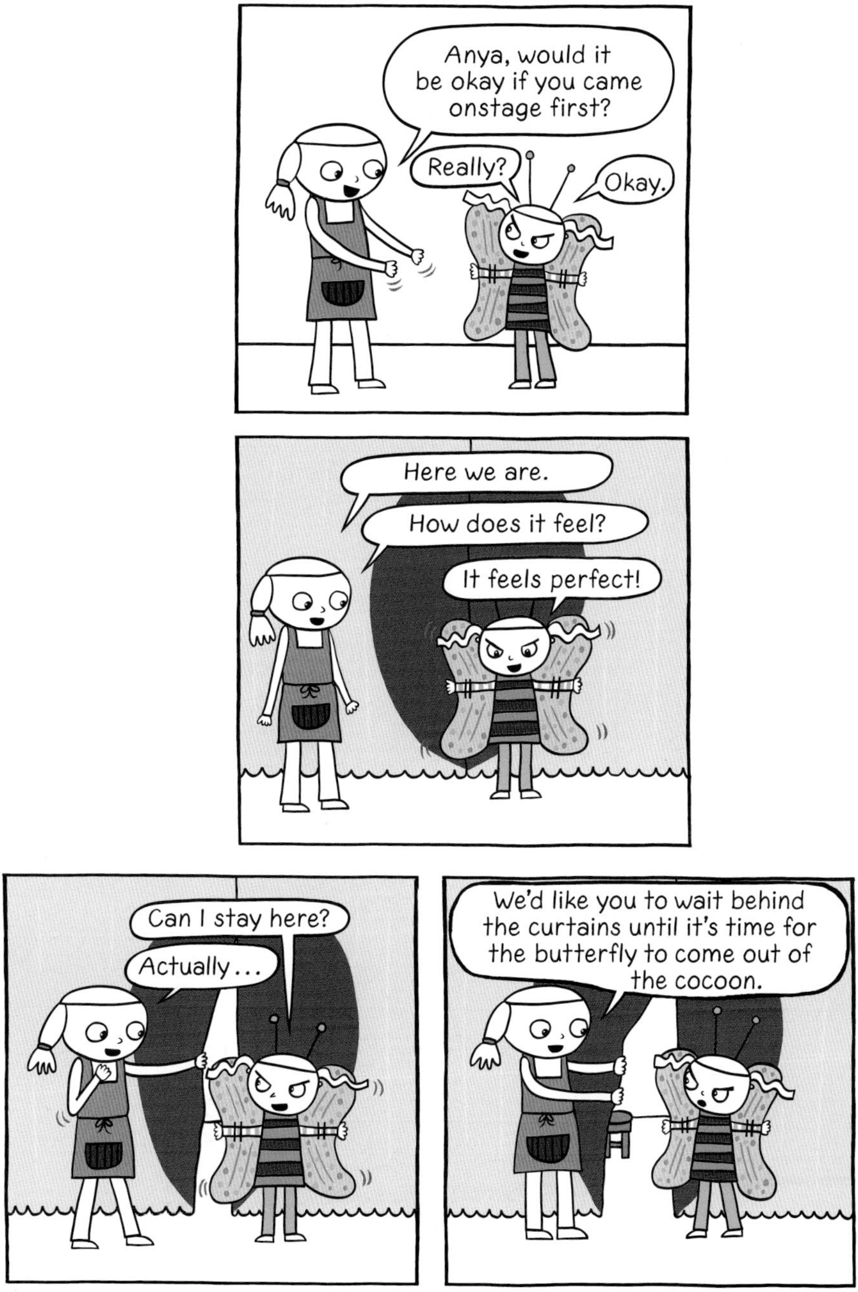
Anya, would it be okay if you came onstage first?
Really?
Okay.
Here we are.
How does it feel?
It feels perfect!
Can I stay here?
Actually...
We'd like you to wait behind the curtains until it's time for the butterfly to come out of the cocoon.

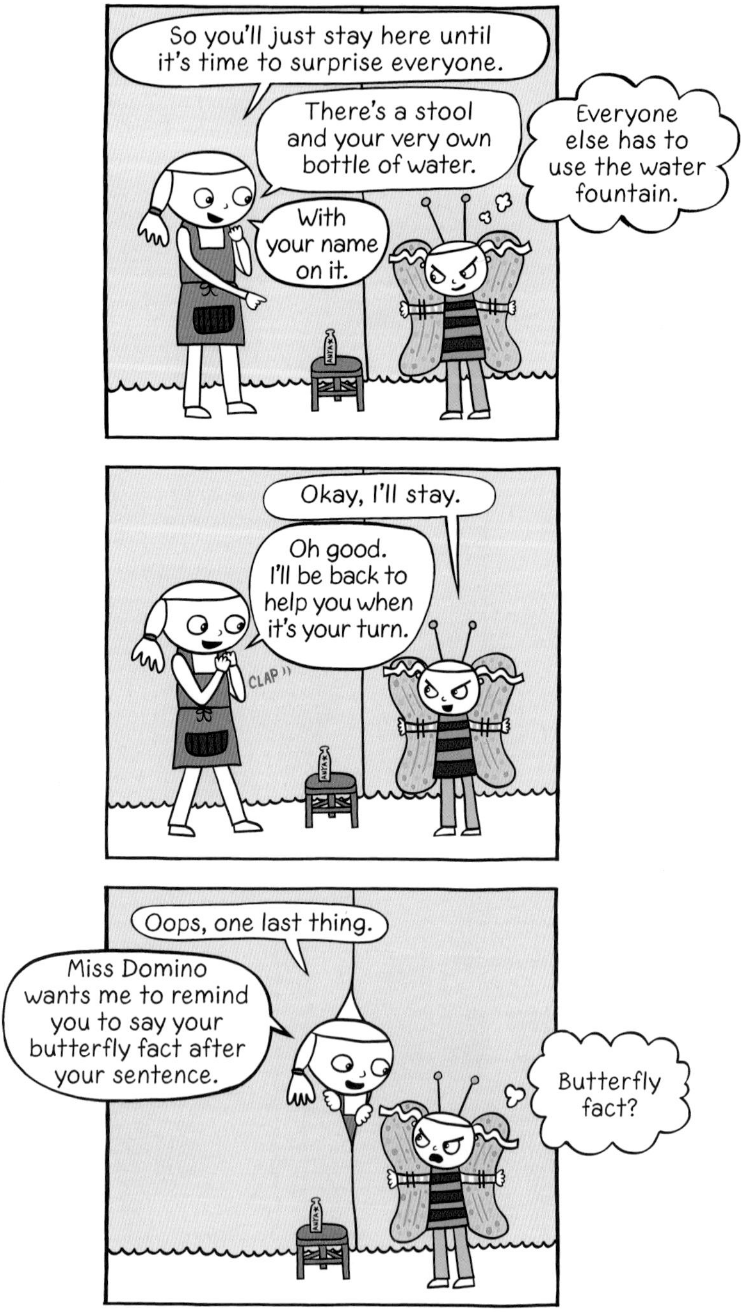
So you'll just stay here until it's time to surprise everyone.
There's a stool and your very own bottle of water.
Everyone else has to use the water fountain.
With your name on it.
Okay, I'll stay.
Oh good. I'll be back to help you when it's your turn.
CLAP
Oops, one last thing.
Miss Domino wants me to remind you to say your butterfly fact after your sentence.
Butterfly fact?

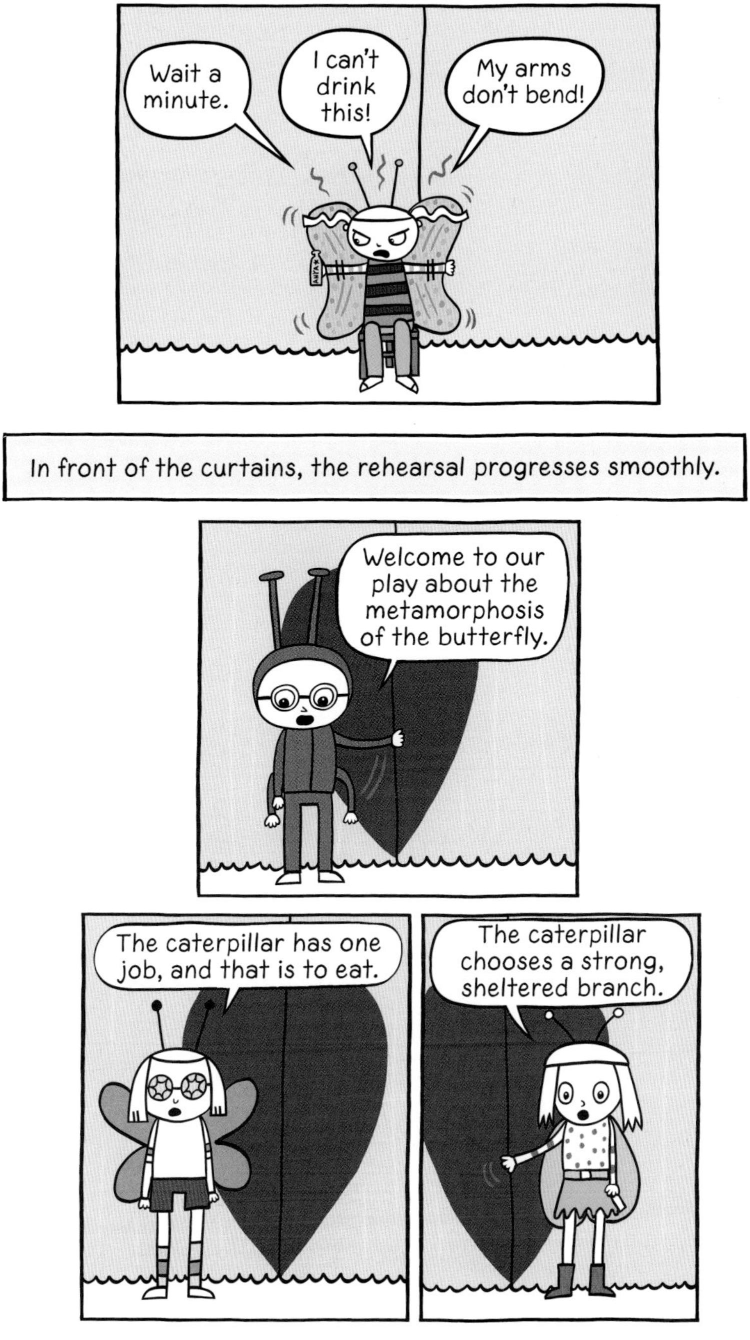
Wait a minute.
I can't drink this!
My arms don't bend!
In front of the curtains, the rehearsal progresses smoothly.
Welcome to our play about the metamorphosis of the butterfly.
The caterpillar has one job, and that is to eat.
The caterpillar chooses a strong, sheltered branch.

Birdie waits patiently.

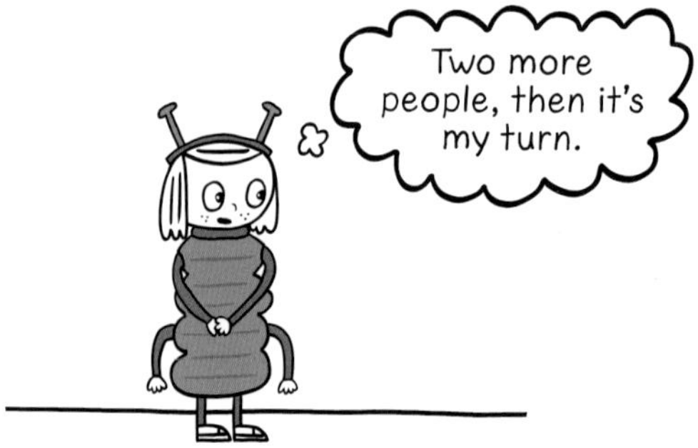
Two more people, then it's my turn.

Finally, it's her big moment onstage.

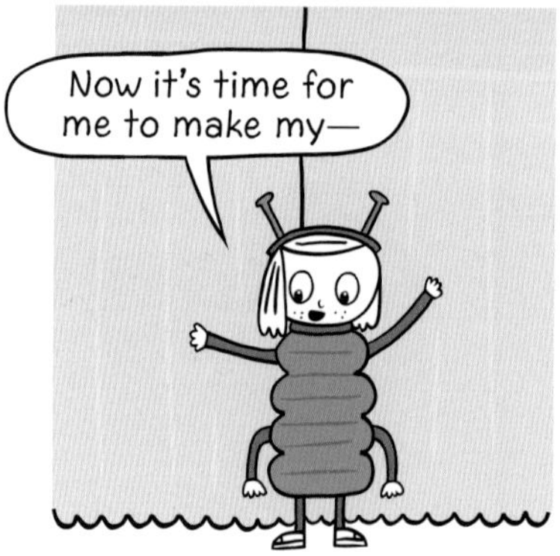
Now it's time for me to make my—

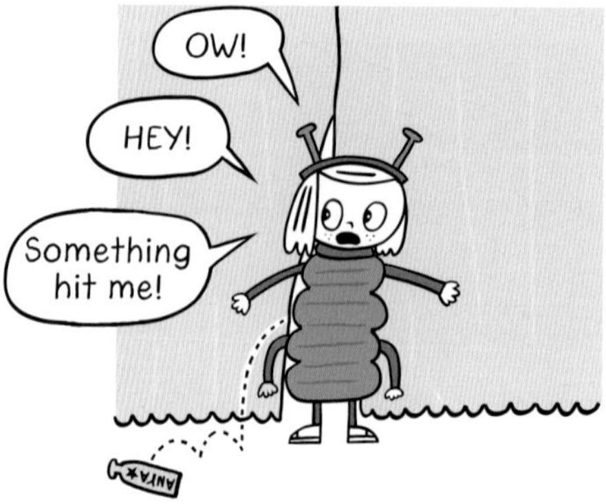
OW!
HEY!
Something hit me!

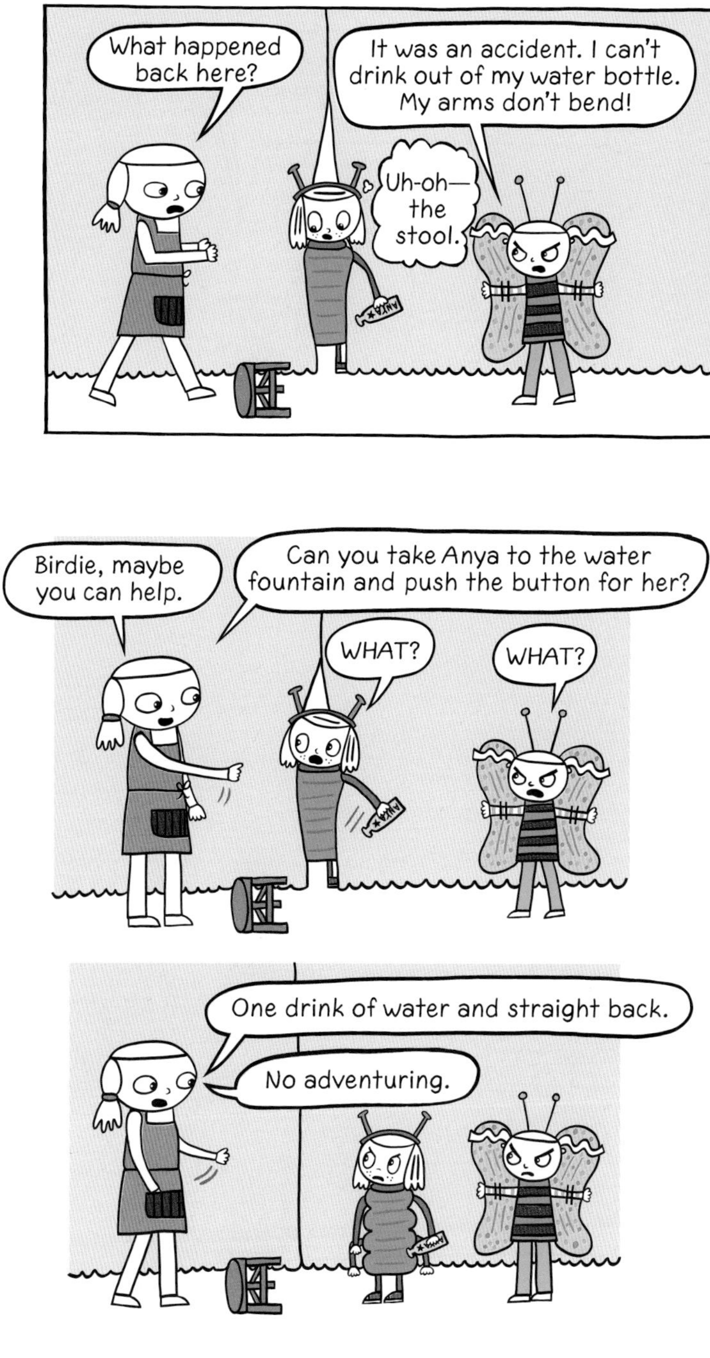
What happened back here?
It was an accident. I can't drink out of my water bottle. My arms don't bend!
Uh-oh— the stool.
ANYA
Birdie, maybe you can help.
Can you take Anya to the water fountain and push the button for her?
WHAT?
WHAT?
One drink of water and straight back.
No adventuring.

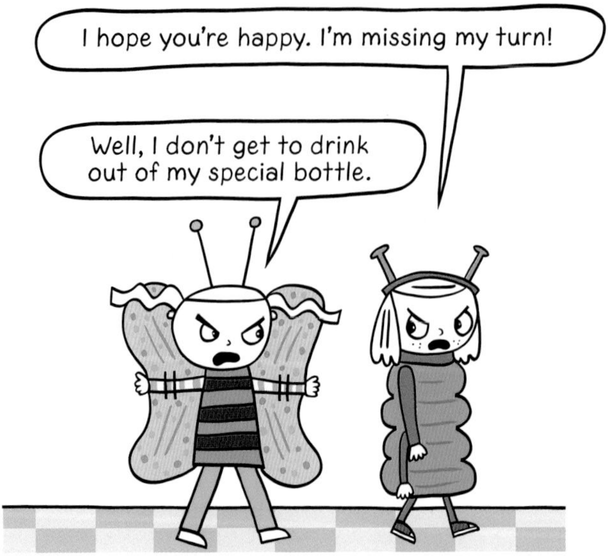
I hope you're happy. I'm missing my turn!
Well, I don't get to drink out of my special bottle.

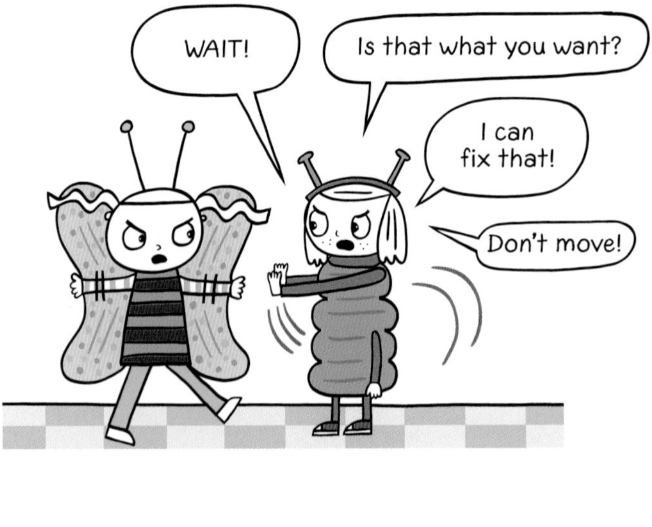
WAIT!
Is that what you want?
I can fix that!
Don't move!

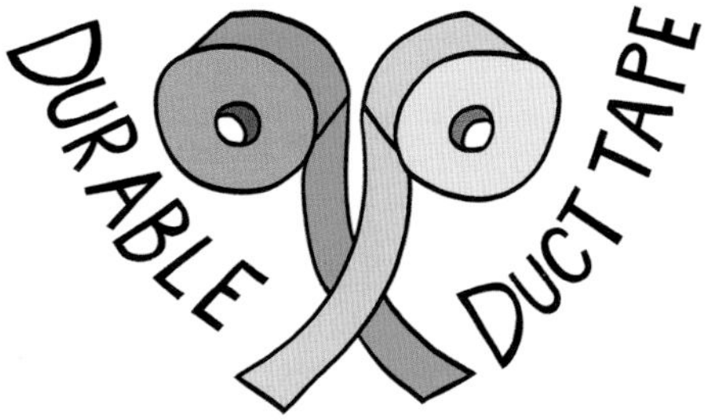
DURABLE
DUCT TAPE

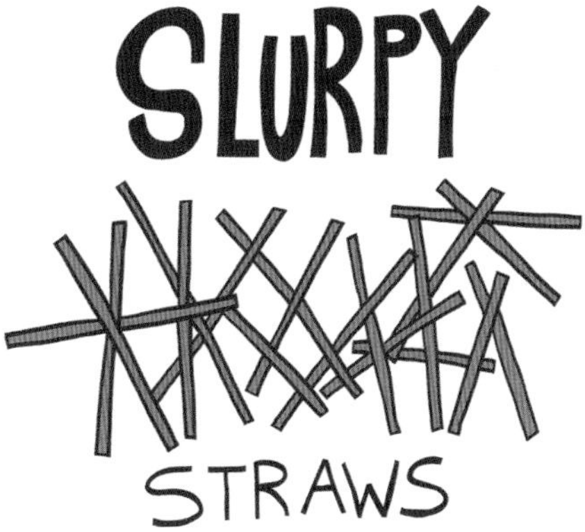
SLURPY
STRAWS

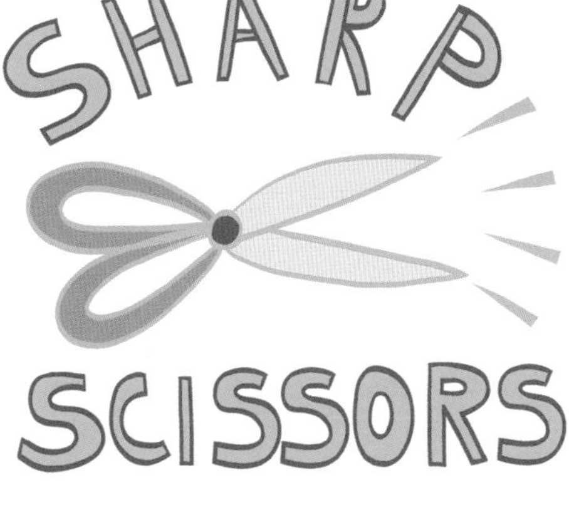
SHARP
SCISSORS

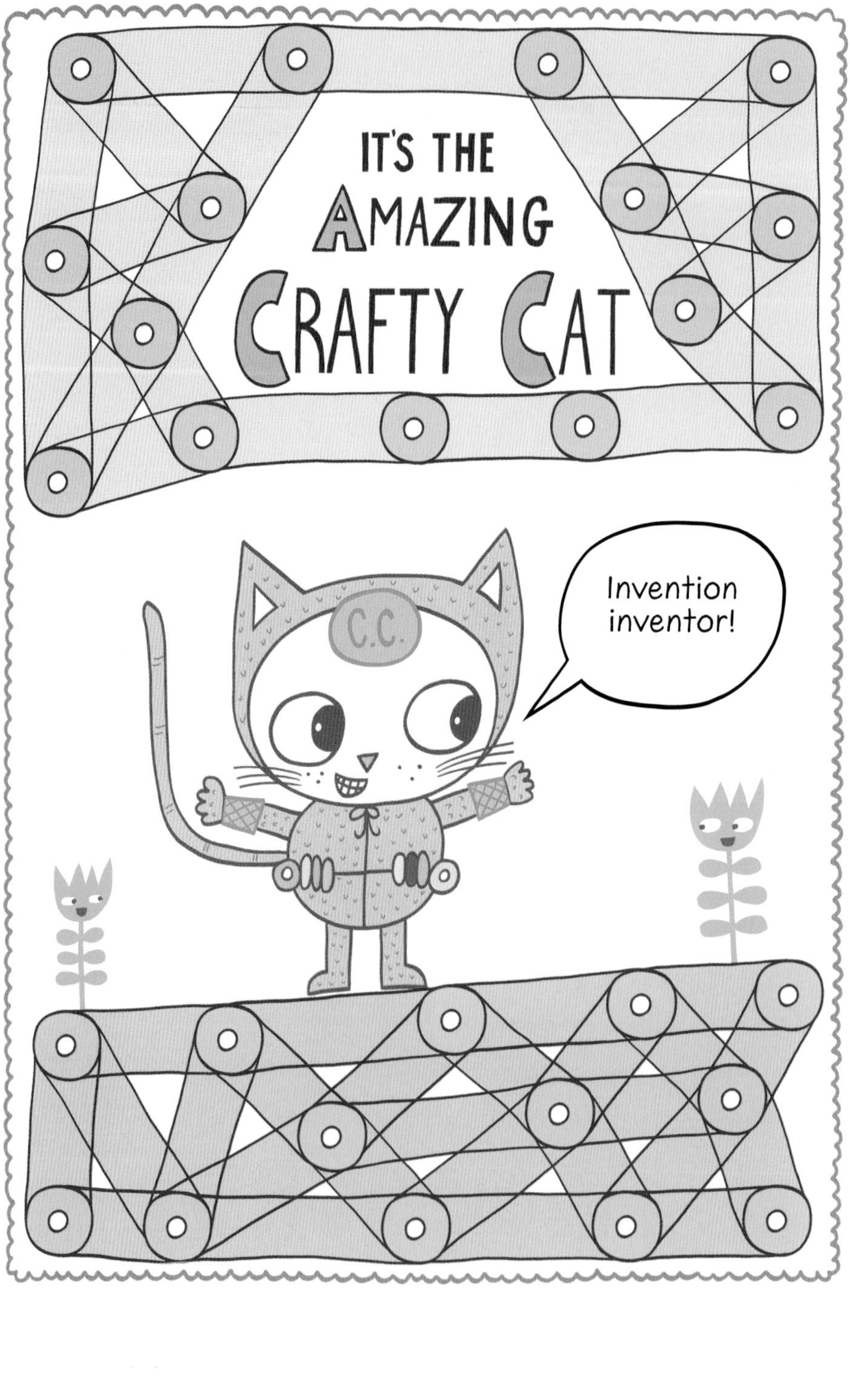
IT'S THE AMAZING CRAFTY CAT
C.C.
Invention inventor!

The transformation is fast—all that is needed is a moment of privacy.

CUSTODIAN
SLAM
Got to get supplies.
This costume was not made for running.

In just minutes, the invention is complete.

SUPPLIES
BENDY STRAWS
SCISSORS
DUCT TAPE
PATH OF WATER
SUCK WATER FROM HERE.
WATER BOTTLE
ANYA

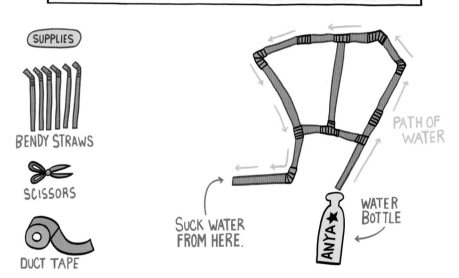

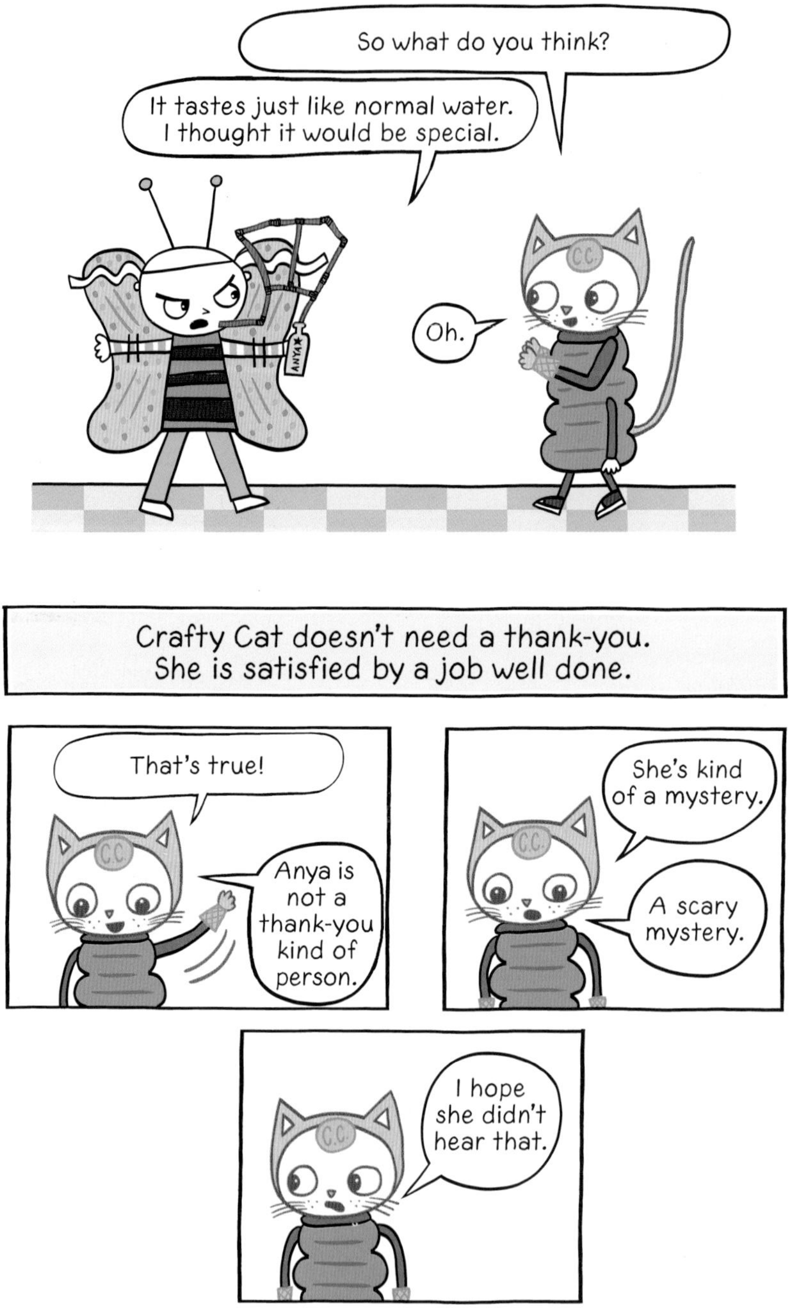
So what do you think?
It tastes just like normal water. I thought it would be special.
ANYA★
Oh.
Crafty Cat doesn't need a thank-you. She is satisfied by a job well done.
That's true!
Anya is not a thank-you kind of person.
She's kind of a mystery.
A scary mystery.
I hope she didn't hear that.

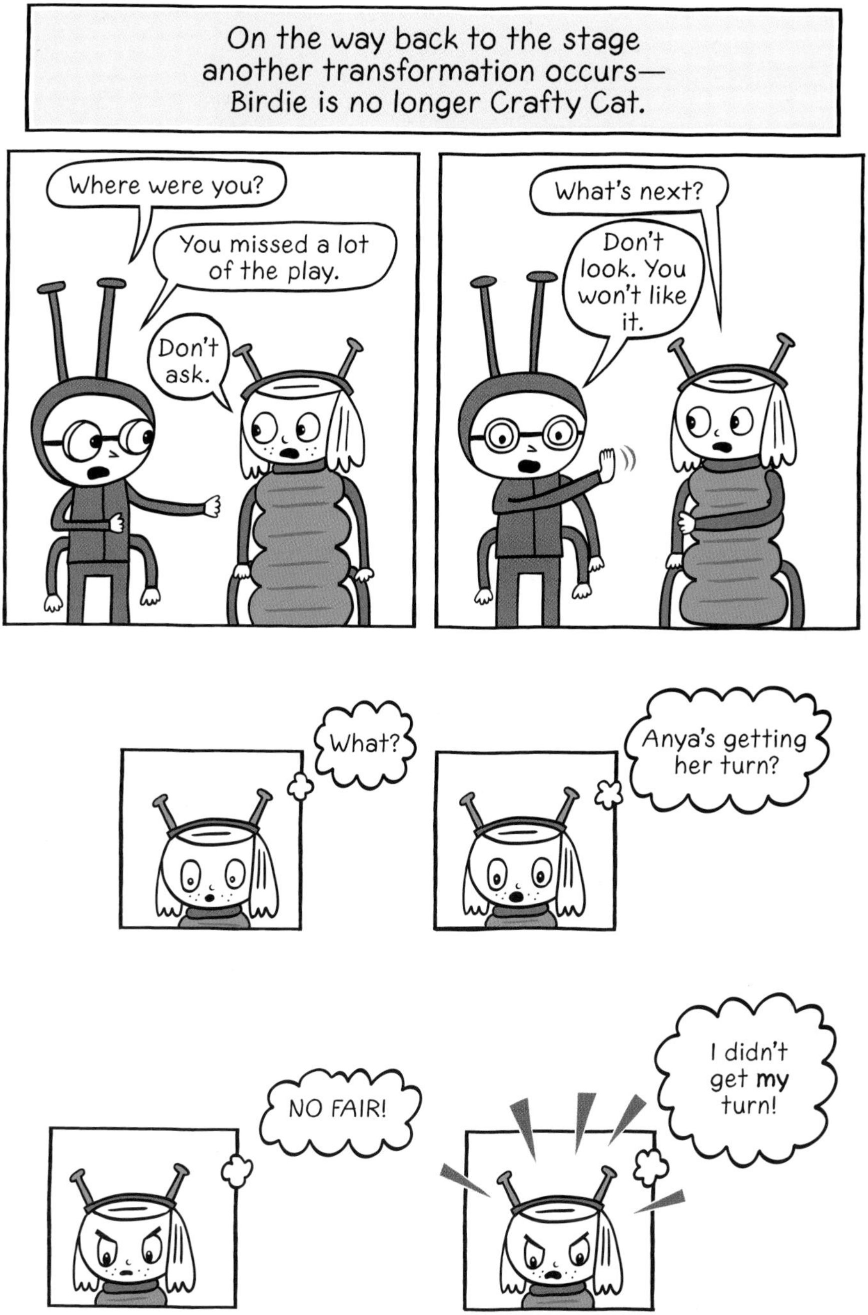
On the way back to the stage another transformation occurs— Birdie is no longer Crafty Cat.
Where were you?
You missed a lot of the play.
Don't ask.
What's next?
Don't look. You won't like it.
What?
Anya's getting her turn?
NO FAIR!
I didn't get **my** turn!

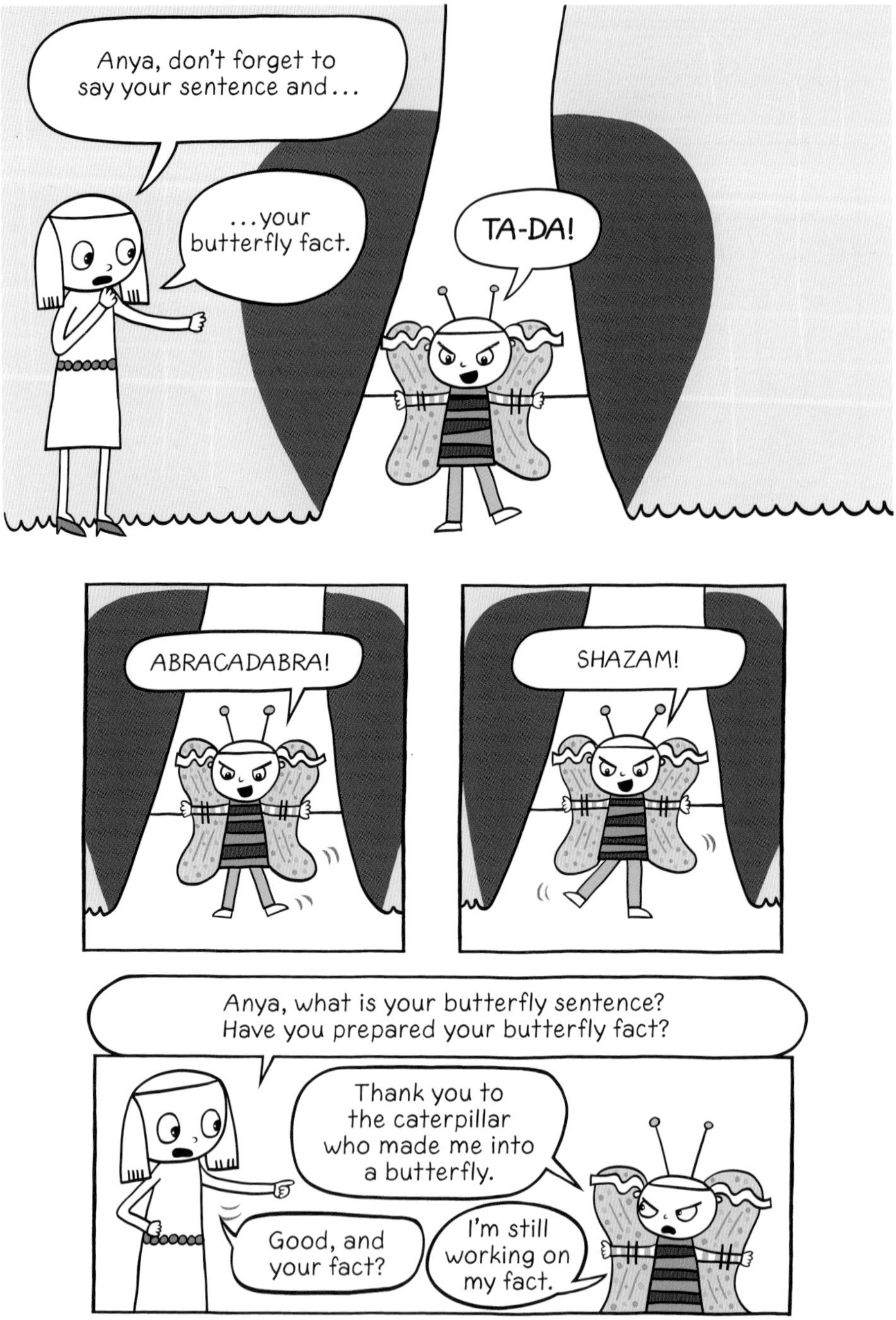
Anya, don't forget to say your sentence and...
...your butterfly fact.
TA-DA!
ABRACADABRA!
SHAZAM!
Anya, what is your butterfly sentence? Have you prepared your butterfly fact?
Thank you to the caterpillar who made me into a butterfly.
Good, and your fact?
I'm still working on my fact.

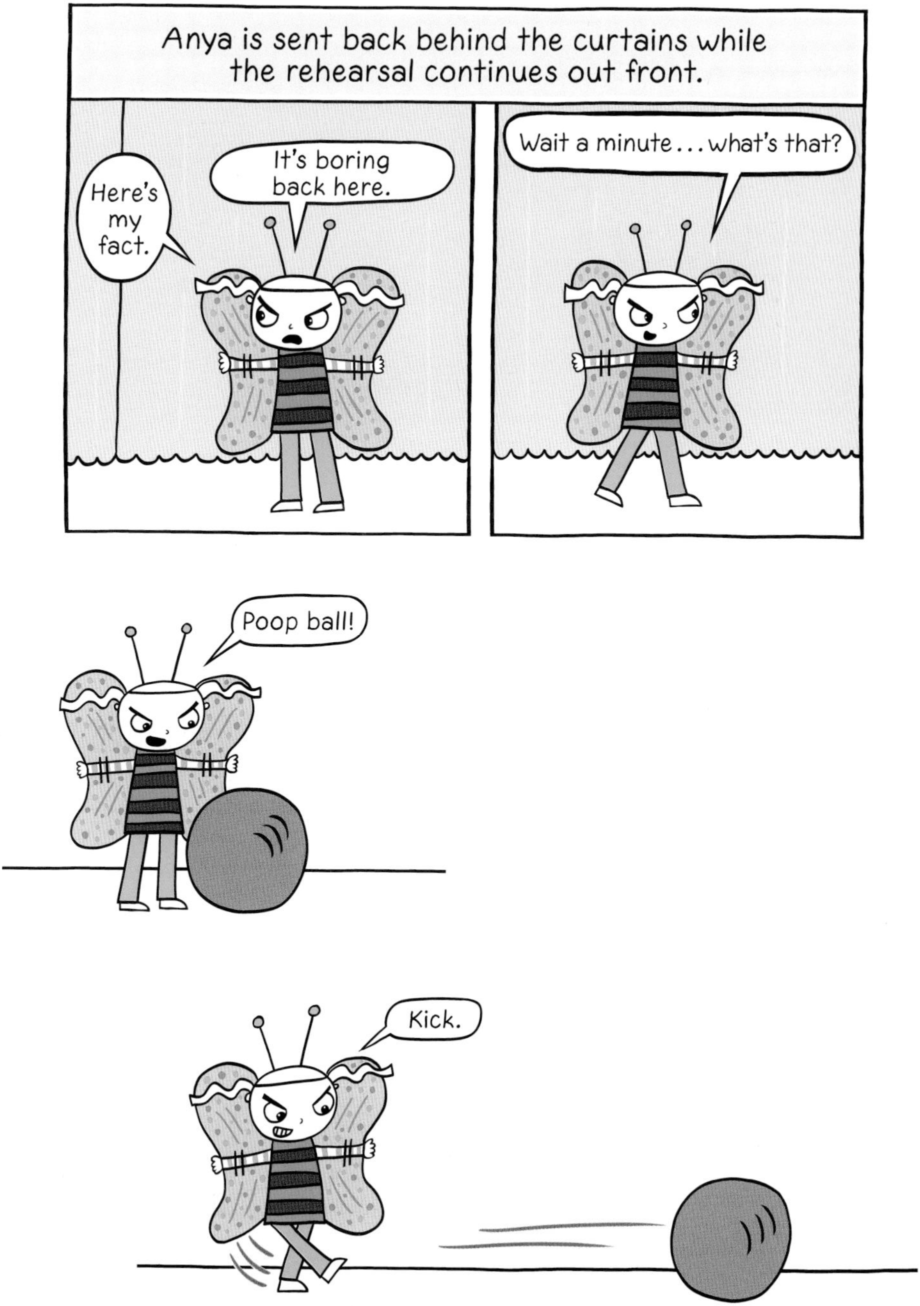
Anya is sent back behind the curtains while the rehearsal continues out front.
It's boring back here.
Here's my fact.
Wait a minute... what's that?
Poop ball!
Kick.

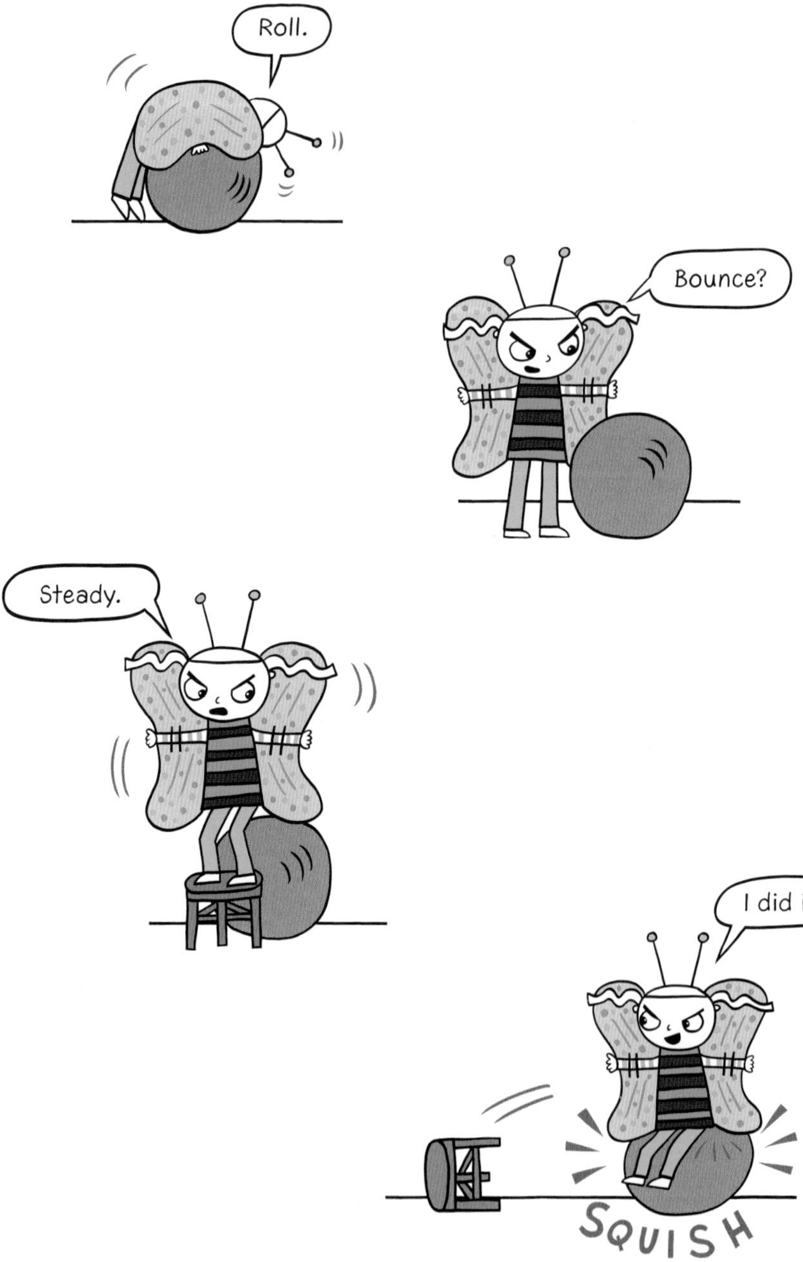
Roll.
Bounce?
Steady.
I did it!
SQUISH

HA! HAAA!
BOING

NO! NO! NO!
WOOSH

SPLAT
AAAH!

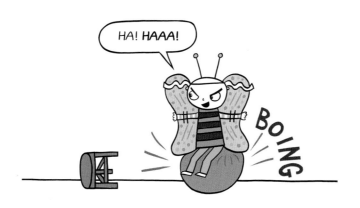

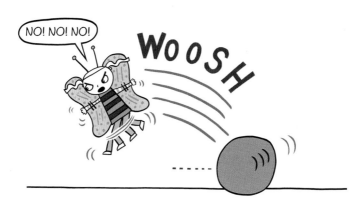

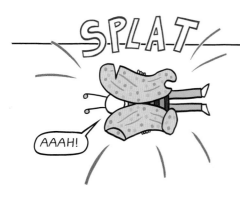

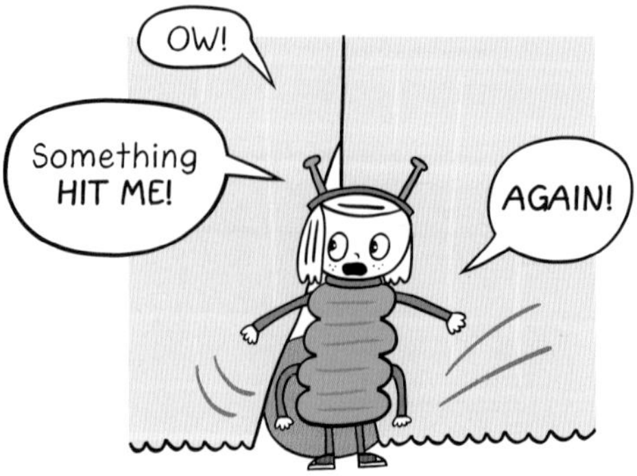
OW!
Something HIT ME!
AGAIN!

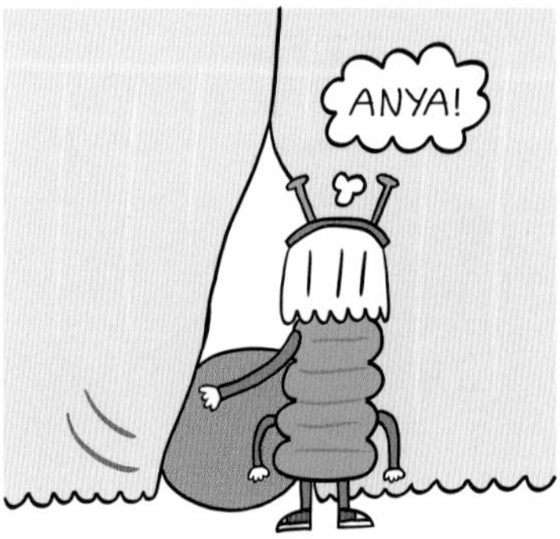
ANYA!

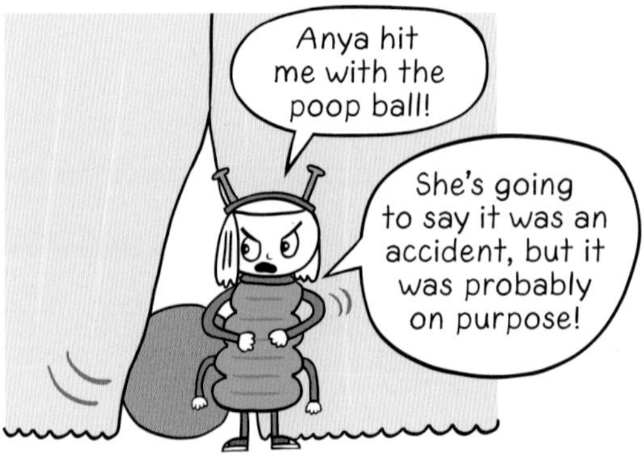
Anya hit me with the poop ball!
She's going to say it was an accident, but it was probably on purpose!

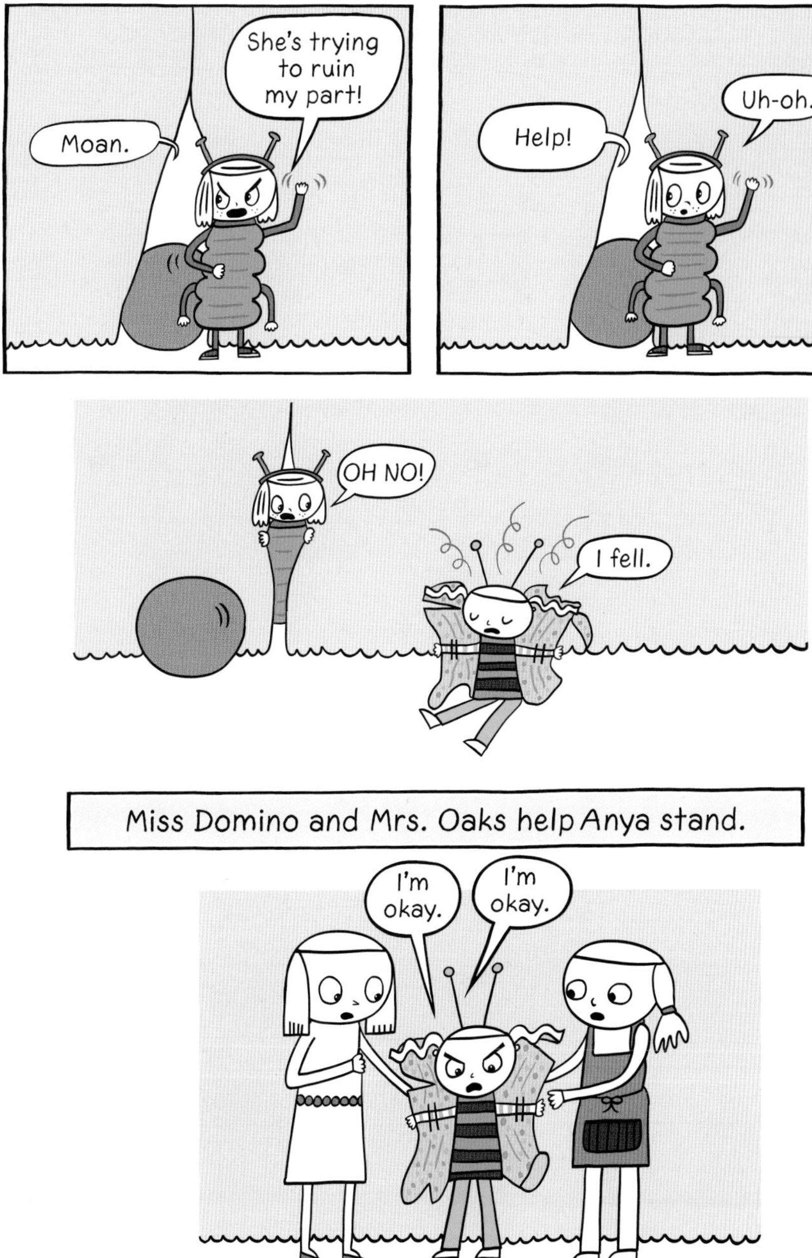
She's trying to ruin my part!
Moan.
Help!
Uh-oh.
OH NO!
I fell.
Miss Domino and Mrs. Oaks help Anya stand.
I'm okay.
I'm okay.

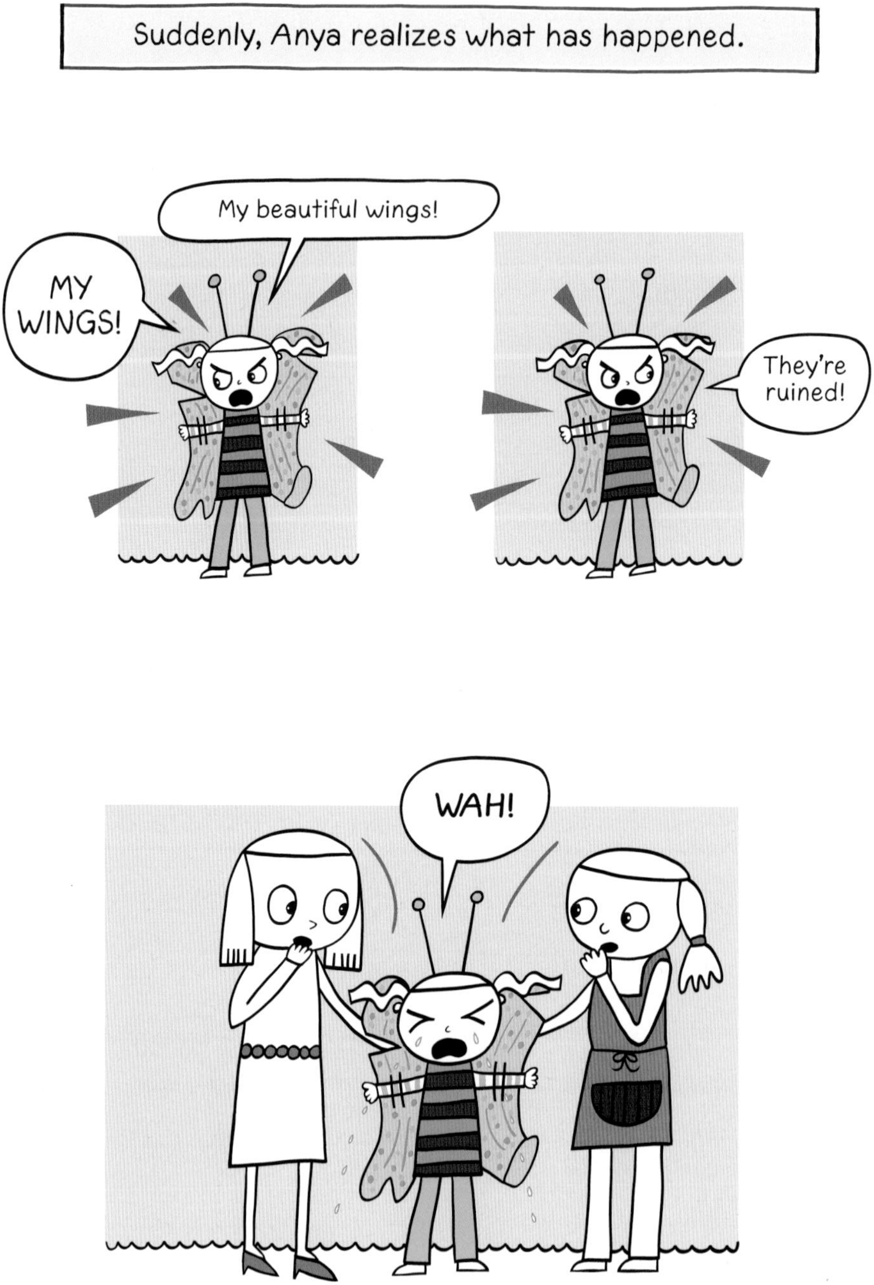
Suddenly, Anya realizes what has happened.
MY WINGS!
My beautiful wings!
They're ruined!
WAH!

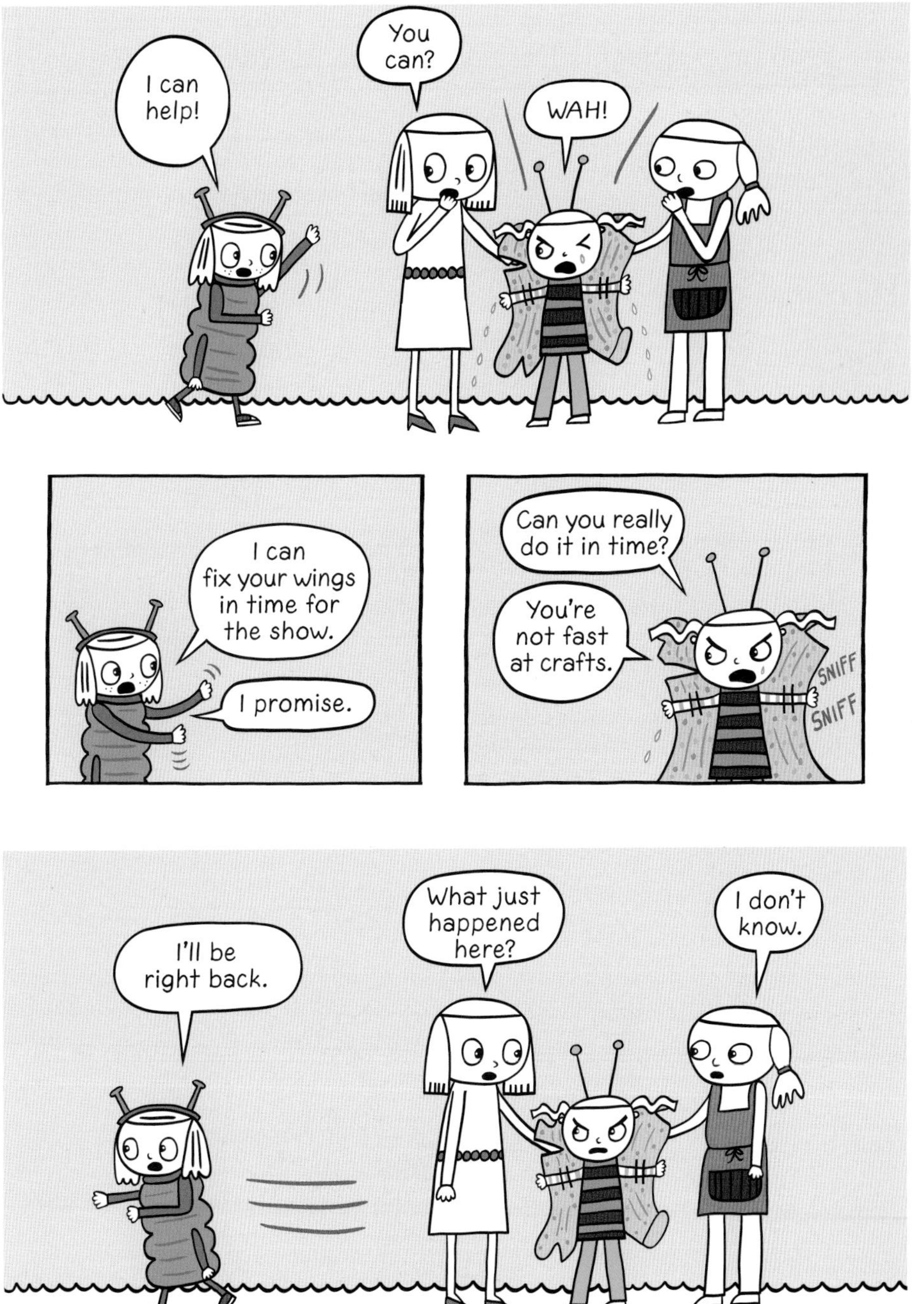
I can help!
You can?
WAH!
I can fix your wings in time for the show.
I promise.
Can you really do it in time?
You're not fast at crafts.
SNIFF
SNIFF
I'll be right back.
What just happened here?
I don't know.

How exciting! Is this another job for Crafty Cat?

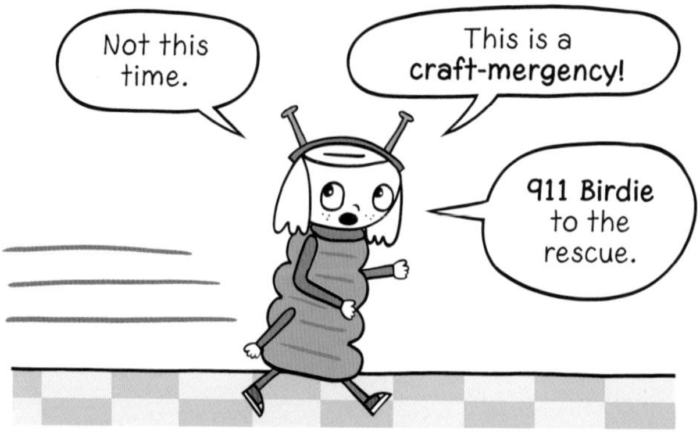
Not this time.
This is a **craft-mergency!**
911 Birdie to the rescue.

Birdie gathers the needed supplies and races back to her patient.

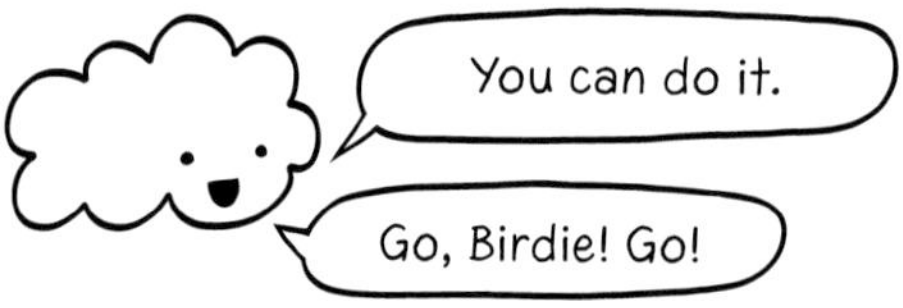
You can do it.
Go, Birdie! Go!

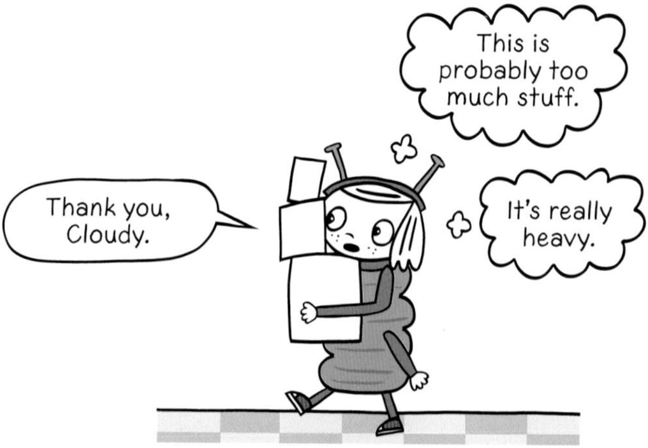
This is probably too much stuff.
Thank you, Cloudy.
It's really heavy.

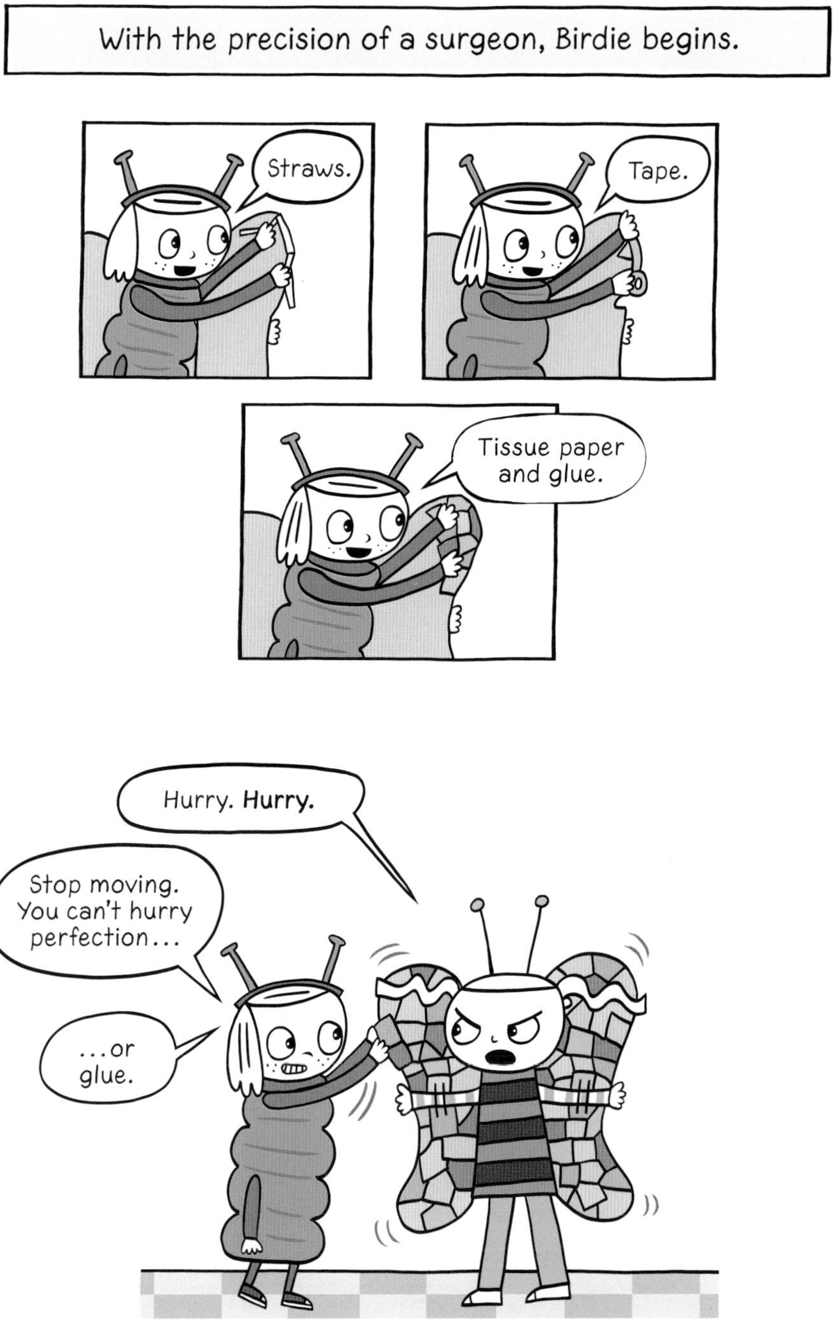
With the precision of a surgeon, Birdie begins.
Straws.
Tape.
Tissue paper and glue.
Hurry. **Hurry.**
Stop moving. You can't hurry perfection...
...or glue.

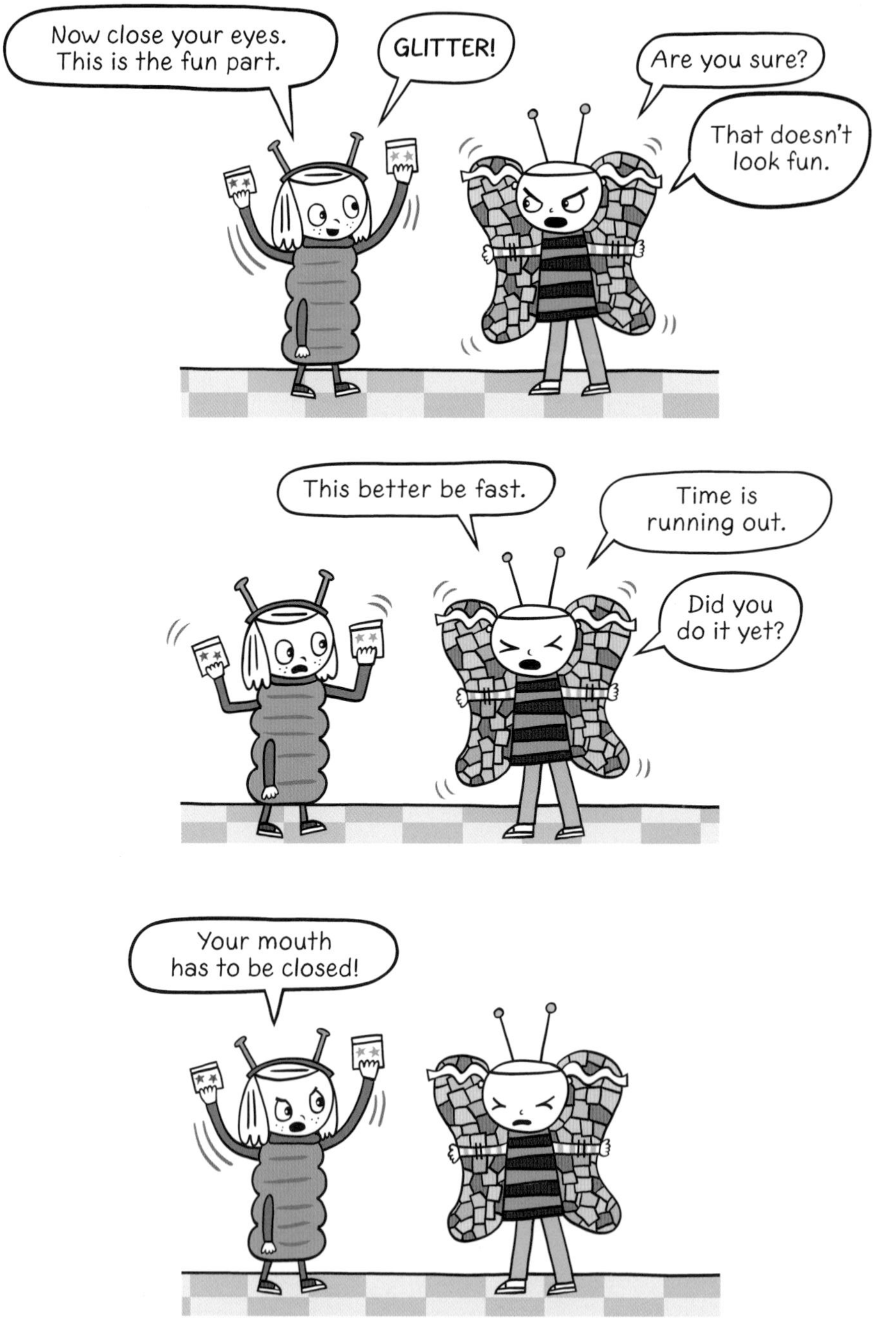
Now close your eyes. This is the fun part.
GLITTER!
Are you sure?
That doesn't look fun.
This better be fast.
Time is running out.
Did you do it yet?
Your mouth has to be closed!

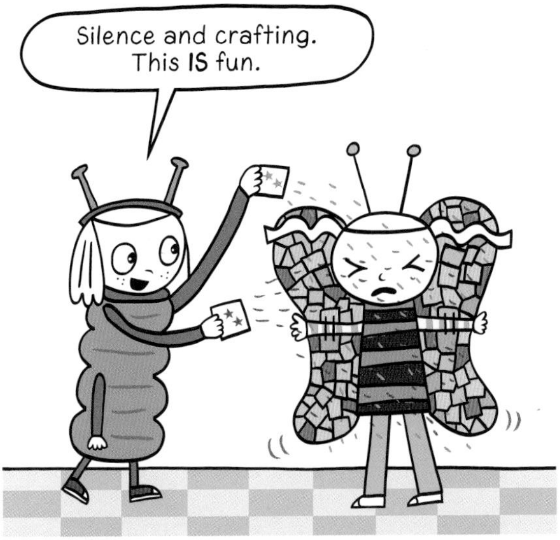
Silence and crafting.
This **IS** fun.

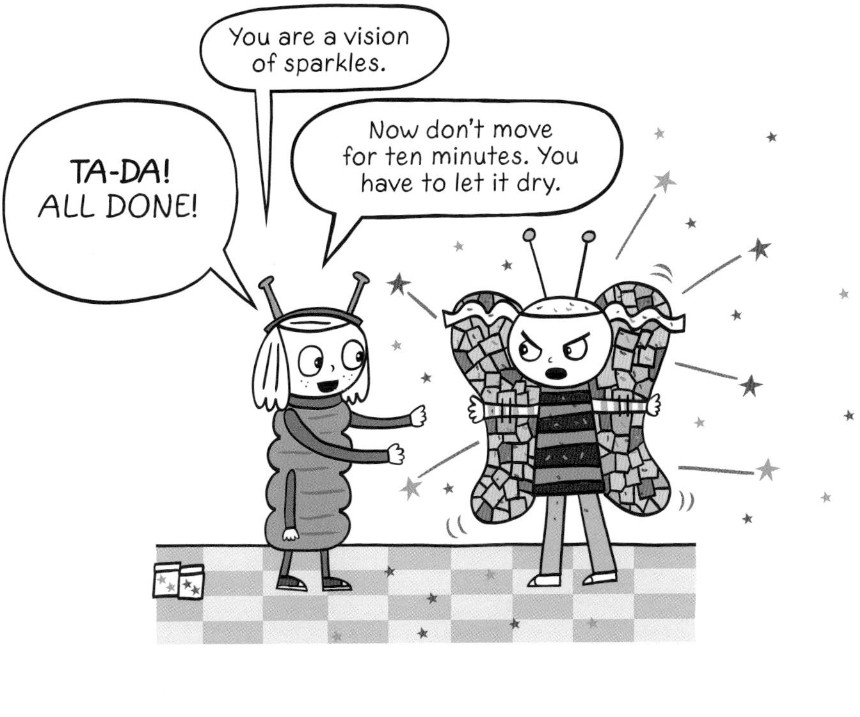
TA-DA!
ALL DONE!
You are a vision
of sparkles.
Now don't move
for ten minutes. You
have to let it dry.

The show starts, and for the first time ever,
Birdie gets to say her entire speech.

Now it's time for me
to make my cocoon.

I did
it!

Anya waits motionless behind the curtains.
Waiting. And waiting! AND waiting!

That glue
better dry
fast!

It's almost my turn.

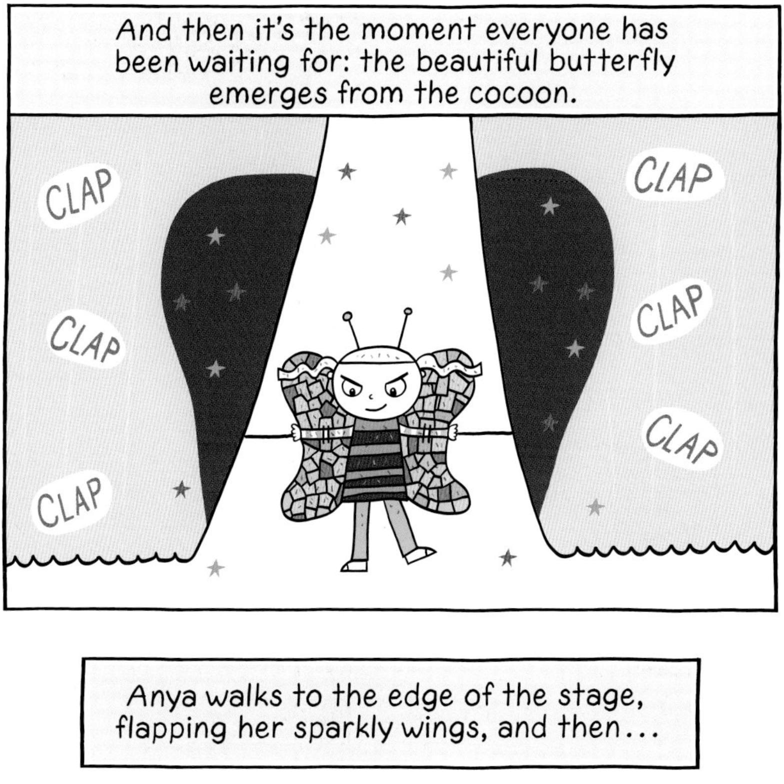
And then it's the moment everyone has been waiting for: the beautiful butterfly emerges from the cocoon.
CLAP
CLAP
CLAP
CLAP
CLAP
CLAP

Anya walks to the edge of the stage, flapping her sparkly wings, and then...

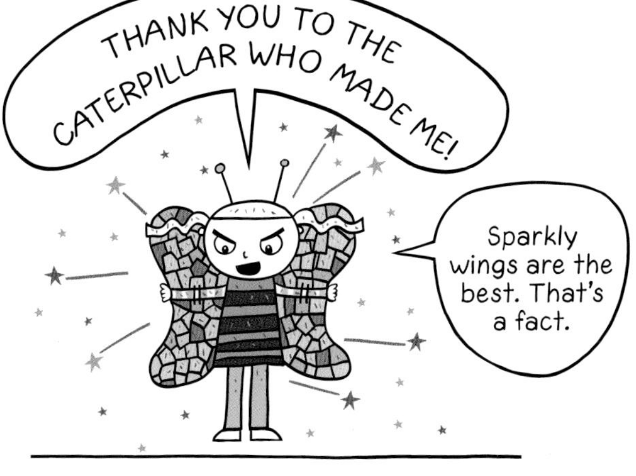
THANK YOU TO THE CATERPILLAR WHO MADE ME!
Sparkly wings are the best. That's a fact.

Everyone claps, but Miss Domino claps the loudest, and she looks right at Birdie.

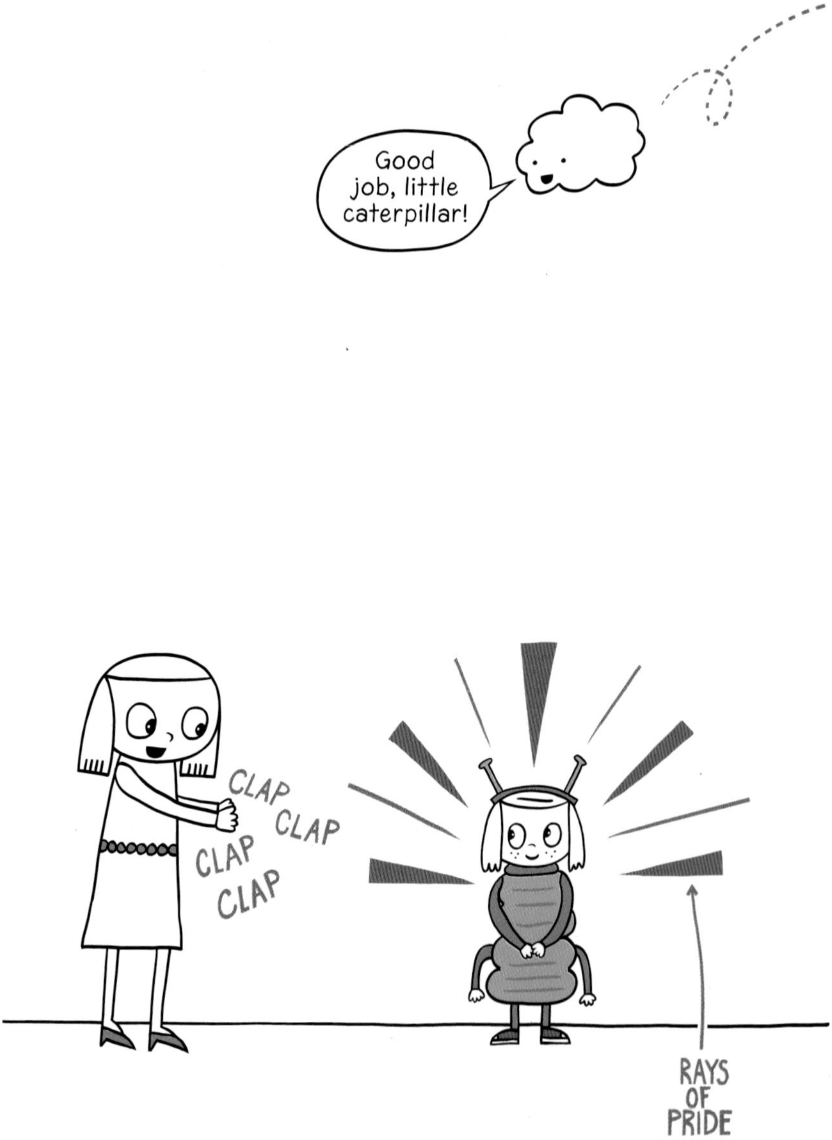
Good job, little caterpillar!
CLAP CLAP CLAP CLAP
RAYS OF PRIDE

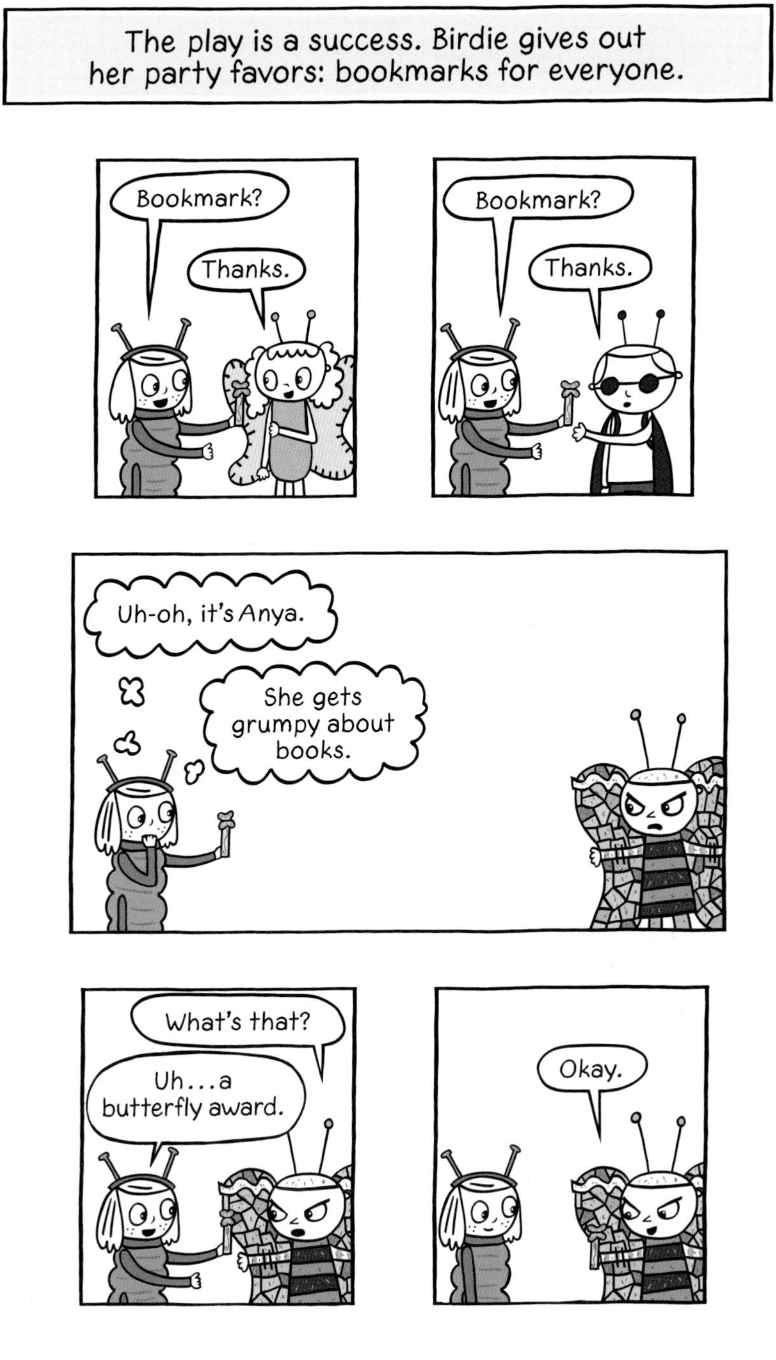
The play is a success. Birdie gives out her party favors: bookmarks for everyone.
Bookmark?
Thanks.
Bookmark?
Thanks.
Uh-oh, it's Anya.
She gets grumpy about books.
What's that?
Uh...a butterfly award.
Okay.

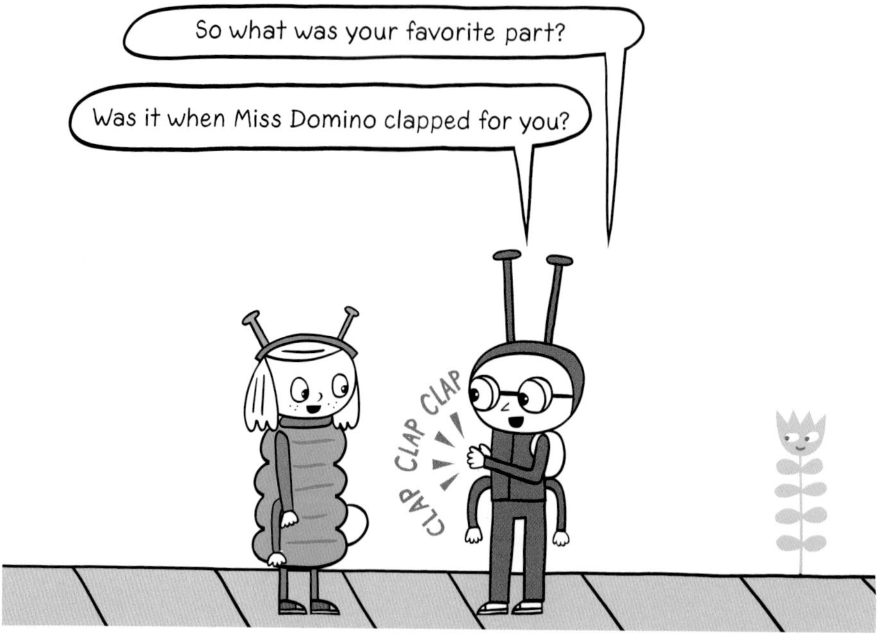
So what was your favorite part?
Was it when Miss Domino clapped for you?
CLAP CLAP CLAP

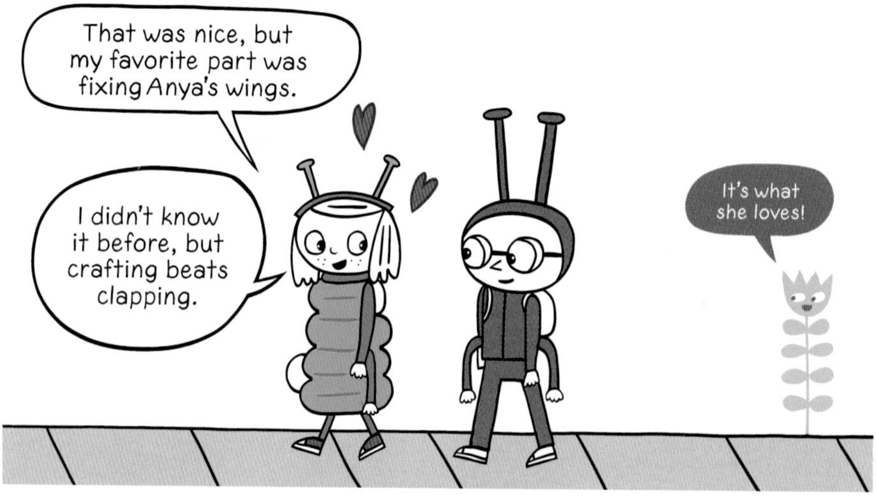
That was nice, but my favorite part was fixing Anya's wings.
I didn't know it before, but crafting beats clapping.
It's what she loves!

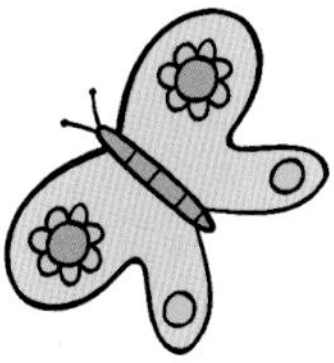

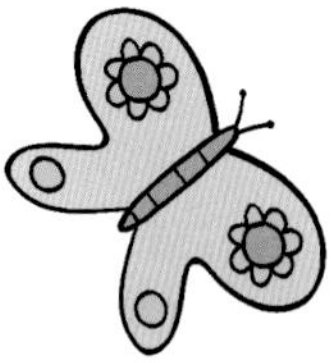

GET YOUR PAWS READY
IT'S CRAFTY TIME

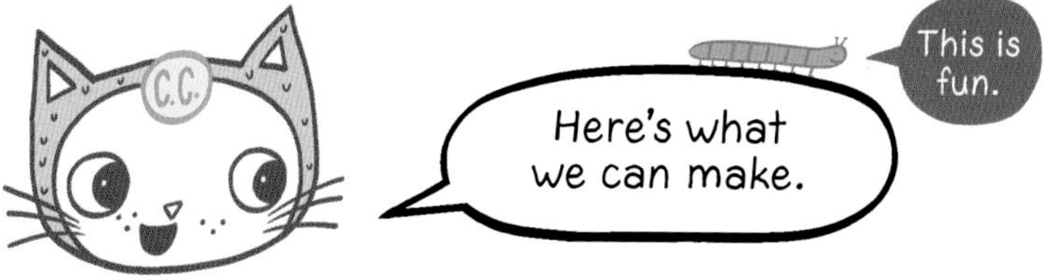
C.C.
This is fun.
Here's what we can make.

BUTTERFLY HAIR CLIP

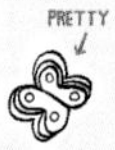
PRETTY

SUPPLIES

- -Cardstock
- -Photocopier
- -Scissors
- -Plain or Pretty Paper
- -Hair Clip
- -Stapler
- -Colored Pencils or Markers

BUTTERFLY WITH MOVING WINGS

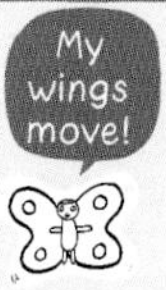
My wings move!

SUPPLIES

- -Paper
- -Photocopier
- -Scissors
- -Glue Stick
- -Tape
- -Colored Pencils or Markers

BUTTERFLY LANTERN

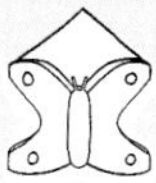

SUPPLIES

- -Paper
- -Photocopier
- -Scissors
- -String
- -Tape
- -Colored Pencils or Markers

CATERPILLAR LANTERN

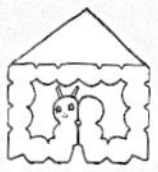

SUPPLIES

- -Paper
- -Photocopier
- -Scissors
- -String
- -Tape
- -Colored Pencils or Markers

BUTTERFLY / CATERPILLAR BOOKMARK

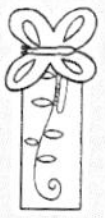

SUPPLIES

- -Cardstock
- -Photocopier
- -Scissors
- -Glue Stick
- -Colored Pencils or Markers

BUTTERFLY HAIRCLIP

1. PHOTOCOPY this template onto CARDSTOCK.

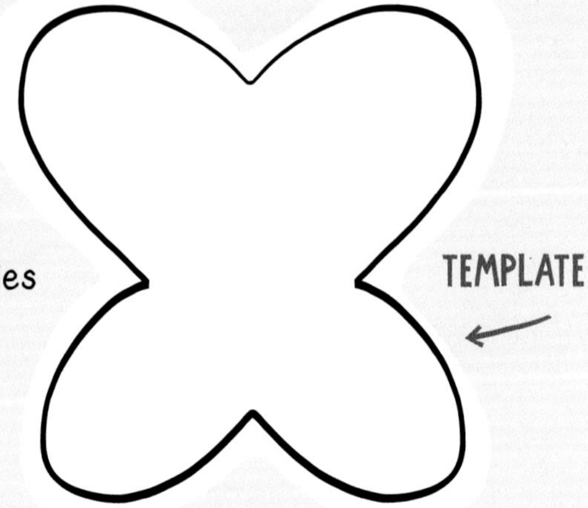
TEMPLATE

2. CUT out your CARDSTOCK template.

3. Use your template to TRACE three butterflies onto PLAIN PAPER or PRETTY PAPER.

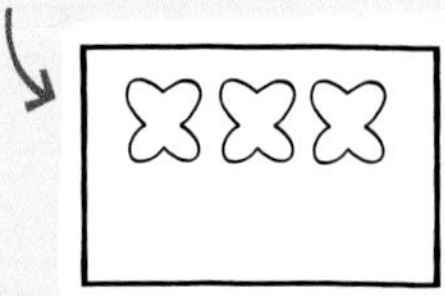

4. CUT out the three butterflies you traced.

5. FOLD each butterfly in half to make a crease.

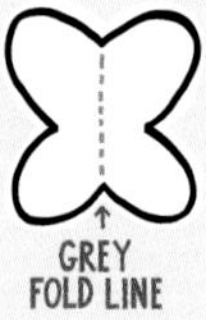
GREY
FOLD LINE

6. DECORATE your butterflies.

7. STACK the three butterflies together and STAPLE them on crease.

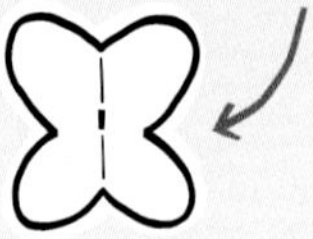

8. TAPE to a HAIR CLIP.

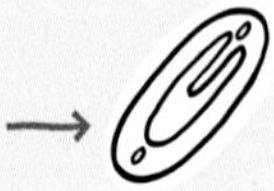

9. FOLD up wings.

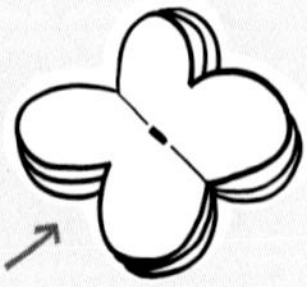

BUTTERFLY WITH MOVING WINGS

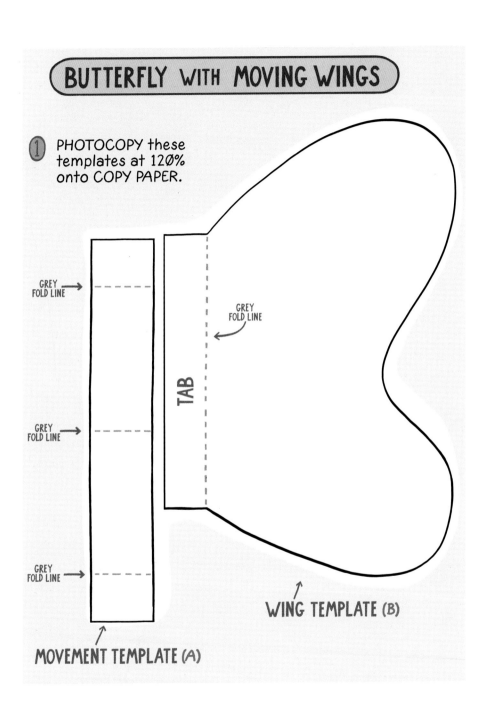

① PHOTOCOPY these templates at 120% onto COPY PAPER.

GREY FOLD LINE →

GREY FOLD LINE ←

TAB

GREY FOLD LINE →

GREY FOLD LINE →

WING TEMPLATE (B)

MOVEMENT TEMPLATE (A)

② PHOTOCOPY these templates onto COPY PAPER.

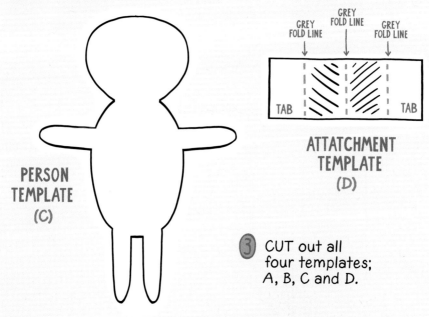

PERSON TEMPLATE (C)

GREY FOLD LINE **GREY FOLD LINE** **GREY FOLD LINE**

TAB TAB

ATTATCHMENT TEMPLATE (D)

③ CUT out all four templates; A, B, C and D.

④ FOLD a piece of PLAIN PAPER in half.

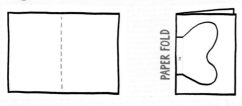

PAPER FOLD

TRACE the wing template (B) on the FOLDED PAPER and CUT out.

⑤

GREY FOLD LINE

TAB

FOLD up the wings along the fold line.

⑥ Your wings should now look like this:

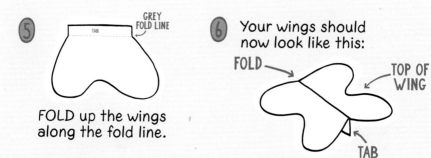

FOLD

TOP OF WING

TAB

⑦ DECORATE the wings and the person template (C).

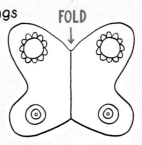

FOLD

Hi.

Now it's time to put everything together.

⑧ FOLD the attachment template (D) along its fold lines. GLUE the backs together and FOLD out the tabs on either side.

↑ GLUE TOGETHER

⑨ TURN your person over and TAPE or GLUE the attachment template (D) to his or her back.

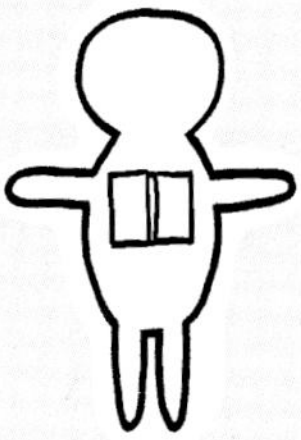

⑩ OPEN your wings.

FOLD

Put GLUE on the shaded area.

SHADED AREA

11 SLIP the tab on the back of your person into the folded space in the middle of the wings. PRESS the wing tabs so they stick together.

I like it here!

12 TURN your butterfly over.

FOLD the movement template (A) to look like this:

You will be TAPING or GLUING these parts only.

13 ATTACH the movement template (A) to the back of the wings.

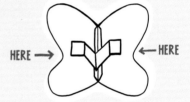

HERE → ← HERE

14 How to Move Your Butterfly:

PULL the movement tab back and forth while holding the back of your butterfly.

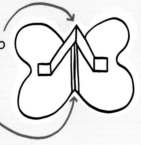

I can fly.

BUTTERFLY LANTERN

FINISHED LANTERN

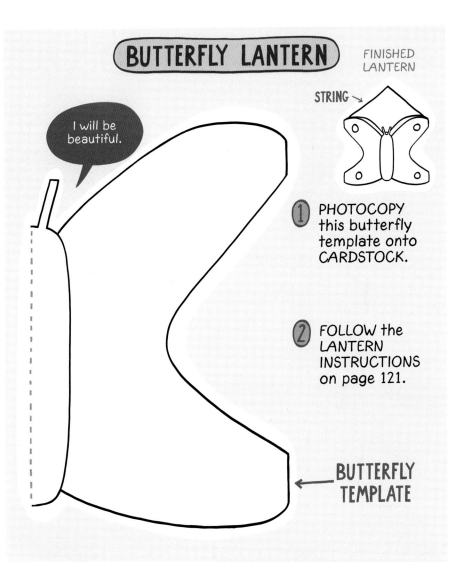

I will be beautiful.

STRING

① PHOTOCOPY this butterfly template onto CARDSTOCK.

② FOLLOW the LANTERN INSTRUCTIONS on page 121.

← BUTTERFLY TEMPLATE

Your butterfly lantern will look like this when it is open:

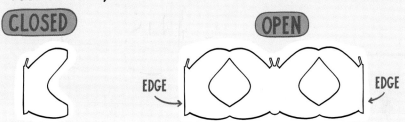

CLOSED

OPEN

EDGE

EDGE

CATERPILLAR LANTERN

FINISHED
LANTERN

STRING

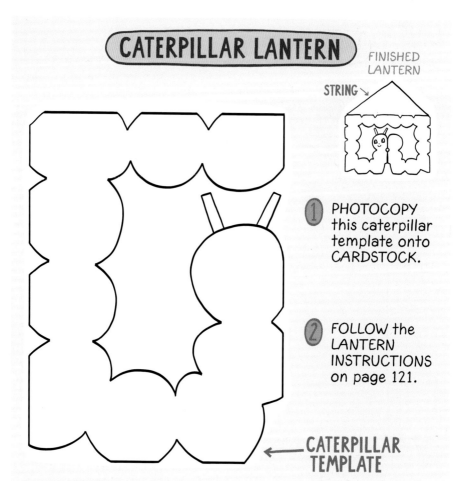

1 PHOTOCOPY
this caterpillar
template onto
CARDSTOCK.

2 FOLLOW the
LANTERN
INSTRUCTIONS
on page 121.

← CATERPILLAR
TEMPLATE

Your caterpillar lantern will look like this when it is open:

CLOSED

OPEN

LANTERN INSTRUCTIONS

1 FOLD an 8½ x 11 piece of PAPER in fourths accordian-style.

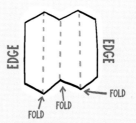

EDGE EDGE

FOLD

FOLD FOLD

2 Now it is skinny.

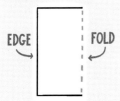

EDGE FOLD

3 PLACE the BUTTERFLY or CATERPILLAR template on top of the FOLDED PAPER and TRACE the pattern.

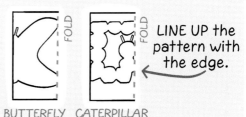

FOLD FOLD

LINE UP the pattern with the edge.

BUTTERFLY CATERPILLAR

4 CUT out the design. Now it looks like this:

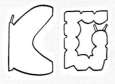

5 OPEN the lantern and DECORATE it.

6 TAPE the edges of your lantern together.

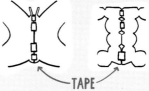

TAPE

7 Be sure to CUT the extra pairs of antennas off your caterpillar lantern. There should be one pair of antennas in the front and one in the back.

8 ATTACH a STRING and HANG UP your lantern.

BUTTERFLY/CATERPILLAR BOOKMARK

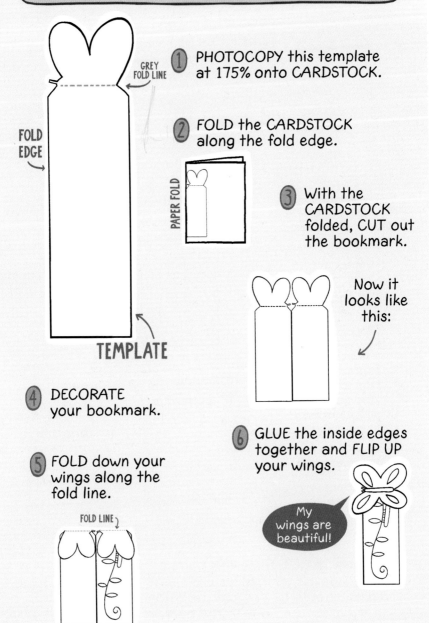

GREY FOLD LINE

FOLD EDGE

PAPER FOLD

TEMPLATE

1. PHOTOCOPY this template at 175% onto CARDSTOCK.

2. FOLD the CARDSTOCK along the fold edge.

3. With the CARDSTOCK folded, CUT out the bookmark.

Now it looks like this:

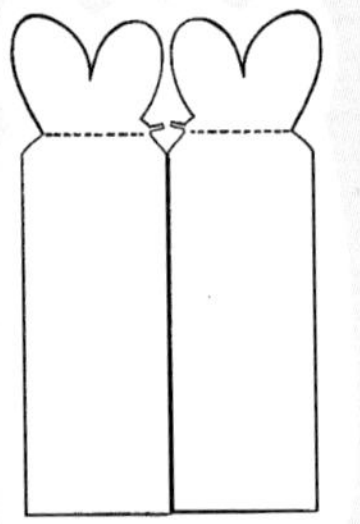

4. DECORATE your bookmark.

5. FOLD down your wings along the fold line.

FOLD LINE

6. GLUE the inside edges together and FLIP UP your wings.

My wings are beautiful!

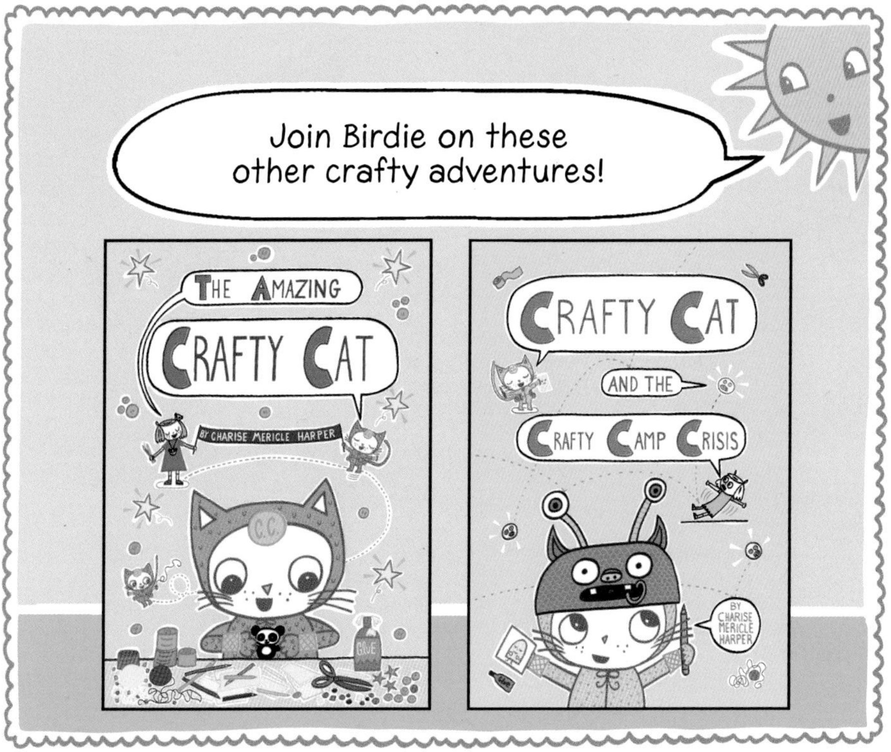
Join Birdie on these other crafty adventures!
THE AMAZING CRAFTY CAT
BY CHARISE MERICLE HARPER
GLUE
CRAFTY CAT AND THE CRAFTY CAMP CRISIS
BY CHARISE MERICLE HARPER

First Second

Published by First Second
First Second is an imprint of Roaring Brook Press, a division of
Holtzbrinck Publishing Holdings Limited Partnership
175 Fifth Avenue, New York, NY 10010

Library of Congress Control Number: 2017906597

ISBN: 978-1-62672-487-7

First edition 2018
Book design by Joyana McDiarmid
Printed in China by Toppan Leefing Printing Ltd.,
Dongguan City, Guangdong Province
1 3 5 7 9 10 8 6 4 2

Sketched on an iPad Pro, inked and colored on
a Cintiq in Photoshop with a digital nib.